Ferelith spent three years studying for her law degree and at the classes in forensic medicine learned a great deal that she would rather, at first, not have known. But she made another of her lifelong friends, this time a woman.

Elspeth Baxter was a medical student and held Ferelith's head as she vomited up the contents of her stomach after a particularly graphic lecture of death from violence.

'I didn't mind "Death in its Medico-legal relations", "Toxicology" or even "Lunacy Certificates,"' said Ferelith. 'In fact, they were extremely interesting lectures but this . . . and those pictures.'

'Not a patch on the real thing, my dear,' said Elspeth as she carefully held Ferelith's hair away from the rim of the toilet bowl. 'Why are you taking this class?'

'I want to be an advocate,' she replied.

THE QUALITY OF MERCY

EILEEN RAMSAY

WARNER BOOKS

A *Warner* Book

First published in Great Britain in 1997
by Little, Brown and Company
This edition published in 1997 by Warner Books

Copyright © Eileen Ramsay 1997

The moral right of the author has been asserted.

A CIP catalogue record for this book
is available from the British Library.

ISBN 0 7515 1849 2

Typeset in Palatino by
Palimpsest Book Production Limited,
Polmont, Stirlingshire
Printed and bound in Great Britain by
Clays Ltd, St Ives plc

Warner Books
A Division of
Little, Brown and Company (UK)
Brettenham House
Lancaster Place
London WC2E 7EN

For my mother –
another bonnie fechter,
and in memory of my father

Acknowledgements

I would like to thank the following members of the legal profession for all their help while I was researching this book. They may now stop dodging behind the aspidistras when I enter a room, unless, of course, they wish to continue to do so. The Right Honourable Lord Frazer of Carmyllie; The Right Honourable Lord Weir; William Berry W.S.; Sheriff Robin McEwen; Mike McGinley; Graham McNicol; Sandy Ingram; Hugh Annan; Jim Robertson and Fiona Raitt of the Faculty of Law, the University of Dundee; Mrs Maria McGuire; and very special thanks to my friend Marian Gilmour, a wonderful advocate in two languages.

Prologue

1933 Edinburgh

BLAIR KNEW IT was not going to work. Ferelith could exert herself until she was blue in the face. Mother had set her mind, and more importantly her heart, against her. Grimly he kept smiling while his heart crumbled into little bits inside him. What could he do? He loved his mother who, since his father's tragic early death in the Great War, had devoted her whole life to him. And yet, at the same time, and with an even fiercer passion, he loved the girl who was so bravely fighting a losing battle against the tide of inexplicable antagonism that flowed across the room towards her from the tiny, but oh-so-elegant, figure of his mother.

Ferelith soldiered on. He knew her so well: he could see how near to tears she was and her soft west-coast accent got stronger and stronger as she struggled against the clipped vowels of the older woman.

'Do you know, Mother?' Blair was determined to help. 'One of our professors says he wouldn't doubt that one day Ferelith might well be Lord Chancellor.'

'Oh, Lord Advocate would be enough,' laughed Ferelith, but Blair's mother did not smile.

'In my day girls stayed at home to look after their families.'

'But I have no family,' said Ferelith quietly, 'and so I must earn a living.'

'Shall we have lunch?'

In four seemingly neutral little words, Helena Crawford managed to convey her dislike, her distrust, her implacable opposition to this girl. Why? Why? What had Ferelith done? Or was it what Ferelith was?

No, it would never work until Mother was forced to see that unless she accepted this working-class girl from a Glasgow orphanage, she would lose her son too.

I can't give her up, Blair decided, as he sipped a very fine pre-lunch sherry.

Sometimes his feelings for Ferelith frightened him. Since that day two years ago when he had walked into the large lecture hall in the university and seen her standing there like a terrified rabbit caught in the gaze of a headlight, she had been more important than eating or sleeping, and far more important than his studies. She was part of him, and how it had happened he could not understand. Their backgrounds were so different. His was privileged: nannies, governesses, servants who anticipated every wish of the fatherless little boy, Eton but not Oxford. He had never worked hard enough. Why should he? He had inherited an estate and the fortune to support it on his eighteenth birthday. He had never wanted anything enough to work for it, not until Ferelith. And why Ferelith?

She had inherited nothing on her eighteenth birthday. There had been nothing to inherit. She had been brought up in an orphanage in Glasgow where one of the sisters of the religious teaching order had recognized her not inconsiderable brain and had fought for the girl's right to further education. Who her parents were and why she had been in the home Ferelith did not know. Blair did not care. The skinny girl with the badly cut hair, the obviously second-hand clothes and the bitten nails was his future. He was not given to introspection. He marvelled at the kismet that had made Ferelith as familiar to him as the skin on his face and he accepted his fate.

Ferelith did not, at first, approve of his plan, the simple but so obvious little plan that had occurred to him somewhere between the sherry and the port his mother had insisted on offering him, because *Grandpapa always had port, dear.*

'We can't, Blair. It's against everything I've ever been taught to respect. We'll wait: she'll come round when she sees how much we love one another.'

Blair's heart gave a sickening lurch inside him. Dear God, how he wished that were true.

'She doesn't care,' he said quietly, and in saying that and admitting that, he grew up. 'My mother has had her own way all her life. You can't believe how much my grandfather spoiled her. She will never accept you because she has not written a nice, brainy, skinny, working-class Catholic orphan into her life script.'

'When she sees that we mean to continue friends . . .'

'I don't mean to continue friends . . . at least I do, but I want us to continue as husband and wife. During that ghastly lunch I saw so clearly that you mean more to me than she does. I love her. I'm sorry that she has chosen to be as self-centred as she is and maybe that was Grandfather's fault and my father's. I don't think he ever refused her anything either. It's not good for children to get their own way all the time. I shall be very strict with all of ours.'

Ferelith laughed and the ferocious scowl eased from his handsome face. 'We're going to have children, are we?'

'Yes, five.'

'After I become Lord Advocate or before, or are you going to have them?'

'Don't laugh. We can do this, Ferelith. I can support you. We'll get married because I need you so much and you need me. With my money, and my name, it will be easier for you, and with your brains, spacing five children between court cases should be easy.'

She was angry. He had forgotten how very sensitive she was about money. She thought about it, or the lack of it, all the time. He never considered it for a moment. It continued to flow when he wanted it just as the mighty Forth flowed through his fertile acres.

'I did not fall in love with you because of your name.'

'I know. That's why I fell in love with you, though. There you stood in that ghastly frock Mother Superior found in the poor box and you said your name. Ferelith, a fairy princess. You cast a spell on me. It will remain until I die and even after death.'

He was silent and it was her turn to wonder. How sensitive and romantic he was! If her life depended on it, she could not tell him that her love would continue through all time. She would want to say it: she would say it in so many ways but never never with words. But she would not marry him to ease her way through law school.

'You have just been kidnapped, Miss Gallagher. I don't think you noticed that we are now on the road to Gretna Green. I am going to marry you to save your good name because I have absolutely no intention of stopping this car until we reach the border. There I shall take you with or without benefit of clergy or blacksmith or whatever, and

please don't get into a Holy Roman snit because
you can get things sorted out with your priest when
we get back to university. Hell, we'll need to find
an apartment. I can't take you into Residence.'

'You're being very childish, Blair. This isn't the
Middle Ages.'

'Oh, Ferelith, Ferelith. I aged a hundred years this
afternoon. I am older than time. Marry me. You
want to, don't you, and really, what does it matter
whether you marry me before or after graduation.
That's surely academic. And if you marry me, you
can keep me at work because if you are in the same
room, even better in the same bed, then I won't
spend all my studying time writing sonnets to your
funny little nose. You owe me a good education.'

'I couldn't hurt Sister Anthony Joseph.'

'You won't. She understands more about life and
love than you do.'

Five hours later Mr and Mrs Blair Crawford sat
down to dinner in the dining room of the best
hotel they could find. Five hours and ten minutes
later they were in the hotel's best bedroom strewing
clothes feverishly across the floor as they made
for the bed. Neither of them was prepared for
the intensity of their feelings, for the overpow-
ering wildness of their mutual passion. Amazed,
exhausted, satisfied, at last they fell asleep.

It was the last good night's sleep either of them
was to have for quite some time.

They woke late the next morning. Ferelith lay on
the bed and laughed as her naked husband averted
his eyes from the body he had so much enjoyed
during the night, and covered her with the sheet
before sprinting for the bathroom and his dressing
gown. Dear God, how sweet and innocent he was.

If he had grown a hundred years older in one afternoon in his mother's opulent home, my God, the night had made her as old as time itself. At last she knew all the secrets. He had invaded her very body. He had conquered her and by conquering he had been conquered. Modestly she hid herself under the sheet and waited while he shaved.

They went down hand in hand to the dining room. There were two men seated at a table in the corner. They were not eating. They were not speaking. They were just sitting as if they were waiting. They stood up as Ferelith and Blair entered.

Blair stopped. 'Oh, no,' he said, and he blushed a bright red. 'This is totally unacceptable.'

Ferelith felt her stomach contract. A second, a lifetime ago, it had felt light and soft and so fulfilled and now, now . . . Such a feeling of foreboding. Oh, God, no. Don't let it be spoiled.

'Blair?' she asked tremulously.

'Mr Crawford, Blair, please.' The older of the two men held out his hand in supplication.

Blair pushed the hand aside. 'This is really insupportable . . .' he began.

'Will you listen, you bloody young fool?'

Blair stared in embarrassed anger and humiliation at his mother's lawyer. 'How dare you follow us, McAndliss. I can't understand. I don't . . . I mean why would Mother even think I was doing this? We said nothing.'

He thought back to the luncheon. He had been, he decided, very mature, very civilized. He had kissed his mother goodbye with the usual throwaway lines. 'I'll see you soon, darling. I'll pop home for a weekend.' He had been as he always was. She could have suspected nothing. But she had. He turned back to the senior man. 'You will crawl back to my mother and tell her that Ferelith is now my wife and . . .'

Sinclair McAndliss looked at the young couple. It was not his job to spare them, even to wish that he did not have to do this cruel thing. And there was only one way to do it.

'She's your sister, laddie,' said the lawyer baldly. 'My God, Blair, I told Helena a dozen times, a thousand times to warn you, to alert you.'

Blair sat down abruptly and clung to the table top as if it was a lifeline. This could not be happening. He could not look at Ferelith. No, no, it was not true. To what depths would his mother dive to get her own way?

'My mother is insane,' he said. 'My sister? My father was killed in action in 1914. Ferelith . . .'

'Was born in 1914 in Bombay, India, the daughter of one Niamh Gallagher, spinster, of Cork. Niamh had worked for an army family as a nanny but apart from her employer who was blameless, the only man she met alone was one Major Winterton. The birth certificate of Miss Gallagher says 'Father Unknown'. Even in death Niamh Gallagher refused to betray her lover, but there was an investigation and it could not have been anyone else. When the pregnancy was discovered your father shot himself, laddie. He was no hero, dying in battle, but a cold-blooded seducer. Why ever did you think your grandfather insisted that you change your name?'

'My name?' Blair looked at the lawyer. He had no idea what he was talking about.

'You were born Blair Winterton, laddie. Your mother was so ashamed of your father that she had her name and yours legally changed after the war. She said it was for continuity in the estate, a condition of your grandfather's will, that you could only inherit if you had his name. I'm sorry, Blair, but there is no doubt at all in my mind that your father, Major the Honourable Archie Winterton, and Mrs . . . Miss Gallagher's father were one and the same man.'

Mr and Mrs Blair Crawford looked at him in misery and then in horror at one another and then looked away, each embarrassed by the other's presence.

And then with horrifying abruptness, Mrs Crawford was violently sick all over the beautiful starched linen cloth on the hotel's best table. Blair rushed to help her but she threw him off as if she could no longer bear his touch. Last night his hands had inflamed her. Now . . . She turned and ran weeping from the room.

1

1913 Fife

CRITICALLY, HELENA WINTERTON examined her image in the full-length mirror. She was displeased with what she saw. Breasts far too large for fashion and disagreeably full of milk, and no waistline that she could discern, no matter how hard she sucked in the stomach that, to her eyes, looked too soft and round.

Was there nothing that would tighten up this overstretched skin? Baby was a poppet and she absolutely adored every hair on his precious little head, but he had cost her.

Her skin was not the only part of her life that demanded firm treatment. Archie, darling Archie. Helena smiled despite herself and felt that too familiar frisson of excitement in her lower belly. No, really she had been just the teeniest bit dishonest in telling Archie that dear Doctor Ferguson advised against the renewing of . . . how could she put it . . . connubial relations just yet. Archie was so patient and so undemanding. But no, she did not want another baby, at least not for a year or two; and it seemed as if Baby had started on the first day of her honeymoon and she could not, would not, risk another pregnancy immediately after his so stressful and painful birth.

She would, however, manage to *reward* her dearest Archie for his forbearance before he left for India.

There. She had said it. Before *he* left for India. She had made the decision then. When Major the Honourable Archie Winterton sailed with his regiment to Bombay in a few short weeks, Mrs Helena Crawford Winterton would not be with him.

Imperiously Helena rang the bell for her maid.

'Quick, Bessie. Ask Nanny to bring Baby. I want to feed him before I dress for dinner: I must see Sir Gordon before Major Winterton returns.'

Helena ignored the tightening of Bessie's lips. Nanny would fume and fuss at the disruption of her precious charge's schedule and might even have the audacity to defy her mistress. Well, she would see who ruled in this house. Helena wrapped herself in her brocade dressing gown and sat in the wing chair by the fire.

Bessie, without the baby, hurried into the room. She bobbed a curtsey to her mistress.

'Mrs Hendry says as Baby is asleep . . .' She stopped before the glint in her young mistress's eye.

'Go upstairs, Bessie, and bring me Baby before I leak all over this chair. I am dressing for dinner and I have no intention of jumping up after the fish to attend to my son.'

Mrs Hendry herself brought Baby. He had not fretted at being wakened from a sound sleep. Really, he was so like Archie in nature. Even at two months old Helena could see the signs of patience and courtesy exhibited so often by her darling Archie. She smiled sweetly at the discomfited nanny.

'I know how we hate to disrupt Precious's schedule, Nanny, but I must talk to Sir Gordon before dinner, and see, Baby is so greedy and so good-natured: he doesn't at all mind dining early. Do you my precious?' she added to the baby as she pressed his beautiful little head against her full breast.

The baby looked up at her out of one eye. His little rosebud mouth was already fastened on her nipple and he was swallowing noisily. Nanny bent over and inserted a finger between his nose and the full softness of his mother's breast.

'Try to keep his nose clear, Mrs Winterton. Baby has the teeniest little cold.'

Helena smiled. 'Yes, poor lamb,' she said. 'You may go, Mrs Hendry. His grandpapa will want to see him. His papa will return him to the nurseries before he himself dresses for dinner.'

Mrs Hendry frowned but apart from registering strong disapproval there was nothing she could do. At least the Major might remember that what went in one end of a tiny baby almost immediately came out the other.

Helena felt the frost in the atmosphere and she regretted it, because really it was so much more pleasant when everyone was happy; but she was the mistress of this estate and had been since she had persuaded her father to dispense with the services of her governess on her fifteenth birthday. She held her breast away from the baby's nose and Mrs Hendry was forced to remove her finger.

'You won't let him be jiggled about too much, Madame?' Mrs Hendry asked anxiously. 'Sir Gordon has a terrible habit of playing too strenuously with him after his feed.'

'I don't think even the most indulgent of grandpapas will court being vomited over too often, Nanny. Sir Gordon has become a very paragon among grandfathers, hasn't he, my sweet?'

Helena lifted the baby and burped him on her shoulder before transferring him to the other breast.

She said nothing but she could see how annoyed Mrs Hendry was that she was becoming such an expert mother. Really there was absolutely nothing to it. Why the whole business had been wrapped in such a veil of secrecy and old wives' tales, she could not imagine. Babies were just like horses. They needed to be fed, watered, housed, and loved, and when they were old enough, exercised and disciplined. She smiled complacent dismissal and Mrs Hendry was forced to leave.

Helena enjoyed these minutes alone with her son. As soon as he was weaned, and unfortunately he would have to be weaned if she was to enjoy any of the season, Mrs Hendry would rule supreme. There would be fewer excuses to steal him away, fewer moments when she could hold him like this and nuzzle his soft little neck with her face, smelling the milky warm smell of him, watching the little mouth open in an enormous yawn that wrinkled up the tiny little nose.

'Come along, Precious, before I change my mind and decide that you shall have a sister before the year is out. We will wait, Poppet, just for a few years and then we will see.'

Helena laid the baby down on the settee from where he contentedly watched her as she buttoned up her robe. That done she pulled a brush through her red-gold hair and bit her lips to give them a little colour. Then she picked the baby up, wrapped him in the finest of Shetland shawls, and hurried out to her father's rooms.

Sir Gordon Crawford was reading the racing results in the morning's papers. He never bet on any horse he had not seen but enjoyed making and losing paper fortunes with his butler. He looked up when an imperious knock announced his daughter and only child, and when he saw that she carried his precious grandson, he jumped from the chair with even more alacrity than he would have shown had it been only his daughter who stood there.

'Come in my darling girl and give that heavy child to me.'

Helena was quite happy to hand the baby over to his grandfather and to take the chair beside the fire, the chair she had always sat in when she came to this very special room. At first they talked about the baby and how amazingly he seemed to have grown since his grandfather had last seen him – only that morning.

'You are the cleverest of clever little mothers, my darling,' said Sir Gordon, 'and what your dear mamma would have made of this poppet . . .'

'They do grow quickly,' Helena interrupted his fond musings, 'but he's so delicate, Father, and he has a nasty cold in his poor little nose.'

'He is trying to breathe through his mouth, Helena. Damn it, if he don't sound like that ghastly boot boy with his constant catarrh.'

The baby, caring nothing at all for the sensibilities of anyone but his all-important self, looked into the face of Sir Gordon Crawford and rid himself of an almighty belch.

'Your boot boy is a paragon of gentility compared to that, Papa,' said Helena and they gazed in complacent wonder at this precious child.

'I will miss him so,' said Sir Gordon, 'and you too, my dear.'

'Actually, Papa, that's one of the reasons I wanted to see you before Archie comes home.' Helena knew she had to be very careful. Her father adored her but he believed implicitly that a woman's place was with her husband. She could not merely tell him that she was bored to tears with India, where almost every young officer had a lovely young wife and where the conversation was always of bridge, tennis, servants, and babies. Till the arrival of her son, all four subjects had wearied Helena immeasurably.

'I'm so torn, Papa. You see, life has changed in these past few months and now I have Baby to consider. I have two duties and which is the predominant one – my duty as a wife or my duty as a mother? It was so hard to leave you when I married Archie but that was a clear cut decision: my duty lay with my husband and, although it broke my heart, I went.' She stopped and stole a look at her fond father out of her red-gold eyelashes. Yes, he had been affected by thoughts of her broken heart, her bravery. 'I think Baby is too small,' she went on, 'too delicate to sail to India, and then he has this cold. Surely it would be better to let the winter pass before making such a long voyage?'

Half an hour later Helena almost skipped back along the passage to her rooms. Sir Gordon, totally besotted with his male heir, was firmly on her side.

When she reached her bedroom Helena put the baby down in the middle of the pink satin coverlet on her bed, and he watched her as she moved across the room to her wardrobes.

'Now what shall we wear, Precious?' she asked as she pulled dress after dress from the cavernous interiors and piled them on the day bed.

She went back to the dressing table, picked up a heavy silver-backed brush and pulled it through her hair.

There was a tap at the door and there stood Bessie, a pile of the baby's linen in her arms. 'I thought I'd change Baby, Mrs Winterton. The Major is in his bath, Madame. He said as how he wouldn't disturb you while you were with Sir Gordon.'

'Thank you, Bessie,' said Helena. She waited while the girl dealt quickly and surely with the infant. When he was ready she would take him and show him off to Archie. Archie, bless his heart, no matter how seductive he thought her in her satin peignoir, would remain in his bath while they chatted. She would leave the baby in his dressing room: Archie would relish the privilege of returning him to the dragon upstairs.

'You're a good girl,' she said as she picked up her son. 'I'm throwing out all those dresses. I'm sure I can't get into one. Perhaps you and your sisters can find a use for them.'

She smiled and went out, leaving the girl standing there looking from the door to the heaped pile of satins and laces with a dazed expression on her face.

Niamh Gallagher was frightened. She was standing at the quayside in her best, her only, coat, and in the bag she had in her hand was everything she owned. That was not much with which to be travelling halfway across the world. One dress, her best, one nightgown stitched by herself and therefore nothing really to be too proud about, two pairs of drawers – one for wearing, one for keeping in case of an accident, a second pair of knitted stockings, a Sunday petticoat with a fine edging of exquisite Limerick lace, and her extra bodice which she had been told, with some glee, would 'crucify her in the heat' but had still to be worn for decency's sake. She had the shoes she stood up in, a shawl, two linen handkerchiefs, a meagre collection of toilet articles that included her Aunt Maeve's tortoiseshell-backed hairbrush, and a prayer book. Niamh was a decent Catholic girl.

Niamh looked at the ship and then back at the town. No matter how hard she tried she could not force her legs to follow one another up that gangplank.

'May I help you?'

Niamh looked up through a mist of tears and saw a soldier shimmering in the sun. He was so tall that she had to look up into his face. It was a nice face, a kind face, and if only that voice had not issued from that face . . . she would have been reassured. But the voice was the voice of the gentry, of the lords and the landlords, and before this moment Niamh had only ever heard it raised in anger.

The voice soothed Niamh Gallagher's frightened heart and she looked straight into his fine eyes and fell instantly and irrevocably in love, and so Niamh smiled and spoke.

'Oh, I'm that nervous, sir, of getting on that boat, but haven't I a grand job waiting for me at the other side of the ocean.'

'Off to India, are you?'

'Yes, sir. I'm to be a nursemaid, sir.' To her surprise Niamh heard herself rattling on as if she and the officer were social equals and he interested in what she had to say. 'My mistress doesn't want a black person looking after her children, and I'm sure she can't be blamed for that because they can't be the same as us now, sir, can they, or they wouldn't be black. Still and all though, how she thinks I'll be better and me never having touched a babby in all my born days, I do not know.'

He smiled at her prejudices. India would teach her a great deal. 'Oh, well, ladies who have just had babies get strange notions, do they not? Let me take your bag and help you aboard. If this is your first voyage no wonder you are a little hesitant about trusting yourself to a ship.'

'Oh, sure I've no worries about the ship, sir. It's all that water.'

He laughed heartily and Niamh basked in the new and heady sensation of being laughed with and not at. She had not known she was funny.

'It'll be full of sharks and things,' she hazarded a guess. He was a soldier and a gentleman and therefore would know.

'In some parts, but really one is in much more danger from a carriage or one of these ghastly new motor vehicles in the middle of town than from a shark in the middle of the ocean. Ships seldom sink, you know.'

She was aboard the ship and had not felt herself walking up that strange thing called a gangway. There were several people standing there and Niamh felt their looks of displeasure. She flushed with embarrassment. 'You and your tongue, Niamh Gallagher. It'll be the death of you, so it will.' She wanted to hurry away and hide: a nursemaid had no business laughing with a gentleman even though the gentleman had initiated the conversation.

He sensed her panic. 'Don't run off. The Purser here will show you where you are to go, Miss . . . ?'

'Gallagher, sir. Niamh Gallagher.' She curtseyed quickly.

'*Bon voyage*, Miss Gallagher,' he said, and he replaced his cap and half bowed. Almost, Niamh felt, as if I were a lady.

'This way, Miss Gallagher,' ordered a voice that was not pleasant and not at all friendly, and Niamh began to follow the querulous tones away from the gangplank and down into the depths of the ship. At

the top of the iron stairs that led to the steerage she
turned and saw that the soldier was still standing
there. Once more the sun prevented her from seeing
him properly. His tall slim figure was surrounded
by light.

'Like God,' thought the good Catholic irreverently. 'He's like God.'

Niamh was sharing a cabin with one other girl
and an older unmarried woman. They too were in
service but *Mrs* McCann was very superior: after all,
was she not a nanny and her charge the daughter of
an Honourable, who was in turn the daughter of a
real live lord. Mary Gibson was, like Niamh, going
out as a nursemaid but whereas Niamh was to be in
full charge of the three children of Captain and Mrs
Butler, Mary was joining a large happy household
where there were two other nursemaids under the
overall care of a Registered Nanny.

'My madame has money,' Mary whispered to
Niamh as they lay in their bunks that night, trying
to accustom themselves to the rolling of the ship.
'When I went to the big house for my interview,
do you know, the housekeeper told me there were
seventeen inside servants and goodness knows how
many outside and more hired in from the village
when my madame comes home with her children.
Can you imagine, Niamh, seventeen people to look
after two. What would they find to do all day?
You don't think someone holds your drawers for
you to step into if you're rich, do you?' At the
hilarious picture conjured up by Mary's words the
girls choked with laughter. 'The rich aren't like you
and me, are they?' continued Mary when she could
speak. 'I wonder why.'

'It's not your place to criticize your elders and
betters, my girls,' said Mrs McCann. 'What would

a lady born and bred know about cleaning fireplaces or blackleading grates or washing and ironing, and aren't they all too delicate to turn a mangle anyway?'

Niamh tried to hear if there was any humour in the voice. Surely Mrs McCann wasn't serious. She, Niamh, couldn't really see dirt as any respecter of any person, rich or poor. She was, however, sensible enough not to argue with Mrs McCann. She fell asleep.

The next few weeks were sheer hell as Mrs McCann and then poor Mary fell victim to seasickness. Niamh could quite cheerfully have abandoned Mrs McCann to welter in her own vomit but Mary was different. She could not abandon Mary.

'You're a good girl, Niamh Gallagher,' whispered Mrs McCann when the ship stopped trying to capsize itself and began to cut a straight furrow through the ocean. The sun, which had dazzled Niamh as she had embarked, having hidden itself for most of their journey down the length of the British Isles and out into the Mediterranean, now blazed out in splendour. Mrs McCann was finally able to sit up a little on that small part of the deck not reserved for the wives and children of the army officers travelling with them out to India. She grasped Niamh's calloused hand in her soft ones. 'Should you ever need help you have only to ask.'

Niamh smiled but said nothing, content just to sit and feel a slight breeze blow around her face. She loved watching the women on the deck. How beautiful their dresses were. She opened the top button at the neck of her dress and rolled up her sleeves.

'Poor things,' she said to Mrs McCann. 'They're dying in this heat and they're too hemmed in by restrictions to make themselves comfortable.'

'Ladies have standards, Niamh, and we would all be the better for adopting some of them.'

'Surely only the ones that make sense,' said Niamh pertly. 'I'm going for a stroll, Mrs McCann. I've paid my fare same as them and God's good clean air belongs to everyone.'

She walked off on to the main deck and leaned over the side of the ship, fascinated by the great surge of water that spread out from the sides of the ship like corn falling at the sweep of the reaper. She was mesmerized by the precision of the great sweeps of the waves, at the way the sun found every separate drop of water and turned them all to liquid silver.

Archie Winterton saw her there as he stood immaculately dressed in tropical kit. He had seen Helena sometimes like that, her neck exposed to the sun, her sleeves rolled up, her hair unbound. Longing for his wife and for his new baby son filled him.

'Miss Gallagher?'

She turned and saw him and he saw her eyes fill with pleasure as she smiled. 'Good day to you, sir,' she said. 'Is this not wonderful after that storm?'

'It is indeed. I hope you were not made unwell by the violent rolling of the ship.'

'Oh, not me, sir, which is just as well since poor Mary and Mrs McCann were unable to lift their heads from their pillows.'

'Mary and Mrs McCann?'

'My roommates, or should I say cabin mates? I am become very knowledgeable about boats, I mean ships, sir. Mary is an Irish girl like myself but unfortunately for me she is to stay in Bombay. There are five children in her family but two other nursemaids and isn't Mrs McCann, who has never been near an altar with a man in her life, a nanny. She has been to India before and has just taken her Master Thomas home to prep school and is now back for three years. She has told me everything I need to know.'

'Well, that is good. And what did she feel that you ought to know, Miss Gallagher?'

'Daft things about protecting my head from the sun's rays and wearing two bodices to mop up the sweat. An important thing she taught me is that I should not talk alone to officers and gentlemen, sir.' She looked up boldly and laughed into his eyes. 'But didn't I know that already,' she finished breathlessly, and turned back to her contemplation of the ocean. 'There's just something about the ocean though. Does it not make us and our problems and our little peculiarities small?'

He looked at her strangely. She really was the oddest young woman. He could not place her in society. Her position was menial, her clothes were poor, but her manner was assured and her accent, although Irish, was not so strong that he could not understand it. 'Are you going out as a governess, Miss Gallagher? You have a remarkable turn of phrase, if you will excuse my boldness, for a nursemaid.'

'Wasn't my old cousin, Maeve, that brought me up, not housekeeper to the parish priest, sir. He was a good man and kept me when my parents died. I went to school till I was fourteen, would you believe, and then I stayed at the parish house because really, wasn't Maeve crippled half the time with the rheumatism. You read an awful lot of books, sir, when you are alone with an old man who spends most of his time on his knees in prayer and an old woman who can't get on her knees at all.'

'And why have you left them?'

The laughter was gone from her face and he was sad to see it go. It lit up the rather austere thin features and made her almost pretty. With more money, Niamh Gallagher could have been beautiful.

'Maeve is dead and the old man has been retired. Was the Bishop got me this job and I hope I don't disappoint them. I know nothing at all about children.'

'There's not much to know. Feed them and water them, like horses, and keep them clean. I should think that would do it. Oh, yes, and discipline and affection.'

She laughed at his absurdity and he laughed back.

'Affection the least important, is it, sir?'

Suddenly he was serious. 'No, Miss Gallagher, affection is always primary.'

'You have children, sir?'

In his mind he saw Baby and his gummy open-mouthed grin: he could feel the child's small warm body and he could almost breathe in that special clean smell of new baby.

'One. A little boy.'

She looked round. The deck was full of small children and nursemaids. She put her hand up to close the buttons at her throat. 'Are they here then?'

'No. They are not here.' He put out his hand and touched her hair gently. 'We go ashore at Aden, Miss Gallagher. I would advise you, if Mrs McCann has not, to buy a hat at Firpo's.'

He nodded his head and turned and walked away, conscious of the looks of displeasure from the dowagers under their awnings, and he cursed himself for his stupidity.

'Oh God, Helena, how can I bear one year alone. It's not a month yet and I ache for you and for Baby.'

He went down to his cabin where he wrote yet another passionate letter to his wife. He poured out all his love for her and his longing, and his need to see his son grow.

Many children survive admirably in India. The ship echoes to the sounds of their games and their tears. Hire an army of competent nursemaids and join,
Your most loving and most desolate,
Archie

For the rest of the voyage Archie resolved to stay close to those brother officers who were also unaccompanied, in most cases because they were unmarried, and in their company he was able to forget the clinging of soft arms. He took to retiring immediately after dinner before the military band began to play for dancing, and in his cabin he read and studied and wrote to Helena. He did not see Miss Gallagher again until they reached Aden.

Like most of the returning military he wanted to go to Firpo's for new tropicals. He forgot that he had encouraged Niamh to go ashore. There she was, the first of the non-military passengers to disembark, her red hair flying like a standard.

'That saucy madame is about to get sunstroke.'

General McWhirter's wife had come up behind him. Strange how so large a lady could move so quietly.

'If she does, Ma'am, Captain Butler's wife should be ashamed of herself for not warning a simple girl of the strength of a tropical sun.'

'Simple, Archie?' she said coyly. 'Her eyes are too bold and her demeanour not at all what poor Mrs Butler has been led to expect.'

'She has an education,' he said. 'It must gall her to have to suffer fools gladly.'

She laughed, taking no offence. She knew that he was referring to the many empty-headed young socialites on their way out to India to catch a husband. 'So Caroline has hired a governess and a nursemaid in one. How very astute are the Scottish. Now take me ashore. I must guard you for Helena: it really was very naughty of her to abandon such a divinely handsome man.'

He gave her his arm. 'Helena trusts me, Ma'am.'

She looked up at him. 'Helena never was a very clever girl and dreadfully spoiled, of course. You should have been much more stern, Archie. A woman's place is with her husband.'

'Baby was unwell . . .' he said, beginning to make excuses.

'Nonsense. She never did deserve you, Archie, but I shall save you for her.'

He laughed. He had dreamed about Helena and the dream had been so strong that he had almost felt her in his arms: he did not need guarding.

'Your obedient servant, Mrs McWhirter,' he said and gave her his arm.

Niamh saw them go ashore, the tall, handsome young officer with the lovely voice and the fat, raddled-looking old lady who had had half the girls on board crying with vexation and exasperation before they had reached the Mediterranean.

She felt the sun on her head and knew that its rays were turning her head to gold. He admired her hair. She could feel his eyes on her. He was a mystery. He was married and he had a child but why were they not with him? He loved the boy: she knew nothing of parental love but there had been something in his voice, something in his eyes when he had spoken of the child. Was it love, regret?

Suddenly she knew that she wished that he would think of her the way he thought of his son. She wanted to mean something to him but no, stupid Niamh, she told herself, he is as far above you as the stars that shine on this ocean at night, and as untouchable. Don't be misled by a courtesy, a kindness. You mean nothing and can mean nothing to him. Buy your hat and hide your golden hair.

2

IT WAS THE heat. She would never get used to it. No matter how many bodices she wore to sop up all the sweat, her dress was still soaked after the slightest exertion, and running after the three spoiled brats that Mrs Butler fondly called her 'darling little people' could never be classed as slight exertion. Niamh's palms itched to make painful contact with any part of the small solid bodies that daily made her miserable existence even more of a hell. She had absolutely no idea how to interest or control them, and the imps of Satan knew it. They had figured her out accurately within a few hours of her being admitted into their spacious, airy nurseries. To give Mrs Butler her due, she had chosen the most pleasant rooms in the house for her children and any breeze that was to be found in Calcutta found its way into the eyrie on the top floor of the large house on Alexandra Court.

Niamh sighed and buttoned up, right to the very high neck, the third of the dresses she had worn that day. Whether Mrs Butler was kind or whether she could not bear to see her children's nursemaid look unkempt, Niamh did not know, but within twenty-four hours of her being in the house, the durzi had been sent for, and dress after dress had hurried from his clever brown fingers. Because he was kind as well as talented the dresses, though fashioned from the cheapest cottons available, were also very flattering to the young girl. Ibrar would sit cross-legged on the verandah and, although he was paid only to make the simplest summer frock, he would embroider an exquisite flower or an initial, and once, even her name. He had ripped that out though, for its formation and pronunciation made no sense to him at all.

'This does not make sense to my way of thinking, Missy,' he said, as he had tried painstakingly to hide the marks where the strange letters had been set.

'Sure it makes little sense to me either, Mr Ibrar,' Niamh had consoled him, 'but then it's Irish, not English, and aren't we both glad of that.'

'In that case, Miss Neeeeve,' he had laughed, proving to her that even brown men have a sense of humour, 'we will rework the unpronounceable word.'

Niamh often wondered if Mrs Butler was wrong about how to handle the Indian climate. She had wonderful ideas for handling the entire subcontinent, and these, and her modern ideas for the upbringing of children, received no favour from her nursemaid.

'Sure doesn't she say the children are flowers that need to be given space to grow,' she informed Major Archie Winterton when, to her great joy, she encountered him on the Maidan, that great stretch of park through the middle of Calcutta. Calcutta, teeming city of the subcontinent, and yet not one brown or black face showed itself anywhere on the Maidan. The Maidan was for the Raj. Archie Winterton accepted this and Niamh had not yet realized it.

Archie had dismounted and was leading his horse along the path as he and Niamh followed the antics of the children. 'A little judicious pruning seems in order,' he said as he watched these spoiled unruly children and compared them with the spoiled unruly borders of his father-in-law's gardens at home: he did not think of his absent wife in terms of discipline.

'Wasn't it you who said all they needed was affection and food, like horses. Sure your horse here is far more the gentleman than young Tom.'

Archie laughed. 'I did mention discipline, Miss Gallagher, and there is a vast difference between affection and indulgence. The former helps the growth, the latter stunts it.'

'It will be my hand stunts these three I'm telling you, Major.'

She sounded serious and Archie looked at her in alarm. She would lose her place if she attempted physically to discipline Captain Butler's children. 'You need a little space away from the children, Miss Gallagher. You do have some free time?'

'Oh, aye. Wednesday and Sunday afternoons and Wednesday evening until ten, but I put one foot in front of the other and I'm sweating like Father Murphy's pig.'

He laughed. He could never see Helena or girls like her admitting to such human failings. 'There are many beautiful buildings in the town that are cool and quite safe for a European, Miss Gallagher. And what of other girls? There must be some your own age. Your friends from the ship, for instance?'

'Isn't that always the way of friendship, Major? There's Mary now moved to Delhi and Mrs McCann still in Bombay. But in the letter I had from Mary she informs me that she is to go to the Hills at the same time as my family and that will be a joy to me.'

The Hills. Everyone who was able would go to the Hills to escape this appalling heat of the Plains. He was to go to Simla himself.

'Mrs Butler has taken a house called the Deodars. I

think that's poplar trees. Won't it be nice to sit under the shade of a real tree?'

At that moment, five-year-old Tom gave his four-year-old sister a violent push and she fell on to the red gravel with a yell that sent resting birds from the tops of the trees that lined the walk. Were not these real trees, Miss Gallagher? he thought, but he said nothing.

Niamh and Archie started forward and Niamh picked up the squalling child who rewarded her with a kick in the stomach. She took a deep controlling breath but said nothing to the little girl. She turned to the soldier. 'Aren't they the little angels, Major?' she said. 'Well, it's been nice talking to you. No, please,' she said in some fear as he reached for Tom, 'I can handle them myself. We'll just go home now and do some arithmetic. I shall give Tom problems to do. If there are three horrible children and one of them, a boy five years old, is carried off by a jackal, how many nice little girls are left?'

At this picture of his future Tom too started to bawl and Archie retreated cowardly leaving Niamh with her charges.

It was not the first time he had seen her since their arrival in India. The life of the military, at least for the officers, in Calcutta was fairly restricted. Everyone knew and entertained everyone else of similiar rank or met them at the various dinner parties, bridge parties, lawn parties, tennis parties. He had not been surprised to see Niamh with her charges at Mrs Butler's tennis afternoon, but he had surprised himself and his host by claiming the acquaintanceship of the outward voyage and introducing himself. Niamh herself had handled the situation better than he had done. She had been polite but not servile, had stood chatting for a moment and had even laughed at his reminding her of her fear of *all that water*, and had moved away from him as soon as possible and had never looked his way again. Oh, she knew how to behave all right, better than her employer who, annoyed that her nursemaid was on easy terms with one of her most important guests, had come forward to make herself better known. For Archie Winterton, although he had not two pennies of his own to rub together, was the second son of an Earl and therefore was Major the Honourable Archie Winterton. Even better, he was the husband of the beautiful Helena who would come soon, everyone agreed, with her beautiful clothes paid for out of her father's vast fortune which grew ever larger as his companies sold more and more Scotch whisky to an ever-expanding market.

Mrs McWhirter had assured everyone that the marriage was not in trouble. The young couple had taken their first furlough and gone home so that Helena could give birth to her son in her father's magnificent Fife home, and unfortunately the baby had contracted a cold and had been deemed unfit for the long ocean voyage. Mrs McWhirter, who had little patience for the Helena Wintertons of this world and vast sympathy for the Archies, lied like the proverbial trooper in her attempts to make sure that Helena's return to Calcutta and her duty would be an easy one.

'The dear child was devastated,' she told every cocktail party guest, 'but what is the use of employing the best and most expensive medical men and then ignoring what they say?'

No one was left in any doubt that Helena and her son would join her husband in a few months, after – although Mrs McWhirter did not tell Calcutta this

– the London season, which was so much more fun than life in Calcutta.

And although Mrs McWhirter had kept her own counsel, Calcutta had decided that since the Honourable Archie Winterton had refused any of the lures cast to him by sophisticated women of his own class, who knew how to play the game of dalliance, he was unlikely to be caught by an Irish servant girl.

Archie remounted and cantered along the Maidan, raising a cloud of brick-red dust as he went. It settled lightly on his polished boots: it seeped into the creases of his immaculate jodhpurs. Later he found it on his very skin under the handmade, skintight shirt, and he laughed, for dust, like the constant smell of evacuated bowels, was an integral part of this great land. And later, as he sat in the hip bath and allowed Aboubakir to sluice him with warm water, he thought not of Helena and her milk-white skin, but of Niamh Gallagher. Her skin, under her clothes, would be soft and white like Helena's, but today it would be covered by a thin mist of powdery red dust and he hoped she had a nice deep bath to sit in while a servant washed it all away.

3

'I LOVE YOU, Archie. I've loved you since that first moment.'

Archie Winterton opened his eyes and looked at the girl who lay so trustingly beside him and he groaned in self-induced pain.

'Oh dear God, Niamh, this should never have happened. I never meant it to happen.' He started up from the soft bed of mosses and pine needles where they had been lying and turned away from her to straighten his clothes.

Niamh propped herself up on her elbow and pulled at his legs. 'But Archie, dear, it's all right since we love each other.' She saw the look of mingled despair and disgust in his eyes and hurried to her feet, pulling down her skirts and rearranging her bodices. 'Archie, you do love me, don't you? You couldn't do that to me and not . . .'

'We did it to each other, Niamh, but yes, I started it, I suppose and, oh my poor little girl, I am to blame. I am so dreadfully sorry.'

'My Aunt Maeve said this happened when young people were in love, Archie. We should have waited till we were wed but . . .'

She was not a stupid woman. Why did she not understand? How could he make her understand?

He held her arms and forced her to look at him. 'Niamh, I am already married. I told you that.' He could not tell her that when he had entered her he had thought only of Helena, Helena, Helena.

'I know,' she said simply, 'and it's a mortal

sin, sure, but we won't let it happen again till we're married. I wish we didn't have to wait . . .' She blushed. 'I mean wait to get married, Archie, but . . .'

'I am married, Niamh,' he said again as slowly and deliberately as he could. 'I have a son, and my wife and child will join me here soon.'

'Oh, the rich can get divorced and I've never been married before and so it will be all right. Your wife won't mind, Archie. Sure if she minded at all, she'd be here, wouldn't she? Everyone says so.'

He dropped his arms and stepped back as if he had been struck. 'If she minded at all . . .' Was that true? No, Helena loved him. It was just that she had been so spoiled all her life that she could not, no matter how hard she tried, put anyone else first. It was not her fault. Sir Gordon was to blame. Helena was a sweet, pretty little thing who had no idea how much loving her hurt him.

'We have to go back, Niamh. I'm sorry. I was an undisciplined oaf and I should be shot . . .' Another horrifying thought leapt into his overactive mind. 'We must hope there will be no serious repercussions' – except that you have taken an innocent girl's virginity, he accused himself – 'but we must never see one another again.' He turned away and began to walk back towards the settlement and she hurried after him and threw her arms around him. He could not wrest her free without hurting her and they stood there on the path, the world crumbling around them.

Niamh screamed and wailed and wept and threw herself down at his feet begging. Every word, every tear, every moan, pierced his heart and his brain.

Far below them one of the dilapidated buses that daily carried at least one hundred people at a time

up the untarred roads that turned into mudslides in
the monsoon months of July and August, lurched
like an ungainly slug around a hairpin bend. What
was the area called, this beautiful country from
Simla to Kashmir? Had his bearer said Kulu? Archie
looked but did not see dusty, winding hilly land,
perfect for ponies, not for battered buses. He saw
only Niamh.

My God, how had he let this happen? He had
deliberately, yes, deliberately, he could admit it
now, sought her out. She needed a friend, he had
told himself. The Butlers demanded more than
Shylock's pound of flesh: she was worked too hard
and she was superior in education to most of the
nursemaids with whom she came in contact, and
inferior in position to any other girl with whom she
might have struck up a friendship. How rigidly
we hem ourselves in with rules and regulations,
he had thought. Here she is, articulate, intelligent,
with more than a smattering of education and yet no
girl of her own age will deign to make her a friend.
Helena, the same age, and not nearly so well-read,
would not even have noticed her. But then, he told
himself brutally, were Helena here, you would not
have noticed her either.

'I will chat to her at tennis parties as she marshalls
her charges,' he had said and then he had found
himself telling her that should she find herself in the
Army and Navy Stores on Wednesday afternoons,
she might also find him there. He would buy her an
ice – an ice as if she were a small child. He would
not take her to tea as if she were a woman.

He had watched her lick the tart lemon ice and
such a feeling of lust had attacked him that he had
been unable to rise from the table. He had sent her
away. He had been, for him, unbelievably rude.

'You are attacking that like a schoolboy, Miss Gallagher. You should really learn to eat ices like a lady if you want to attract a man.'

She had not been a bit dismayed. 'Sure, isn't this the only way to eat ice cream,' she had said, 'but if it's that fat old lady that's just come in you don't want to see me, Major, you only had to say.'

And she had gone from the table before Mrs McWhirter could come bearing down on them to ask what in the name of heaven he thought he was doing.

'An ice,' he would have laughed. 'Is there anything more innocent than an ice and the child needs at least one friend in Calcutta.'

And he could so assuredly have laughed it off.

But how had that meeting led to this? It had been inevitable, like night following day, like the sun rising morning after morning and painting the tips of the Himalayas with pink and lilac and gold.

He pulled her arms from his legs and forced her to her feet. 'I did not mean to hurt you, Niamh. I will help you to find another position or I will help you return to Ireland, whichever you wish. Oh my poor girl, I cannot ask you to understand, but I love my wife. I never meant to dishonour her or you . . .'

She looked up at him again through her tears and as he stood there the Indian sun filtered through the trees and sent a halo of light around his head. Her knight in shining golden armour. Her knight with feet of clay. A red-hot rage surged through her. He had taken her virginity, the only gift a poor girl could give to the man she loved and he had thrown her sacrifice in her face. She would have preferred that he lie to her. He should be saying that he loved her: he should be making plans to get out of the entanglement of a loveless marriage but

'*I love my wife and I have dishonoured her by loving you*'
was what he was saying.

'I'll tell her,' she said and wrenched herself free.
'I'll tell your precious Helena.'

For a moment she glared with her lovely eyes into
his troubled ones and then she turned and raced
away from him down the hill. He started after her,
his hand held out in a supplicating gesture and then
he stopped and watched her slip and slide down the
slope. He made as if to go after her. If she stumbled
she would fall and could hurt herself quite badly,
as badly as he had already hurt her. He had ruined
her young life.

'Oh God, Niamh, I never meant to hurt you,'
he yelled down the slope at the slithering, slid-
ing figure.

He had meant only to be her friend: it had never
occurred to him that he would become her lover.
He was Helena's lover, Helena's husband, the father
of Helena's son. He was a swine. And Niamh,
hurt, betrayed, was going to write to Helena. Was
she right? Did Helena really love him? She wrote
wonderful, loving letters, promising that maybe
next month, maybe when Baby had cut this oh-
so-troublesome tooth . . . when Papa had got over
this latest painful bout of the gout that attacked him
no matter how he restricted his appetites . . .

Dear God, it was over. Niamh, his career, his
marriage, his chance to teach the little chap . . . Oh,
God, what about the little chap?

Archie saw very clearly the only decent and
honourable thing to do.

And he did it.

4

1931 Glasgow

FERELITH GALLAGHER LOVED the old Convent. Sometimes she pretended that she lived there alone, apart that is, from the hordes of servants who were needed to keep one young girl in comfort. Her imagination was so strong that, with no trouble at all, she could dress the simple nuns, who scurried around all day, in the black dresses and white aprons that all the maids wore in the B movies she loved to watch every Saturday afternoon. Whenever she had a free moment she would take her notebook or the novel she was reading down to the ruined castle that stood at the farthest edge of the orphanage property, and she would sit there amid the crumbling and overgrown stones and imagine that she was a princess or a missing heiress, and one day soon a handsome knight on a white horse was going to come riding up the path to rescue her. He would need to come soon or the end of this year of 1931 would see her, like all the other orphaned girls, in domestic service, or, if they were like Ferelith and had a brain, working in a shop as a cashier.

Ferelith's knight in shining armour was an old nun in a black serge dress and a starched white wimple. While her princess mooned away the hours in her ruined castle, Sister Anthony Joseph fought for her future.

'We have never put a girl through university

before, Sister. I shudder to think what the Bishop would say.' That was Reverend Mother.

Sister Anthony Joseph, who had known the Bishop since the days when together they had purloined apples from the trees in their neighbour's garden, wished with a sigh that dear Reverend Mother would remember that Tom might be a bishop but he was also a man and perfectly approachable and reasonable.

'Ferelith Gallagher has an unusually gimp brain, Reverend Mother, and the dear Bishop would not want it wasted.'

Reverend Mother, who addressed the Bishop as 'my Lord Bishop' but knew perfectly well that dear Sister Anthony Joseph called him Tom when they were alone together, asserted her authority.

'That unusually gimp brain, as you put it, Sister, makes her spend most of the time when she should be helping with tasks sitting on a cold stone in that ruin we should knock down, and she will no doubt be troubled with piles in later life. Girls marry, if they do not enter religious life and for that certainly Ferelith has no aptitude. It would be scandalous were we to waste our precious resources on a girl who will no doubt marry as soon as she obtains a degree if not before. Besides she has never once mentioned a desire for further education.'

Sister Anthony decided not to attack with 'surely an educated woman makes a better mother than one who has not had the benefit of education' because she wasn't sure that that made any sense.

'Ferelith has not expressed an ambition, Reverend Mother, because girls are not encouraged to do so and that, surely, is wrong. Mr Smith, her English teacher, says that she could be a teacher. We could send her to Craiglockhart.'

'The Sacred Heart?' Reverend Mother emitted a very faint and superior sniff. 'Educated women.' Alas, even the truly religious have their moments of weakness.

'They turn out educated ladies, Reverend Mother. Ferelith is clever and, although she does not realize it, she is very pretty. She will marry. I have absolutely no doubt about that, but she could also teach nice Catholic boys and girls for a few years before she takes her skills to a marriage. A perfect scenario, I think.'

'I think that I do not know how you managed to persuade me to let her do Highers. We had a conversation not unlike this then and you said how your precious Ferelith could get a better job were she better educated, and be a credit to the orphanage.'

'And I meant it, Reverend Mother, but I did not then know how clever she actually is. What a credit a university degree would be to the work you have done all these years.'

Reverend Mother looked at the elderly nun. She was not a fool and she knew she was being flattered but she was not immune to flattery and besides, she did have the best interests of the children, or at least what she considered to be their best interests, very much at heart. 'I will pray for guidance, Sister. We will both pray.'

Sister Anthony Joseph bowed her head and smiled. The game was now 'deuce' and she could get the advantage – if she could get to Tom. And time was running out for Ferelith. She should be applying to universities and so far she had not even thought of further education.

At that very moment Ferelith Gallagher was sitting in her crumbling fortress which, with no trouble at all, she had turned into the warm, dry stately rooms of Buckingham Palace, and she was promising the King that she would head a coalition government and that she would work with Ramsay MacDonald and Mr Baldwin in the best interests of Britain and the Empire. The King was moved and invited her to tea. That's when Ferelith's imagination failed. Did the King have bread and jam sandwiches for tea as she did or did kings eat more exotic foods? She remembered the picture of their majesties in the last Pathé newsreel she had seen. They certainly ate something, both being exceptionally well padded. Mind you, Sister Anthony was well padded and as far as Ferelith could discover, ate nothing at all.

The coldness of the stone on which she was perched finally got through her heavy skirt and thick knickers and she rubbed at her backside to warm it up and get the blood flowing again. She sighed. To be Prime Minister, surely you needed education and you needed to be a boy. Mr Smith said she could go to university. That would take care of the education bit. But, as Sister Mary Immaculate said every day, 'Pigs might fly and we'd have to shoot bacon.'

'If I was Lady Astor,' Ferelith solemnly told a ladybird that was crawling along the stone she had just vacated, 'I would force them to make me Prime Minister. Why is she content just to be the first female Member of Parliament?' At the word 'just' Ferelith laughed at her own nonsense. Just, just a Member of Parliament. My God, in 1931 that was wonderful. 'And I'll do it too. I'll, I'll . . . I'll go and clean the lavatory before Reverend Mother discovers it isn't done.'

Even her agile imagination balked at turning the cleaning of a lavatory into a romantic scenario. A lavatory was a lavatory and this one was particularly well-used, since there were eighteen girls and

twenty-three boys in the home. The nuns, if they *had*
human attributes (and Ferelith was unsure of this),
used a lavatory in a different part of the sprawling
old house. Since, however, this one was cleaned
at least once a day, cleaning it was really not too
onerous a task.

'How nice to find you on your knees.' The sar-
castic voice of Reverend Mother startled her. 'And
without a book too, or do you have one hidden under
your pinny?'

'No, Reverend Mother,' said Ferelith, jumping to
her feet. 'At least, I have one under my apron but
it's not hidden, just there for safety.'

'A life of a saint, no doubt,' said Reverend Mother
drily. 'I would like to see you in my office. Fifteen
minutes and change your frock. You have cleaned
more of the floor with that one than with your
washcloth.'

Ferelith curtseyed and looked ruefully at the
simple cotton dress she had put on to spare her
school uniform. How had it got wet? A much greater
question, one that set her heart beating fearfully, was
what did Reverend Mother want with her? She could
not be really angry. Had she been angry her rapier
tongue would have been flashing cruelly but she had
been, for Reverend Mother, almost friendly, almost
human. Oh, if only she could see Sister Anthony
Joseph.

Fifteen minutes later, tidy and clean, she stood
outside Reverend Mother's office waiting to be
admitted, and told herself it was the all-permeating
smell of cabbage cooking for the midday dinner that
was making her stomach heave.

'Come.'

She opened the door and the smell of beeswax
coming out fought with the smell of cabbage coming

in. Ferelith loved this room, although she had never yet enjoyed any occasion when she had been in it. Now she tried to take comfort from the heavy, beautifully-polished antique furniture, the shelves of leather-bound books, the delicate painting of an Italian Madonna and child.

'Sit down, Ferelith, and tell me what you would like to do with the rest of your life.'

The bald question startled the girl. She had almost hoped to be taken to task yet again for some contravention of the rules. Only that morning, drawn by the fresh call of the early morning air, she had gone for a walk outside the grounds among the neighbouring fields. Only Sister Glenn had seen her and Ferelith had begged the old nun to keep her secret.

'Don't tell Reverend Mother,' she had said clasping the elderly woman's frail work-worn hands.

Sister Glenn had shrugged her off and turned to her milk churns. 'Reverend Mother? Sure it's God I came to serve.'

No, Sister Glenn had not betrayed her.

'Well, Ferelith. Sister Anthony Joseph says you have some ambition to enter a university?'

'I have? I mean I have.' Until that moment Ferelith had never considered a university education no matter what Mr Smith said. Universities were not for orphans, and certainly not for female ones. 'I love learning, Reverend Mother.'

'For the sake of learning, child, or for the greater glory of God?'

Ca va sans dire, said Ferelith to herself but she dared not say it aloud. It was her favourite French phrase. 'I believe God wants me to make the best use of the brain He has given me, Reverend Mother.'

The nun looked at her sceptically. 'We should make you a lawyer.'

A lawyer. The only lawyer Ferelith had ever read about or heard about was Portia in *The Merchant of Venice* and Shakespeare's heroine had surely only pretended to be a lawyer. But, guessing rightly that Reverend Mother did not really expect an answer, Ferelith said nothing.

'Sister Anthony seems to think that you will not throw away an expensive education on Holy Matrimony, although it is said that if a woman is educated it helps her family. I am also aware that, as far as your future is concerned, I am, one might say, outgunned, since Sister has the ear of the dear Bishop. You are a clever girl, Ferelith, and I will have no objection to helping to finance your education, but I would ask you to consider very carefully what you want to do with the rest of your life. You have no vocation for the religious life. As far as I can see, all you want to do is to sit in that damp old castle and read trashy novels.' She paused to give Ferelith a chance to defend herself but the girl merely blushed furiously and hung her head, and Reverend Mother remembered another young girl a lifetime ago who had lain in the grass on the top of a hill and read what her mother had called trash. It was the spirit of that young girl who now smiled at Ferelith.

'Just don't believe that life is like your books, my dear,' she said with a real and pitying tenderness. 'Now go to the chapel and pray for guidance.'

'Yes, Reverend Mother,' said Ferelith, and fled.

She could not pray. She knelt in the chapel and waited for the peace to wash over her and eventually it did and her stomach stopped heaving and the blood slowed its mad race around her body.

University. What would Mr Smith say and did she want to go and where? She had never been anywhere but this convent. Sometimes she hated it but mostly she loved it and she was well aware of its security. All decisions were taken from her: what to wear, when to eat, when to sleep, when to work, when to pray. Could she go to Glasgow University and come home here to the blessedly familiar every night with her books? Yes, that's what she would do.

She worked it all out and then, with great glee, shared her plans with Sister Anthony Joseph.

'Not a good idea, Ferelith,' said the old nun decisively. 'Far too disturbing for the other children and too restrictive for you. A hostel is what you want, or a university residence, but first we need to get you into a university. What would you like to study?'

And Ferelith had stared at her blankly. 'I don't know,' she had finally admitted.

'Pray for guidance, child, for you must have a compelling reason for the Bishop and for Reverend Mother. Education costs money. Besides, you're a girl, and men will think it's wasted on you.'

Ferelith nodded respectfully at this simple truth but then she thought, no, Mr Smith is a man, and he doesn't think education is wasted on women.

'It's your only way out of the trap of poverty. With a decent education, you can go anywhere, speak to anyone, be anything.'

At school next day Ferelith looked in her favourite teacher's fat unwieldy dictionary.

'Lawyer, member of the legal profession, especially attorney or solicitor.'

Sounds dull, she thought.

'Solicitor. One who solicits (rare); member of the legal profession competent to advise clients and instruct and prepare cases for barristers but not to appear as advocate . . .' I don't like the sound of solicit. I'm never going to ask for anything that a person isn't willing to give me. Besides I'd hate to do all the work and have someone else walk off with the glory.

'Advocate. One who pleads for another. Faculty of Advocates. Scotch Bar. Lord Advocate. Principal law officer of the Crown in Scotland.'

Later she was to tell Sister Anthony that she had enjoyed an experience not unlike that of the blessed Saint Paul on his road to Damascus: she felt rightly that the sister would enjoy the religious parallel.

'It was as if a light went on in my head, Sister, and I knew, suddenly, that I wanted to study law.'

The classroom was empty. She stood up and struck a histrionic pose. 'Well, Reverend Mother, you hit the nail on the head. It is now beautifully crystal clear. I want to be an advocate: I want to plead for others as Sister Anthony Joseph has always pleaded for me. I want to be the top advocate, and I shall fight for the downtrodden, especially women and orphans. Education wasted on me indeed. I shall be hailed as the new Portia in the press but I won't need to pretend to be a man. I shall be beautiful, feminine, and devastating.' She caught a mental picture of her skinny undersized frame and giggled. 'Well, feminine and devastating can't be too bad.'

She argued her first case against Reverend Mother and won. Ferelith Gallagher, orphan, would be allowed to go to university.

'We must try to get you into Glasgow where we can keep an eye on you.'

Ferelith immediately began to pray that Glasgow would not accept her and, at the same time, applied for admittance to the University of Edinburgh. A few anxious months later, she stood with an acceptance in her hand. After the first few moments of euphoria she felt her knees begin to tremble. Why had she not been open and confiding?

Now what do I say to Reverend Mother?

'Why did you apply to Edinburgh, Ferelith?' asked the old voice so gently that Ferelith felt like a criminal. 'Why did you mislead us?' She shook her head as if the weight of disappointment was unbearable.

'I'm sorry, Reverend Mother, but I thought it was time that I became a little independent.'

'And you thought we would not understand?' The gentle voice chided: the calm, sweet unlined face with its straggly white hairs creeping out from the edge of the wimple gazed at her. 'Well, we must see what we can do about Edinburgh. Independence but safety. Ferelith, it is unlikely that you will find anyone like you at the University, not among the girls anyway. You are an orphan. You have spent your entire life in a convent, ordered around by bells. Apart from limited school work, you have never in your life had to think for yourself and now you want to go out into the world and you think you can survive on your own. My dear child, you are a little minnow and the sea is full of sharks. We will find a nice safe bowl in which our own little minnow can swim happily – a hostel, I think, run by a religious order.'

Ferelith left Reverend Mother's study and went to the chapel as she had been bid but she did not pray. She was too angry. A minnow, was she? She wanted out, she wanted to be free, to make mistakes if necessary. What could possibly happen to her that would be so awful?

She had spent her entire life in an institution: she did not want to exchange a Glasgow orphanage for an Edinburgh Catholic hostel. She wanted a

Residence. The fascinating information sheets from the university told her that there were five suitable residences on East Suffolk Road for female students. Each had a common room, a dining room, a library and, holy of holies, separate study bedrooms and all for the (*gulp, gulp*) mere bagatelle of fifty guineas for the session of three terms. In all her life Miss Gallagher had personally handled no more than a shilling. Where was she to find one guinea, let alone fifty?

In October, when she was enjoying her first classes at the University of Edinburgh, she agreed that it was probably just as well that her guardians had decided that she should exchange one convent for another: the shock of finding herself, at seventeen, on her own might have been just too much. At Springhill Gardens she had her own room, an unimagined luxury for someone who had spent every night of her life in a large dormitory with girls of all ages. The room was plain and sparsely furnished but to the young girl it was wonderful. A bed, a small wardrobe that held her spare frock, her coat and her outdoor shoes, a dressing table for her three sets of underwear and her two nightdresses, a chair and a table for her books. There was an electric light hanging from the ceiling and a small lamp on the table. On the bare highly-polished linoleum floor there was a rag rug, but the glory of all glories was the window which looked out over the garden to the street beyond. The hostel was within walking distance of the University and, for economy's sake, Ferelith decided that it was within walking distance of everywhere else in the city she might want to visit. And she resolved to explore everything – castle, parks, museums, old town, new town, everywhere. She walked everywhere and became fitter and stronger as the months passed. She still looked frail but she blessed the fact that from some unknown parent she had inherited an iron constitution. The food at the hostel was plain but substantial and, if her lecture room was full of cold and flu germs, by the time she had walked back home the friendly Edinburgh winds had blown them all away.

The other residents were a pathetic mixture of women who had, for the most part, been badly treated by circumstance. Annie Black had spent almost her entire life, woman and child, in the care of the Sisters. Her mind had been damaged by some early childhood experience and she was only relaxed and at ease when a nun, any nun, in dark dress and starched wimple was within her sight: then she felt safe.

Sister Frances told Ferelith not to speak to Peggy Wilson and, therefore, naturally, if there was any free time at all, Ferelith longed to hear Peggy's stories, of the men she had loved, of the children she had conceived and lost, and even of a king she had met once and who had smiled at her and kissed her hand.

'Don't listen to her blethers, lassie,' screeched old Annie. 'Kissed her hand indeed. Wasn't she in service and didn't she near spill gravy all over the old king and he held the gravy boat and her hand to save his best suit. Kissed her hand, indeed.'

Tears had started in Peggy's eyes and Ferelith had soothed her. 'I'm sure he kissed your hand when he held it, Peggy. Sister Anthony Joseph saw him once and said he was a most gallant old gentleman.'

Dorothy Johnston wanted desperately to enter the religious life and although she appeared to Ferelith to be totally dedicated and even holy, no convent –

for no doubt viable reasons that they did not care to divulge to Miss Gallagher – would take her and so she stayed in the hostel and earned her keep by doing clerical work.

Ferelith looked at them and mourned for them and for the countless others whom life had condemned to live in the shadows. She was living in the shadows a bit herself, getting up in the morning, washing, dressing, running downstairs to eat her breakfast with the other strange residents who, one and all, warned her every morning to look out for the dangers that lurked in the Edinburgh streets waiting to pounce. And then, as she walked along past the castle, she saw only the beautiful skyline of this most lovely of cities and heard only the ghostly murmurings of the long dead. Did they warn her too of danger? No, they welcomed her. She was one of them. She was beginning to love as they had loved and she would fight as they had fought, perhaps with different weapons and for different causes, but always against injustice.

She walked briskly around the ancient city and she dreamed her dreams of yesterday's heroes and vowed to become one of tomorrow's, and perhaps it was the animation in her usually still face that excited and captivated Blair Crawford. He did not reason: he merely accepted that he had met his ideal mate. She was so unlike anyone he had ever known but it was as if he had known her always.

'Hello,' he said. 'Just up?'

'I beg your pardon?' Ferelith thought that he was asking her if she had just got up out of bed. Sister Anthony Joseph had warned her of young men like the one standing gazing down at her so foolishly.

'Up?' he asked again. 'I'm second year. I thought you looked as if you were new: you know, just up.'

Ferelith laughed. 'I thought you were being rude,' she said and he laughed at her consternation. 'The Sisters warned me about boys like you.'

'The Sisters?'

'Nuns. Religious. I was brought up in an orphanage.'

A warning bell tried to ring in his head but he ignored it. 'It must be quite awful not to have parents. My father died in the war but I still have my mother.' As he spoke he thought of his mother who wore only grey or black because she was still in mourning for her husband, his mother who had sent him away when he was seven years old and whom he saw very rarely, his mother whom he adored and wanted desperately to please. He frowned and Ferelith noticed the frown.

'I think it's the not knowing who you are or wondering why no one wanted you that hurts,' she said after much quiet thought.

'And not being loved, surely that hurts?'

Ferelith considered the question and he laughed a little as he saw how seriously she was preparing her answer.

'I have never really felt unloved,' she said at last. 'There are all kinds of love, aren't there?'

Blair remembered his strong tall grandfather: he felt the remembered harshness of his beard as he had hugged the small boy, smelled the oddly lovable smell of horse and leather, tobacco smoke and whisky, and very old tweed.

'My grandfather loved me very much,' he said.

They stood looking at one another, saying nothing.

'Would you like a cup of tea?' he asked, because suddenly he was afraid that if he did not keep her she would fly away like a little bird and he knew that he could not bear never to see her again. And so it began.

* * *

Ferelith Gallagher learned almost as much from Blair Crawford as she learned from her books and her lecturers. She learned without knowing that she was learning because her sheltered upbringing had made her like a sponge and she was ready to soak up everything and anything with which she came into contact. It was good that the first man she met was Blair for, although he was expensively educated and widely travelled, he had a quality of innocence and goodness that matched her own. He knew music, art, and books and he opened the world of the arts up to her and she was eager to learn. His taste became her taste. Beethoven was God, his orchestral music the sublimest and *Fidelio* the greatest opera ever written. They sat through *Fidelio*: she understood not a word and was secretly disappointed that there were no beautiful gowns or luxurious sets, but she wept, she knew not why, at Florestan's magnificent aria, and marvelled at the genius of the mind that could write such glorious music and not be able to hear it.

'We have our own musical genius here at the University,' Blair told her. 'Professor Donald Tovey has the Reid seat of music and he is acknowledged everywhere as one of the greatest musicians and composers of the twentieth century. I really can't understand why his concerts aren't packed like sardine tins. We take him too much for granted, I suppose. Now you shall accompany me on Sundays to the Reid Concerts. Students get in for sixpence, and what a sixpennyworth it is. On Mondays we have the Scottish Orchestra at the Usher Hall. You must join the Musical Society. Can you sing?'

'No.'

He looked at her sceptically. His music teachers had told him that the entire human race was born musical; but then there had been a chap at school whom even Ferelith's church St Cecilia would have found a challenge.

'Too bad but never mind, you can appreciate. It's only two and six a year and members get discount tickets for Reid and Scottish Orchestra Concerts. Do you play golf?'

Ferelith laughed, a laugh that made him think of clean clear water tumbling over the white stones in a Highland burn. He could not believe the effect this young woman was having on him.

'Blair Crawford. Orphans don't play golf: rich young men play golf.'

He blushed furiously and at once she felt sorry for him.

'I'll beat your socks off on the tennis courts though.'

'You're on. We have a marvellous athletic union and some of it has come out of the dark ages: I mean we do concede that women can play hockey, tennis, and golf, even boating. Join the tennis club. I'm afraid it's possibly a bit more expensive than hockey.'

It was, but Reverend Mother agreed that physical activity was very good for young bodies that she fondly imagined would otherwise spend too much time sitting at desks studying.

'You will have seven and six for hockey in the winter and spring, Ferelith, and you'll have twelve and six for tennis. Sister Glenn will make your clothes. Department store prices are scandalous.'

Department store prices did not concern Blair Crawford. Nor did study, as far as Ferelith could see. He asked her to join several other societies and he always had tickets for every dance and social, concert and play.

'When do you study?' she asked him innocently one November afternoon as they struggled against the Edinburgh wind down the Mound to the art galleries.

'Oh, I will. I really learn best if I give it a real go just before the exams, otherwise if I waste time studying now, I've forgotten it by the time I sit down trembling in the examination hall.'

Never in her life had she heard such nonsense, thought Ferelith, and she had not yet learned to guard her tongue. 'You're fooling yourself, Blair. You haven't forgotten it: you just haven't learned it.'

'We all learn differently,' he said rather huffily and immediately she changed the subject. She could not bear to hurt him.

'I'm sorry,' she said, tucking her hand into his arm. 'You're quite right. When you swim in a small pool you tend to think you know everything. I think I'm in for some shocks at university.'

Immediately he smiled again. 'No shocks today,' he said. 'Just some awfully nice pictures and then high tea at Crammond.'

'My parents bought some rather nice French impressionist stuff,' he told her as they wandered Saturday after rainy Saturday around the art galleries, 'but I must confess to an admiration for these fellows called the Glasgow School or the Glasgow Boys. They're not all Scots, they didn't even all live in Glasgow, but every single one of them was a frequent visitor to studios near, well I think but I can't be sure, the area around Sauchiehall Street and St Vincent Street. Shall we take the train through some day and see some of it? They're actually almost completely ignored by the art world, in a sort of limbo. You know "Limbo", good Catholic that you are, the place where you just hang around and wait for delivery. James Guthrie and John Lavery have both been bought by Mummy and I do wish she was brave enough to adopt some of the others because the world will, one day.'

They did go through to Glasgow and she adopted the paintings of E.A. Hornel, Alexander Davidson, and Duncan MacKellar: why steep oneself in the undoubted glories of France or Italy when there were paintings like these? She was, after all, a Scot, or was she? For the first time, faced with Blair and his background of hundreds of years in the same house on the same plot of land, if 12,000 acres could be called a plot, she wondered who she was.

'It doesn't matter,' said Blair, 'even if you have just sprung, as I think you have, from the head of Zeus, you are you, whole and entire, and I . . .' he shrank on such short acquaintance from saying the word that sat on his tongue begging to be allowed to burst forth into glorious birth, 'and I think you're just wonderful.'

She laughed at him, which was not nice, but then no one had ever told her that she was wonderful before. Quite bright, a daydreamer, woolgatherer, too smart for your own good, my girl – these phrases had been hurled at her many times in seventeen years, but wonderful . . . ?

'Blair Crawford, I am a skinny woolgathering girl from a Glasgow orphanage. I have no father, no mother. Did they die or did they just take one look and say, "Oh no"?'

'No, they did not,' he said intensely, 'and it doesn't matter and you are the nicest thing that has ever happened to me.'

He was so intense, so serious. She looked at him. 'Well then, aren't you the nicest thing that has happened to me too?'

But she did not take him to the orphanage where she had grown up: she did not introduce him to Sister Anthony Joseph. Indeed, there was no mention of him at all in her letters home and she made no effort to let anyone know when she was in Glasgow.

There isn't time, she defended herself, to see paintings and to go to the Convent, and anyway, Blair is not a Catholic and he would be amused and possibly unnerved by sister after sister coming to have a look at him.

She did not, of course, spend all her time with Blair Crawford. She had decided to begin her assault on the great Scottish legal system by taking a degree in modern languages. French was to be her first language with Spanish, of which she knew not one word, as her second. As a practising Catholic she felt that her knowledge of church Latin should surely spin over into Spanish which was, after all, an offshoot. She became heady with excitement at the thought of spending her third year abroad at a French-speaking university.

'Time enough to think of being in gay Paree when you have passed a few exams, miss,' said Reverend Mother drily. 'You will find the intellectual level of your peers at the University *un peu* more advanced than that to which you have sadly become accustomed, miss. You have been the pike in the wee pond, Ferelith,' said the old nun, exhibiting once again her preoccupation with fish. 'Now you are about to become the wee guppie in a tank full of big ones.'

There were lectures and tutorials and so much reading: Desgranges, Molière, La Bruyere, Rousseau,

Hugo, La Fontaine's *Fables*, which she had already read both in English and French, Levy, Duruy, Michelet's *Histoire de France*, Brillat-Savarin, and more. She was intoxicated with the whole idea of university education. There were lectures and discussions, dear God, from Professor Sarolea, Mr Moore and Miss Burns who was a *Docteur de L'Université de Paris*, who thought that the opinions and ideas of mere mortals – and Ferelith Gallagher was surely the merest of the mere – mattered. Mattered? They discussed the History of French Literature and the History of French Civilization in its relation to French Literature; there were interpretations of French authors and translations from French into English and vice versa and lectures on philology and grammar.

Ferelith listened and absorbed and wished that she could sound like Blair.

'It's easy,' he said. 'Think French, think of red wine, champagne, croissants and cheese, *et voila*, and for heaven's sake, Ferelith, relax and rrroll your Rs. That's it. That sounds really . . .'

And he could say no more for he had been going to say seductive. What was she doing to him, this skinny little orphan from Glasgow? He could think of nothing but her, so much so that for the first time ever, he failed all his term's exams and had to spend the Christmas vac with a tutor like a schoolboy.

Ferelith, who had passed her first exams as she would pass all her exams – with consummate ease, spent the holidays earning her board and keep at the orphanage where she had been raised. She loved every minute but whenever she could escape to her castle she wrote letters to Blair in first-year French, but she never posted them. Such flowery expressions of love were surely merely exercises in

her new skills and not for a moment to be taken
seriously.

Reverend Mother and Sister Anthony had been
quite pleased with her scholastic achievements and
they were, at least Sister Anthony was, delighted
that she had become a member of the University
hockey team.

'But, what,' they asked, 'did you do for anyone
besides Miss Gallagher in the past three months?
The word "Catholic" has been singularly absent
from all these wonderful tales of the goings-on at the
Students' Union. Are we to suppose, Ferelith, that
you have not bothered to join the Catholic Students'
Union?'

'I go to Mass and the Sacrament every Sunday,
Reverend Mother, and Confession . . . some Saturday nights.'

It was impossible to tell Blair, when he was taking
her to a party or a dance or a concert, that she really
ought to drop in to the Church, and so she had
got into the habit of going to Confession only on
those weekends when Blair was in Fife seeing his
mother.

Now Reverend Mother was looking at her with
that look which had instilled unbelievable guilt into
generations of Glasgow orphans. Sister Anthony's
mild stare was more understanding, but there was
a hint there too of disappointment that her chick
seemed to care more for the transient delights of the
flesh – if holding hands with a young man during a
Beethoven symphony could be so called – than for
the more lasting delights of a living religious faith.
Reverend Mother reached into her cavernous pocket
and withdrew a small, worn leather purse. She took
out a half-crown.

'This is the annual subscription to the Catholic

Students' Union, Ferelith. I believe it's a shilling entrance fee. It's at twenty-four George Square, young lady, and you will be able to hear Mass daily and also to have the joy of meeting His Grace the Archbishop on many Sunday evenings. I am sure that if you look after the spiritual side of your life, everything else will slot into place quite nicely.'

Ferelith had seen photographs of the Archbishop in the Catholic papers several times and was perfectly sure that such a normal-looking human being would understand that at eighteen she would find Blair Crawford infinitely more attractive than an elderly archbishop, but wisely she did not share this confidence with either of the two sisters on the other side of the table. She promised to mend her wicked ways and to at least join the union.

'A step in the right direction,' conceded Reverend Mother to Sister Anthony Joseph, 'but time will tell how much use your precious chick makes of the facilities.'

5

In FEBRUARY BLAIR contracted a very heavy cold and his mother sent a car, comfortably equipped with hot-water bottles and several blankets, to convey her son from cold and windy Edinburgh to cold and windy Fife. He went without a murmur. He did not often fight with his mother because he usually lost the war. On the few occasions when he did win Mrs Crawford was so miserably unhappy that for weeks Blair felt that he was undoubtedly the world's most ungrateful son. This time though, he wanted to crawl home. He was quite ill.

'I'll come back as soon as I get over this,' he sneezed at Ferelith, who, never having been allowed to submit to ill-health at any time in her short life, had little sympathy for him.

His absence, therefore, meant that she found herself with some free time which could have been used in study.

The half-crown that Reverend Mother had given her stared at her from the edge of her table and so, feeling exceedingly virtuous, Ferelith wrapped herself up against the rigours of the elements, and set off for George Square. It was not too long a walk, just along Lauriston Place, past George Heriot's School For Boys, and then the Infirmary, down Meadow Walk and there it was, but so unrelenting was the rain that she was completely soaked by the time she was blown up the steps and in the front door.

'Hey, wait a minute,' said a very angry voice

whose owner had received most of the excess rain-water from Ferelith's coat all over his immaculate blazer.

'I'm sorry,' gasped Ferelith, ineffectively trying to wipe him dry with her wet hands.

'Stop helping me, please,' he gasped and then started to laugh. His laughter was so pleasant that Ferelith had to laugh too. 'I'm so sorry,' she said again, 'but I didn't see you standing there.'

'The story of my life,' he said ruefully and Ferelith pushed her hair out of her eyes and looked at him.

'I can't believe that,' she said.

He blushed. 'People look at me once they see me,' he said, 'but being so short . . .'

He was smaller than Ferelith and could have been no more than five foot five but he was, there was no other word for it, exceptionally beautiful. He reminded her of someone: it was that nose. That was it! Surely he was like the Italian priest who had holidayed at the orphanage one summer. But he was talking.

'Dominic Regent,' he said. 'Since you have just re-baptized me I feel we can dispense with other introductions.'

'Ferelith Gallagher.'

'I've never seen you before,' he said. 'May I show you around? I'm the secretary.'

The union was full of students, steaming clothes, and laughter. Dominic introduced Ferelith to several of the other students, showed her the room where the chaplain celebrated daily Mass, the library, the other facilities.

'Now a nice hot cup of tea,' he said when the tour was over. 'You can have one on the house tonight while you tell me all about yourself.'

He was easy to talk to and very easy indeed to

look at. She was so aware of his physical appearance. No, it was not really Father Coia, although she could almost be sure that he was of Italian extraction. Perhaps he was Greek. Yes, a statue: he must remind her of a statue . . . or did he resemble a holy picture in a book that she had read in the orphanage?

He became self-conscious as Ferelith gazed at him, and stopped talking. 'It's rude to stare,' he said.

It was Ferelith's turn to blush. 'I'm sorry, Dominic. It's just that you remind me of someone or something, an Italian painting, I think.'

'The Regents are proud to be good Glasgow Scots,' he said, and asked her about herself.

Ferelith continued to watch him as she told him the, to her, very dull story of her life and thought rightly that he would not want to know that he reminded her, not of some strong Greek god, but of the beautiful face of a goddess, or even worse, a fairy in one of the illustrated poetry books she had read to the babies during the Christmas holidays. When she had finished her great tale he told her that he was doing a master's degree in English Literature and that he wanted to be a lawyer.

'Snap.'

'You're reading English Lit. and you want to be a lawyer?'

'I'm studying modern languages and I want to be an advocate.'

'An advocate. A real live Portia. Great heavens. Is the world ready for this?'

'It had better be. We are almost one third of the way through the twentieth century and you men want to keep women —'

'Steady, steady,' he interrupted. 'Not *you men*, some men, and some women too, feisty little Ferelith, prefer the status quo.'

'I can't believe that.'

He smiled at her naivety. 'Come with me to the University Settlement . . .' He saw her look of puzzlement. 'You've never heard of it? Tut, tut. It's the University's own charitable foundation. It's in Kirk O' Field College . . . you must have heard of Kirk O' Fields? You know where Mary Queen of Scots – it is supposed or theorized – blew up, or had blown up, or connived at the blowing up of, her husband. Not that one would blame her. The Settlement is run by a wonderful woman called Miss Drysdale, and there you will see sights, Miss Gallagher, that would make that pretty hair of yours curl, if it didn't already do so.'

He proceeded to tell her of the Settlement and the work among the poor and unemployed of Edinburgh that the University tried to do.

'I go one night a week, sometimes a bit of time at the weekend. What do you think I teach, Miss Gallagher, to the disadvantaged, to the so-called dregs of society?'

She looked at him and she saw well-tailored clothes. She listened to him and she heard a cultured voice, not like Blair's but yet educated. She hazarded a guess. 'Literacy skills?'

'I'm teaching a basic cooking class and coaching football.' He saw her smile and said angrily, 'Now which of those do you find amusing, Miss Gallagher?'

Ferelith blushed when she saw how annoyed he was. 'Actually I didn't find either funny. I was wondering what you would say if I enrolled in your cookery class.'

'I can't believe you weren't taught to cook in an orphanage.'

'I didn't have time: I did my share of scrubbing lavatories but, for some reason, probably because I was always swotting, or as Reverend Mother would say hiding in the ruins, reading rubbish, I have never learned to cook.'

'Then you won't be able to help with my classes, but there's much that needs to be done and if you are going to be an advocate you might as well get to know the people you will be representing one day.'

Blair was not pleased to return to Edinburgh and to find Ferelith immersed, as he called it, in dirt and disease, and on first name terms with people whom he would never, in the course of a day, notice. It was not that he was unsympathetic to the poor and disadvantaged, it was just that he preferred to write a cheque in the calm and beauty of his home and to feel vaguely that he was doing good. Hands-on goodness was not something that he had ever encountered and he very much disliked this weedy effeminate-looking fellow who seemed to be becoming so important to Ferelith. He was furiously angry, and could not really understand why, when Ferelith told him that he and Dominic were very much alike.

'He is so like you, Blair. Well educated, well brought up – his father has a huge business in Glasgow – and he's passionately interested in the arts: music, the theatre, painting.'

'I am not passionately interested in anything, except, perhaps, keeping you away from somewhere where you will encounter depravity.'

'The people at the Settlement want to get away from depravity, Blair. They are poor and jobless and some of them drink and beat their wives and their children but they are trying to make things better and I want to help.'

'Because of your precious Dominic?'

'He introduced me to the Settlement.'

'Decent women don't go there.'

Oh Lord, whether he liked it or not, he was going to have to be dragged screaming and yelling into the twentieth century.

'Oh, Blair, what a prejudiced and muddleheaded thing to say. Come for yourself and see these people. I am so ashamed of all my advantages when I see girls the same age and look at their lives.'

Her advantages? He looked at her and again his heart swelled with love. She had had no advantages but she felt rich compared with others. He was ashamed of himself, and to make amends he promised to go with her on her next visit. It was his first visit and his last. He was unnerved at first by the familiarity with which Ferelith and Dominic were greeted. There was no tugging of forelocks here.

'Dominic! Ferelith! Hey weans, look who's here!'

'Dominic, ye gaun tae play fitba wi' us?'

'Ferelith, show us how tae dae wir hair like that?'

Ferelith introduced him to someone called 'Maggie Broon', a thin pasty-faced girl in a too-big blouse and skirt whose probable good looks were marred by the hunger in her face and the ugly bruise under her eye.

'It wis me dad,' she explained to Blair who was looking at her, dismay and horror written all over his handsome young face. She turned to Ferelith and her own gaunt face lit up. 'I'm walkin' oot, Ferelith. I've a lad, Bert Sturrock. He wis that mad when he saw this bruise. I wis near pleased I got it fer maybe he wouldnae hae spoke.'

Nothing in Blair's sheltered life had equipped him to cope at first hand with poverty and despair. He saw this as a weakness in himself and, to give him credit, never again tried to persuade Ferelith to stop going. He could not imagine his mother in such a setting. She was very good at visiting the poor and destitute on their own estate but was quite sure that the poor would do better if they would just, in her words, *get down to it*. Ferelith, and her friend Dominic, of whom he found himself more and more jealous, would not agree.

'Many of them would like to work, Blair,' argued Dominic, 'but there are no jobs and if there is a job, usually they are too untrained or too unskilled. If they are apathetic it is life that has made them apathetic. You're a good Presbyterian. You read your Bible much more than we Catholics do. You should know my favourite quote. *Without vision the people perish*. The Settlement will give them a little vision.'

'I'm quite happy to give them some money.'

'Gratefully received, I'm sure, but education is better.'

'Then they should have stayed at school,' argued Blair hotly. 'That Maggie Broon . . .' he began and was furious when Ferelith and Dominic laughed at him. 'What's so funny?'

'Your toffy tones saying Broon, you idiot,' said Dominic. 'It's "Brown". Don't you ever speak to the peasants on your boundless acres?'

'Where did you find your friend?' asked Dominic of Ferelith later and was so scorched by her blistering answer that it was some time before he mentioned Blair again.

Ferelith too decided to keep the two young men apart as much as possible. She could not understand what her feelings for Dominic were: friendship, yes, respect, most definitely, affection? What was affection? She knew two young men and each time she saw either one she felt good, but seeing Dominic or thinking about Dominic did not make her go hot and cold all over. It was a warm, pleasant feeling. She could not decide whether the feelings she had for Blair were pleasant or disturbing. As the days and weeks and months passed she even began to wonder if the feelings were this strange thing that the latest films called Love.

The first time he kissed her she felt in no doubt. It had to be love. Nothing else could make her heart do these amazing somersaults, could make the blood rush through her veins so strongly that she felt it must burst out through her skin.

'If music be the food of love, play on,' they demanded of Donald Tovey, and he and the Reid Orchestra unwittingly obliged. Ferelith and Blair, like every other couple discovering the delights of young love, knew that they alone were experiencing these emotions, and that no one anywhere had ever loved and felt quite as they did.

Sometimes Ferelith feared that she was too happy. Perhaps it was an inheritance from her Celtic past but she found it so difficult to accept her life and her love. She would sit in the lovely library at Edinburgh University and, instead of studying her books, she would study the head of Blair Crawford as he struggled to assimilate what she found so easy.

Sometimes he would feel her wide blue gaze and he would look up and they would look at one another as if they had just met and a slow smile of recognition would cross Blair's face.

'Hello, friend of my heart,' he would say, and she would blush and look down at her books again for she, in her turn, could not say the things that came so easily to Blair.

She could love him though, with her eyes and her lips, and by the end of Ferelith's first year everyone, including Dominic, knew *Blair and that funny wee girl from the orphanage are a pair. Inseparable, my darlings, like Siamese twins.*

Everyone knew but the two people who mattered most: Sister Anthony Joseph and Blair's widowed mother, Mrs Helena Crawford. Blair had tried to tell his mother: he had tried to bring the two of them together but Ferelith was afraid and Helena Crawford was . . . difficult.

'Nonsense, darling,' she would say when Blair tried tentatively to tell her that he felt he had met the one woman whom he could really love. 'Now do send Penelope a wire to tell her about the Ball.'

And so it went on until in the summer of 1933, Blair Crawford decided that it was time for him to assert himself and to tell his mother that he loved Ferelith Gallagher. The results, of course, of his decision were disastrous, both for him and for Ferelith, his love, his sweetheart – his sister.

Ferelith had run from Gretna Green to the orphanage in Glasgow and had been welcomed, not with scolding for her wickedness in celebrating a clandestine and unblessed marriage, but with loving arms and countless cups of hot sweet tea.

'I suppose part of the fault is ours,' the old nun had told the heartbroken girl, 'but Reverend Mother thought it best at the time not to tell you what we knew.'

Ferelith heard again the bald statements of the dry-as-dust lawyer. 'Well, for God's sake tell me now,' she had begged.

'You came to us when you were only a few months old, Ferelith. You were supposed to go to Ireland

where, we think, there might have been someone
who had known your mother: there might have
been relatives even. We never did trace anyone.
Anyway, because of the outbreak of the Great War,
the sister who was charged with taking you back,
never got to Ireland at all but stayed in Scotland
and you with her. She knew nothing of your history,
only that you were an orphan and might have Irish
relatives. We knew that you were born in a convent
in Bombay. Sister told us that your mother was a
nursemaid to a British officer's family and,' the nun
hung her head to save Ferelith embarrassment, 'she
got into trouble. The father, your father, was already
married, and there's some talk of a suicide . . . we
were never really told.'

She stood up and, on safer ground now, went to
the window. 'Your mother's employers took a very
un-Christlike attitude and threw her out when it was
discovered that you were on the way. Thanks be to
God she was able to take refuge with an English
nanny she had befriended on the ship out.' She
laughed a little. 'They're not all bad, the English.
The nanny got Miss Gallagher into the Convent but
Niamh, your mother, made no real effort to keep
well. She blamed herself, you see, for the soldier's
death. We believe that he shot himself rather than
face up to the consequences of his actions, well,
their actions. It was all hushed up for his wife's
sake, you see. Apparently, Niamh Gallagher kept
saying, "I told him I'd tell but I never would. I
only said it because I was angry and scared." She
died a few hours after you were born: she wanted
to die, Ferelith. I doubt she even saw you or she
would have made an effort, I'm sure she would.'

'I'm sure,' said Ferelith drily. 'Who decided to
send me back to Ireland?'

'The Mother Superior in Bombay. She could hardly send you to the Major's wife and you were white, you see, all white. The other babies were half-castes. She thought there might be a chance of adoption for you, but who had thoughts of adoption during the war? We kept you and we loved you and when we saw you had a brain we decided that there had to be more than domestic service for you.'

Ferelith smiled at her warmly. Well, she knew who had spent hours fighting for her, fighting that she be singled out. 'You mean *you* saw that I had a brain. I wasn't going to throw it all away, Sister. I love Blair, loved him . . .'

She began to cry again and the old nun rocked her in her arms and soothed her.

'You love him. Of course you still love him and it will be a long time before that love changes itself into a more acceptable and manageable form of love, but don't turn it into hate, Ferelith. Blair is a victim too and he is suffering as you are suffering and we must pray that he too recovers.'

Ferelith had not thought of Blair as another victim of the tragedy and thinking about him and his unhappiness helped her recovery. Then too, this was to be her third year, and the third year of an honours course in language meant a continuous year of study abroad.

Dominic was the only other person in whom Ferelith confided her secret.

'Dearie me, as my old nanny would have said. You poor old thing.' He stopped and then began again. 'And Blair, of course. He must be devastated. Dear God what a shocker. I do feel for you both but it's not the end of the world, little one. Actually, if you had to do something as drastic as marrying less than halfway through your education I suppose

this was the year to do it. You must get away from
Edinburgh, from all the memories. There's a chap,
keeper of the register, a Mr Lyford-Pike. He can
give you a card of introduction abroad. You should
go to Paris, or Rouen, or even Marseilles for a year.
The Honorary Academic Consul there, with whom
Mr L-P will put you in touch, will introduce you
to university circles. You'll have a marvellous time
and I shall miss you unbelievably. I've quite got
used to having you around.'

'Perhaps I should have married you, Dominic.'

'I don't think I'm quite cut out for holy matrimony: couldn't bear howling babies. Who knows
though. I certainly like you better than anyone
else I know and I'm quite sure we're not related.
Oh God, what an insensitive thing to say,' he said
as Ferelith dissolved into tears. Awkwardly he put
his arms around her and she sobbed into another of
his immaculate blazers as she had sobbed into Sister
Anthony's serge front.

'I'm sorry, Ferelith,' he said as she grew calmer.
'I just have no idea what to say and so should have
said nothing. Here.' He handed her his freshly-
laundered handkerchief and she blew her nose
soundly.

'It's not lesson one, is it? How to deal with someone who marries her own brother. Oh, Dominic.
It's a bloody awful nightmare and I wish I could
wake up.'

Who was the first person to work out that working hard is a positive antidote to heartbreak? But
Dominic was right in believing that an even better
way to deal with loss is to get as far away from
the memories as possible. So October 1933 found
Ferelith Gallagher, for so unbelievably beautiful a
moment, Ferelith Crawford, living in France and

studying at the Université de Paris. *Paris is a city for lovers*. Trite. Any city, anywhere, is a city for lovers when the lovers are together. But Paris does have a charm and for Ferelith it had its newness, its excitement, its foreignness ... The smells and sounds of Paris were not the smells and sounds of Glasgow or Edinburgh. She wandered the streets of Paris as she had wandered the streets of Scotland's beautiful capital and she found that once more she was able to breathe and to feel and even to smile. She smiled at the unbelievable beauty of the huge tulips the *concierge* put in all her rooms. She even smiled on the morning that she found herself hungry and, for the first time, really tasted the hot sweet chocolate and the freshly-baked croissants that Madame had prepared for *le petit déjeuner*.

Sister Anthony and Dominic were right again, thought Ferelith as she savoured the textures and aromas. I am coming back to life: nothing will be the same. I am not the same but I am alive. I feel, and oh, dear God, I feel so absolutely awful, so full of despair. Bring it out and look at what has happened, Ferelith, and then put it behind you.

She sat on a park bench and watched Paris going past her: people hurrying to work, to school, to the markets, each with his own secrets, his own desires, fears, loves, hates. All her life she had wondered about her parents. Why had they abandoned her? Had her mother wanted her, had she looked forward to the birth of a child with joy or with fear? And her father? Who was this shadowy person who was responsible for her very existence? She had wondered if he had begot her with love. He must have loved her mother: he had to have loved her mother. Too awful, too awful to be the result of some casual encounter, of rape.

Oh, how she had prayed that it had not been
rape.

She had often sat in classrooms, marked out by her
orphanage uniform, and thought of the other boys
and girls, running home to tea with brothers and
sisters, loving, squabbling, sharing secrets, and she
had wished that there was one, even just one person
to whom she belonged. And all the time there had
been Blair. Blair in his privileged, gilded home. Son
of the same father, her brother, her half-brother. In
his body there were the same genes; in his character
there were the same traits. No wonder that when
they had met she had loved him. Was he not part
of herself? Had she loved the husband, the brother,
or herself that she had found in him?

Ferelith Gallagher cried in Paris. She wept for
the young Ferelith and for Blair and for that Irish
nursemaid. I'm Irish. I'm Scottish. I'm Celtic. At
least now I know something. Was she loose, this
Irish mother? Was she blindly in love with an
unprincipled man? He killed himself. Because of
me? Dear blessed God, what a legacy to leave
me, Father dear. And my mother, like Monsieur
Le Dauphin, turned her head to the wall – and
died. No. No. No. I refuse to accept the blame.

She stood up and blew her nose loudly. She wiped
her eyes with a dry corner of her handkerchief and
she began to walk into her future.

'You loved Blair Crawford, Blair Winterton, whatever his name was,' she said to herself. 'You married
him and . . . you slept with him and it was . . .
beautiful but it's crazy, crazy, insane for he was . . .
is . . . your brother, your brother, the son of your
father, Major the Honourable Archie Winterton. You
have other family out there somewhere, Wintertons
all over the place. Don't cry, don't cry but hide here

in Paris and learn to rrroll your Rs and forget about love. Why the hell couldn't you fall in love with Dominic or Dominic with you?'

Because she was still so badly bruised she did not allow love or even friendship to get close to her in Paris. She sat in a class full of students from all over Europe and she was alone, for she shied away from every approach and after a while fellow students gave up on the prickly Scot with the prickly pride and she was left alone and, she told herself, that was how she wanted it. She filled the year with study and research, very occasional letters to Dominic and more frequent letters to Sister Anthony. To her great sorrow she also missed out on the greatest of France's cultural joys for she could afford to do no more than live quietly.

'I'll come back and go to the opera,' she said each time she passed the beautiful opera house. 'I'll come back and I will tour the chateaux of the Loire valley. But this year is for work, this year is for Sister Anthony and Reverend Mother. I owe them so much and I have to repay it for some other girl.'

'You have learned the French language well, Ferelith,' her tutor, Mireille Lefèvre, told her when she was leaving, 'but of France I think you have learned very little. That is a great regret.'

'I have learned what I needed to know, madame,' said Ferelith. 'It would be good to stay longer, to learn more, to travel, explore a little, but for me it is not the right time.'

'But France has healed a wound, *ma petite*, no?'

'Healed? I don't know. Covered it over so that I no longer wince, madame.'

She returned to Edinburgh for her final year. Dominic had graduated and had gone to study law in

Glasgow and she knew that she would miss him, that the Settlement would miss him. At first she was afraid that she might run into Blair. The cold legal communications from his family's lawyers had said nothing of where he was, how he was, what he was doing. She assumed that, if he had stayed at the University, he had graduated. But although, in Paris, he was constantly in her thoughts, she never mentioned him in her letters to Dominic who, in turn, had written only of his work at the Settlement and of his studies, nothing at all of his personal life, and he had asked no questions about hers.

From Paris she had submitted satisfactory reports on the work covered and had attended lectures on French history. That gave her a head start for her final course in French history. She had sent too a draft of her thesis for the approval of the professor and now she had two full terms to deliver it in its final form. She had decided to study four stages in the development of French medieval prose and was reading Villehardouin, Joinville, Froissart, and Commines, and wished heartily that she did not have to read the old French text, *Chanson de Roland*, as another obligatory part of the final year. France and the French were too romantic.

She kept to her strict regime and the Ferelith Gallagher who graduated in the summer of 1935 was a very changed girl from the naive trusting student who had entered the hallowed halls with such expectation and excitement four years before.

'You're twenty-one now, my child,' reminded Reverend Mother, who had greatly surprised her by turning up to the graduation ceremony with several other sisters including Sister Anthony Joseph, 'and the time has definitely come to sever some of the ties. We will continue to pay for your education until you have received your law degree but this Convent is no longer your home.' She saw the stunned look on Ferelith's face and smiled. 'That's what you wanted, my dear, remember. We are becoming a habit, if you will excuse the unpardonable pun, and it is not a good one. You are on your own, Ferelith. We will watch and we will pray and we will never turn you away from our doors but you must fly the nest, to use an overworked poetic phrase.'

'I don't quite know what to do, to say.'

'Go away again. Take a summer job. Sister Anthony has been writing letters for weeks. Go and see what she has contrived, and good luck and more importantly, God be with you.'

Ferelith fled to Sister Anthony. 'I've been thrown out. I have wanted to be out from under for ever and now that it's come, I'm terrified. Where will I live? I mean how does one go about finding somewhere to live? I can't stay in hostels all my life.'

'Well, you haven't lost your taste for melodrama. You are not being thrown out as you put it: you are being set —'

'Adrift without a paddle,' Ferelith interrupted.

'On your own two feet,' Sister Anthony finished her own sentence. 'I think it is more than time that you left the umbrella of the Church. Next session you must go into a residence and Ferelith, you must put the episode of your marriage behind you. There are other nice men . . .' She saw the mulish look on the young woman's face. 'Ferelith, there are other nice men out there,' she said again. 'You have no friends at all, girls or boys . . . well, except this Dominic. You must allow yourself to open like a flower.'

'No more, Sister. I will never marry: I will devote my whole life to my career,' said Ferelith grandly.

'Oh my, how dreadfully dull. Perhaps you will never marry but don't let it be because you hid away from the chance. Let someone else into your heart, Ferelith. Joy is all the greater when there has been some pain before, believe me.'

Ferelith looked at the nun. The old face smiled with serenity and inner peace. I wish I was like that, she thought, so accepting, not wanting to fight all the time. 'Very well, Sister. How do you want me to start?'

'Join something else: the choir,' she said, then laughed. 'Well, maybe not. Or the debating society. That would be good experience for an advocate. Don't sit alone or always with the lost souls. As an advocate you will deal with lost souls all the time. I should imagine one might go crazy if there was nothing around but human misery.'

'I'll try something but right now I have to do something with the summer. Reverend Mother hasn't even let me unpack.'

'How about a job where you will have to meet lots of different people, some nice some nasty?'

Ferelith sighed. 'You don't give up easily, do you?'

'No,' said Sister Anthony. 'I never give up – ever.'

And so the summer of 1935 found Miss Ferelith Gallagher, M.A. working in a hotel in Rome. There were advantages, she had to admit, in having been brought up by Roman Catholic nuns. Sister Anthony Joseph had a friend at the mother house in Rome, Sister Aquinus, who had a friend who knew someone, who owned a really nice guesthouse and who would be delighted to have cheap, for the entire summer, a law student who spoke good English, satisfactory Spanish, excellent French and who was prepared to learn Italian. Needless to say, the said student was also supposed to work very hard at everything from cleaning rooms to waiting tables.

In Rome she found to her surprise that she was not miserable. The *pensione*, which was within sight of St Peter's, had been a private house, then a convent and then a private house again. The family who owned it had lost their money in the Great War, but not their pride and self-respect, and they had decided to turn their beautiful home into a hotel. All surviving family members who were fit to work did so. The furniture in the rooms was the remaining treasure of a once rich dynasty: the china, glassware, linens, silver were all beautiful and valuable. Guests who had never been accustomed to such treasures in their own homes wrote glowing reports to their friends.

There isn't much furniture but what there is, is magnificent. The bathtubs are medieval but the water is hot and the food, served on translucent porcelain plates, is superb. You must see it before they realize how crazy they are.

And their friends came and they told their friends, and Ferelith worked almost until she dropped. By the end of the summer she found that she had learned passable Italian, she had absorbed an incredible amount of knowledge of Italian painting and music, and she had been adopted by an eccentric group of Italian aristocrats. Pietro Angelosanti, the younger son of the house, did not, however, want her for a sister but for a lover and that was a complication she would have been happy to do without.

'Why are you so cold, Ferelith?' he asked her.

Ferelith looked at him and felt separated from him

by light years. One day he wanted to be a priest; the
next day he was going to audition for the Teatro San
Carlo in Naples where his godfather, a Cardinal, was
a friend of the Director of Music; the next he – like
most Italian boys (and that, thought Ferelith, was
all he was, a boy) – wanted to play football.

They stood together in the central courtyard of
his family home. If she looked up through the
intertwining branches of the huge grapevines she
could see the top of St Peter's Basilica and above that
the stars twinkling in a sky that looked fashioned
from a luscious deep-blue velvet. She looked at him
and he was good to look at. He was much shorter
than Blair and not much taller than Ferelith herself
but he had the muscled body of an athlete and the
classic Roman profile that would look very good on
the stage. She felt nothing and she sighed.

'I'm not cold, Pietro. I'm merely a hundred years
older than you.'

He looked at her, a puzzled expression on his
handsome face. 'You are a little older, yes.'

'I have been married . . .' she began.

He started back from her. 'You have a husband?'

She shook her head. 'I had a husband, Pietro.'
She hesitated. How much should she tell him? How
much did he have the right to know? 'I was married
but . . . there was a problem, and the marriage had
to be annulled. But you have to understand that I
loved my husband. I still love him and I can't just
jump from one relationship to another.'

He smiled at her. 'I am a Roman, Ferelith and
therefore have all the time in the world to wait.
You will let me keep in touch? You are part of our
family now, yes? You will come back to see us, to
help maybe?'

'I promise to come back if you make your debut

at the Teatro San Carlo. I promise to come back
when you are ordained, if you are ordained. I do
not promise to come back when you start playing
football.'

'It is gone,' he said. 'No more football. I will
come to Scotland to the University. You will learn
to love me.'

Ferelith sighed. A lovesick Italian nobleman she
did not need or want. 'Please, Pietro. I have years of
university ahead of me. I don't just want to become
a lawyer. My sights are set much higher. I intend to
read for the Bar: I'm going to be a barrister and try
cases, usually a male prerogative, and I may even
become a judge. Who knows? Maybe I'll be the first
ever female Lord Advocate.'

He laughed at this obvious nonsense. A woman,
and a pretty woman at that, wasting her time in
a man's world when she could do so well in her
own. 'Why do you want to be a lawyer? It is so
unfeminine.'

Ferelith laughed. 'And you are so typically male
and typically Latin.'

Pietro flushed but said nothing. He walked away
from her across the courtyard and then turned and
smiled. 'There is nothing wrong in believing that a
woman is best suited to gracing the house of the
man who loves her. It is God's perfect plan and
we should not throw defiance in the face of the
Almighty, but I do not want to fight with you,
Ferelith. I want to know what draws you to this
so masculine profession.'

She decided to ignore his last adjective.

'I need a career that will use the talents God has
given me. I also want to help other people, especially
. . . well, frankly, I want to help poor people, people
who have had it hard. Then, I find that I have

an extremely good memory, I think clearly and logically and I have a very analytical mind. My teachers tell me I'm good at sifting through masses of information to find the small nuggets in it that are important: I don't get sidetracked by poetic prose or misplaced sentiment. My thinking is precise and, I believe, accurate, and I have the ability to absorb and understand all kinds of information. I hope I'm good at interviewing others, so I should turn this question and answer session on to you, Pietro.'

He looked at her sadly. 'You make yourself sound like a machine and you are not. You are warm and lovely and soft and oh, so desirable. These are God-given talents too. You are throwing away your chances of fulfilment as a woman, Ferelith, for a dream of a cold, lonely office. This dream takes years and what is there at the end when you become this Lord Advocate?'

'Fulfilment as a human being.'

'A barren woman. A barren life, and you must feel the same way yourself or you would not have already married. Or is it that you wish to punish men now that your first dream is over?'

Ferelith tried not to be offended. She looked up at the sky and again she saw the beauty of this eternal city and she smelled the good smells of grapes hanging heavy just above her head. 'He was part of the dream, Pietro, and through no fault of his own, his dream too is shattered.' She turned away from him and walked across the courtyard to the door from where lights and soft music and the mingled smells of wine and garlic and sun-dried tomatoes were creeping through the still night air. At the door she turned again. 'I wanted it all, Pietro, and I will let nothing and no one stand in the way of my chance of getting the part that's left.'

When the door had closed behind her he took out his silver cigarette case and looked sadly at the engraving of his family crest. Then he took out a cigarette and rapped it smartly on the head of the little dragon. 'And what of me, my Lady Advocate?' He lit the cigarette and inhaled deeply and blew the smoke up into the grapes hanging above his head. Never had he been more thankful that he had been born an Italian. It was easy to decide that his best course of action was to pray – for both of them.

6

ON THE TRAIN back across Europe to the Channel ports, Ferelith mused on the fact that a woman's road to worldly success seemed to be like a hurdle race. She, Ferelith Gallagher, wanted to be Lord Advocate. Was this a totally unrealistic aim? She pushed that unworthy thought deep down inside. But still she had to deal with the realities: she was penniless and had no family to support her. To do well in law did one need both family and financial support? As yet she knew little of the august body she hoped to join but the members of it she had seen did seem to be rather special people, all of whom spoke with the same voice and had been to the same schools. Once, and only for a few moments, she had allowed herself to wonder what would have happened had she become pregnant on that one beautiful night; and after she had found from books that the dangers to the baby's mental and physical health were negligible she had, for one second, allowed herself to daydream, and then she had pushed the thought away and had never let it return. There was to be a clean break. She would never see Blair or think of him ever again.

She would keep instead the shadowy figure of a female Lord Advocate before her as something at which to aim. The first hurdle was to get into law school. In 1935, the year in which one Stanley Baldwin formed a National Government, Edinburgh University Law School admitted twenty-seven female students: Ferelith Gallagher was one of them. She stopped humming last year's popular song, 'Blue Moon', and sang either 'Just One of Those Things', or 'I Got Plenty of Nothin' which seemed to sum it all up.

She had enough money saved from her time in Italy to buy her books, which included the *Introduction to the Law of Scotland* by Gloag and Henderson which she carried around for days as if it was as precious as her Bible. This was not because at £2 and two shillings it was the most expensive book she had ever had to buy but because she felt that, like the Bible, the answers to so many questions would be inside if she could but ferret them out. She went from Green and Son, carrying her brown-paper parcel of books, to Patrick Thomson's on the Bridges where she bought a very smart, grey suit and a white blouse which told the world that she was a practising lawyer's clerk, and with her last five and six a knit-wool muffler in the University colours which, thrown nonchalantly around her neck, perfectly completed this grown-up ensemble. Nothing she was now wearing had been stitched by the patient hands of Sister Glenn and, perversely, as soon as she had discarded her home-made cotton knickers she missed them and retrieved them from her wastebasket. Washed and folded up, they were put at the bottom of a drawer against one of Sister Glenn's proverbial rainy days.

The law degree was a part-time course. Ferelith, like all the other prospective law students, had had to find a solicitor who was willing to hire her on a part-time basis and who would teach her the day-to-day running of a legal practice in the hours around her class times. Her professors gave her a good reference and she was hired by an old friend of Docteur Burns, Graham Lord. The work was not well paid but it was certainly not onerous. Mr Lord wondered gently how a knowledge of three European languages would help a solicitor in a firm that dealt mainly with conveyancing and mercantile law. Even so, he promised to instruct her in all parts of the business and profession of procurators of Court and conveyancers in order that she might learn the same – *so far as he knew himself and the said apprentice shall be capable of learning* – but he clearly felt that women were tender flowers to be protected from all the nastiness of life and he found it difficult actually to ask Ferelith to do anything. He even made his junior partner, his great nephew, James, make the morning tea. Ferelith was allowed to keep the stamps which meant that she bought stamps every few months at the Post Office, stamped all Mr Lord's letters and made neat notes of how many stamps she used each day. Little by little, however, she managed to persuade him to allow her at least to read his mail and to do research for him and, since she was not tall and had learned to remain very quiet, he eventually forgot that she was there at all and she was able finally to watch a very conscientious solicitor at work.

Sometimes visiting clients assumed that she was Mr Lord's secretary and made remarks like, 'Mak sure the lassie taks a' this doon, Maister Lord,' and she smiled at them sweetly and did exactly what they wanted.

She heard from Pietro, who wrote her an almost hysterical letter reminding her that Adolph Hitler had polluted the air of glorious Venice by meeting Benito Mussolini there.

Now he has invaded Abyssinia. Did he discuss this action in the shadow of the Frari, whose

austere Franciscan interior houses some of Titian's
major works? Did they talk casually about the
Nuremberg laws against the Jews in the church
of San Giovanni where the immortal Vivaldi
was baptized? Why did the very buildings not
disappear for ever under the Lagoon in protest?
But why should simple stone and paint cry out
against injustice when man does not? I have been
accepted at the Conservatory. Shall I learn to sing
of the glory of God or man?

All her classes, apart from forensic medicine which
she had to take with real medical students, were
in the Old College, and her first class was at 9
a.m. on Wednesday the 16th of October 1935. The
lecturer was Professor Annan and the subject was
accounting. The second day was more interesting.
Professor James Mackintosh introduced his students
to civil law. He promised them practising lawyers as
guest lecturers and the first one was an ancient – to
Ferelith – lawyer called Angus Webster.

'He'll be Lord Advocate one of these days,' other
students said or, 'Wait for it. He's already a K.C.'

'King's Council,' agreed the first student. 'He's
got everything: a fantastic record, a great brain,
impeccable antecedents and bags of money.'

'That's awful,' said Ferelith. 'You mean he's buying his advancement?'

'No, not really, but if you are going to be a judge,
with all that it entails, it doesn't hurt to know the
right people and to have some money. Face it,
Ferelith, law is a closed shop. Every judge just
happens to have a daddy who was a judge, or a
godfather, or his wife's great-uncle.'

Ferelith watched and listened to her first guest
lecturer and wanted to dislike him because he

was one of the men like Blair who seemed to get everything they wanted because of who they were. But she could not. Angus Webster, forty if he was a day, was . . . nice. He was tall, and would be even taller if he stood up straight. He seemed to be one of those gentlemen who had so often bent over to deal with the problems of someone smaller that he had developed a stoop. He was grey and that was to be expected at his age but he was thin, too thin. She wondered if he ate properly and thought of what Sister Glenn at the Convent would have done about fattening him up. His voice, although definitely Scottish public school, was, she had to admit, charming, not at all dry and colourless, and what he had to say, at this first lecture and every other time she heard him, was fascinating.

'You want to leave this university with a degree, Bachelor of Laws – plural, laws, civil and common,' he began. 'You want . . . *Baccalaureus utriusque juris* . . .' Several students began to look rather uncomfortable and he smiled at their consternation – a lecture in Latin, oh, please, no! That's when Ferelith decided that she liked him – and he went back to the King's English, 'Bachelor of both laws. LL.B. As you all *know*' – did he say this with sarcasm or humour? Humour, Ferelith decided – 'it is the Latin convention when abbreviating plural words to repeat the initial letter. We will begin with Civil Law, the laws governing private rights, those rights which belong to every man, woman, and child, whether they be rich or poor.'

I like it, thought Ferelith. He's saying the right words, every woman, every child, poor.

'Since fourteen hundred and twenty-four, gentlemen – sorry, ladies and gentlemen, I will not make that mistake again – five hundred and ten years, think of it, there has been a law in this country of ours that allows free legal aid to the poor among us. Perhaps one or two of you may go on to become advocates' – did he look directly at Ferelith? She thought he did – 'and you will become directly involved with that elderly but still powerful law.'

Ferelith scribbled and scribbled and then, when she realized that her writing was becoming so untidy that she could no longer read it, she sat back and tried to really listen and to absorb. 'I'll read it up later. I'll go over my notes later. Oh, dear God, I am in the right place. At last, at last, I am in the right place.'

It was not all work. She had moved out of the hostel in Springhill Gardens and had taken a room in a student hostel. Again it would have been perfectly simple to keep herself away from everyone and just to work but she was beginning to find that she no longer wanted to be isolated from human contact. Pietro had helped her more than either of them realized. She was still deeply in love with Blair and it was no use to tell herself over and over that he was her brother and that her feelings for him were wrong, even sinful. But she had to admit that she had been stirred ever so slightly by Pietro's admiration. No matter what she said to herself, she was a young woman and she wanted the company, the conversation, the fun of being with other young people.

She decided to continue to attend the Reid Concerts, although the first one clashed with the showing of *The Brothers Karamazov* at the Caley picture house, but she went to the concert, not really for the music but because at a concert one could speak to other concert-goers. She was unlikely to speak to anyone at the pictures.

In 1935 the famous Dr Albert Schweitzer came to the faculty of the University of Edinburgh and even though the title of his first lecture – Problems of Natural Theology and Natural Ethics – did not sound too terribly exciting she decided correctly that everyone who could possibly get into Rainy Hall would be there, and she joined them.

Simon Osborne, also a law student, saw her there but lost her in the press of students and faculty who had come to hear and see the great man. To his delight he saw her again at his next class.

'Well hello, sweetness.' What an odd way to greet a perfect stranger. Sweetness. She smiled: she liked it. 'Come sit beside me,' he continued, 'and tell me why you always look like a startled rabbit.'

Ferelith looked in some surprise at the only other student in the lecture hall. This was going too far. 'I beg your pardon,' she said frostily.

He jumped to his feet and came over to her and she saw that he was about her age and, although by no stretch of the imagination could he be called pretty, he reminded her immediately of Dominic. They were about the same height. This man was slightly taller and broader but there was something about the eyes, the set of the head.

'You have been well brought up,' he said. 'I can tell, and your mother told you never to speak to strange men and I, my love, am very strange. Allow me to introduce myself. My name is Simon Osborne. How do you do? There, we have been formally introduced and now you have to tell me who you are.'

'Ferelith Gallagher,' said Ferelith, holding out her hand.

'Ferelith. But what a totally adorable name. Perfect. I have never heard it before and I'm so pleased because it's obviously a name for a goddess who . . .'

'Looks like a startled rabbit.'

'I was going to say looks like a wood sprite.'

'Really, you can't have it both ways. I can't look like a rabbit and a sprite at the same time.'

He laughed. 'You are going to become a lady advocate, aren't you, I can tell. I shall tell my father to expect you. He is not ready for you but then the poor darling wasn't ready for me either and he coped. Amazing how some class of Scot always manages to cope, isn't it?'

'Do you always talk like this?'

'Only when I am fearfully nervous.'

'There's no need to be nervous around me.'

He looked at her and understood that that was so. He smiled. 'Ferelith Gallagher, I shall adore you for ever. Come and sit beside me and protect me from all the hulking rugby players in this class.'

'Why do you need protecting?'

He looked at her measuringly. 'What an innocent we are. Never mind, sweetness. We shall help one another. Come and tell me where you have been all my life and then after this terribly boring lecture – I can say that because my own dear daddy is the lecturer – I shall take you away for lunch.'

'You are a very strange young man.'

'And you are repeating yourself.'

Ferelith sat beside him during the lecture, which was an introduction to conveyancing, and was surprised to see that he took not one note. She scribbled furiously. Her practice was to make notes as clearly as she could and then to write them up more fully when she got to the library. Only when she was sure that she had a textbook that covered the lecture almost verbatim did she allow herself to relax and just listen and even then she made heading notes. She said nothing however but allowed herself, at the end of the lecture, to be led from the benches.

'Come and meet my pa and then we'll have lunch.'

She hung back, not quite sure if she wanted to be introduced to a lecturer, but Simon propelled her forward and she found herself shaking hands with the lecturer. George Osborne did not look in the least like his son and was also much more reserved. He was very kind though and wished them both luck with their law degrees and invited them to join him for lunch.

'Sorry Dad, Ferelith and I are having lunch together.'

His father smiled. 'That's wonderful, Simon. I do hope I meet you again soon, Miss Gallagher.'

'What a nice man,' she said to Simon later as they walked along George IV Bridge. 'I thought you said he didn't approve of women lawyers.'

'He doesn't but then he has never met a lady lawyer or at least never allowed one near him. Frightfully prejudiced, my pa. But I could see that he most certainly approved of you. Come on, I shall buy you a steak.'

'A steak. You're out of your mind.'

'Don't you like steak?'

Ferelith tried to cast her mind back to a time when she had actually eaten steak. Rome, oh yes, she had eaten steak in Rome.

'Of course I like steak.'

'Then stop complaining. We'll munch away and you can tell me what you thought of the great Schweitzer.'

She turned to him animatedly. 'Oh, were you there? I couldn't believe I was actually in the same room.'

'I feel the same way about being at a concert when Barbirolli conducts but then perhaps that's really because I'm terrified that he's going to be carried away by his enthusiasm and fall off his podium into my waiting arms. What would one do with him?'

'He does beat the air a bit, doesn't he?'

'Philistine.'

Ferelith spent a lot of time with Simon that term. He was as well read and as interested in the arts as Blair but, unlike Blair, he was also very serious about his studies. After their first few meetings he dropped what she called his very jolly pose and was calm and natural. She liked the calm Simon better than the one she felt wore a defensive shell, and became very much at ease with him. She liked especially that, like Dominic, he made no move to touch her: it was like having a friend who just happened to be male, like having, she hated to say it, a brother. This should have been her relationship with Blair. She began to find that it did not hurt so much to think of Blair, to wonder where he was and what had happened to him. She even began to hope that he had met someone else, one of the *correct* young women his mother had picked out for him, and that he had married. She did not mention him to Simon, not that first year or the second.

She enjoyed the freedom of her relationship with Simon, a relationship she could not quite fathom but which she deliberately decided not to try to understand. She spent as much time with him as she had with Dominic and almost as much time as she had with Blair, but her heart did not race as it had when she had been with Blair, she did not find herself yearning for his touch, his kiss. But she was just a little annoyed that he seemed to feel exactly the same about her. She wondered why he never made any effort to touch her. He helped her on with her coat: he pulled her on to moving trams, but his hands never lingered and his eyes never caressed.

'He's like me,' she told herself. 'He works too hard to want to complicate life with love.'

At least once a term she attended a lecture given by Angus Webster and she thought that he definitely was the ideal lawyer. She was, she decided, going to be just like him, knowledgeable, caring and compassionate. He had also a droll sense of humour and sometimes she had the feeling that he was speaking just to her for she understood his humour and would laugh before, as the children in the orphanage had said years before, 'the penny drapped', or realization dawned on her peers.

In her third year, having saved almost every penny she had earned, she left the university residence and moved into a tiny flat in Newington. It was hardly big enough for her and contained a poky living room with a fold-down bed and a table that doubled as a desk, or really a desk that doubled as a table since she spent far more time studying than eating. There was also a pocket-sized kitchen and a lavatory. Ferelith, scrubbing herself nightly in the kitchen sink with water hot from a kettle, thought she was in paradise. For the first time in her life she had a home of her own and she could entertain. She invited Simon to supper and he came bringing flowers, a bottle of wine, and a gilt-framed oil painting.

'Simon, I can't accept that.'

'Don't be silly, sweetness. It's a house-warming present.'

'This isn't a house. It's a minuscule flat.'

'What a good advocate we are practising to be.'

'Don't be facetious.'

'Ferelith my love, you must learn to accept nicely. Giving is easy especially when you have it to give but to accept is an art. I hope this little picture will be the first of many gifts that I will have the pleasure of giving you.'

She turned away from him, troubled. He was her friend. Was he now going to want more than friendship? The painting was obviously valuable.

'I love the flowers, Simon, and we'll share the wine. I've made spaghetti the way I learned to make it in Rome. It's very simple.'

'It's very pungent: the whole of Newington is sharing it with us by default. Now you open the wine and tell me where to hang your present.'

'Simon, please, I can't. It's too much. You must see that.'

He ignored her and went into the kitchenette and began to look through the drawers.

'Well, I shall have to use the heel of my shoe as a hammer. I brought my own nail. On that wall, I think, above the table, and then you will be able to see it all the time. You do like it, don't you? I should hate to think that you loathed it. Pour the wine, sweetness, and Uncle Simon will tell you something about life that your Sister Anthony never told you.'

She did as she was bid and stood watching him take as much time and trouble over hanging the little painting as he did over everything else. He was such an intense person under that silly veneer he affected.

'There.' He stepped off the chair and stood back to admire the effect. 'Entrancing. Brings this . . . charming little nest to life, don't you think?'

'If it was mine, Simon, I should never tire of looking at it.'

'What a perfectly lovely thing to say. Come, some wine. I need some courage for the next part. It's not usually something I have to explain.'

She poured the wine and he moved the room's only other chair around so that they were both looking at the painting.

'Ferelith, you do like me, don't you?'

'Of course, Simon, but . . .'

'I like you too, but that's as far as it goes. No, that's a lie. I think I love you . . .' he felt her tense beside him and laughed, '. . . as much as I can love any woman, sweetness.'

The words sat in the air beside them and Ferelith absorbed them and then coloured furiously. 'Oh, how stupid. It never occurred . . .' She stopped talking, unable to cope with his revelation.

'I hope it's not going to make any difference to us except that I'm a *wee thing* worried about your lack of interest in the male body and yet you're not like me.'

She looked at him. 'No, no I'm not.'

'I cold-bloodedly decided to use you, you know, Ferelith, as a buffer. I used to be beaten up quite regularly by *real* men. Spare me from real men who have to beat the hell out of everything they don't understand or that frightens them. I'm not a threat to anyone. Do and let do, is my motto, but when I saw you at that lecture I recognized you as an answer to a prayer, a prayer for peace. Who hurt you, sweetness? Why are you avoiding any kind of emotion? Why aren't you falling in love with a good, kind, solid man and leaving the pursuit of the law to chase small children all over the place?'

'I did fall in love,' she said simply and told him the whole story.

'Poor you,' he said when she had finished. 'Poor

Blair. Now can you warm up that congealed garlic or shall I run out for fish suppers?'

And that was the only time for several years that they talked about Blair but it was the first of many discussions they had about Ferelith's love life.

'You should meet other people, make other friends, male and female.'

'So should you.'

'Ferelith, I'm not you. I'm not even really sure who I am. Night after night I tell myself that I would be supremely happy if I could love you, I mean really love you, or if I could feel that kind of love for anyone, even for another man. I'm so frightened sometimes. Perhaps I should have been born three hundred years ago.'

'Why on earth would that make a difference?'

'I wouldn't be out of place as someone who worships beauty.'

Again she was reminded of Dominic. Was he like Simon?

'Surely a lover of beauty isn't out of place in this society especially with what is happening in Europe. You do have a strong social conscience too.'

'Perhaps that's my problem.'

'Oh Simon, don't ever regret caring about people.'

There was so much caring to do in the next few years. Pietro wrote despairing letters from Italy about the worsening situation in Europe.

Doesn't the rest of the civilized world see what is happening here, the Jews who disappear overnight, the old men beaten up in the streets? This German is a mad creature and he will not be satisfied until Europe drowns under a sea of blood. I study Cavaradossi and Florestan and I say Verdi and Beethoven have been dead for

many years but the social injustice and political
intrigue of which they wrote is even more alive
in Europe than it ever was.

Ferelith spent three years studying for her law
degree. She had classes at 9 a.m. almost every
day of the week including Saturday, lectures at
2 p.m., at 4 p.m. and at 5 p.m. She learned about
the ownership of inheritable property and about
obligations and contracts. She studied palaeography
so that one day, if necessary, she could help clients
decipher the Scots of ancient documents. Words
like competency, burden of proof, evidence and
procedure, conveyancing, became a natural part of
her vocabulary. At Professor Sydney Smith's classes
in forensic medicine she learned a great deal that she
would rather, at first, not have known, and she made
another of her lifelong friends, this time a woman.

Elspeth Baxter was a medical student and held
Ferelith's head for her as she vomited up the contents of her stomach after a particularly graphic
lecture on death from violence which included the
examination of blood and seminal stains.

'I hate to tell you that the professor was sparing
your maidenly blushes a bit,' Elspeth said matter-
of-factly as she handed over her handkerchief which
she had thoughtfully dipped in cold water.

'I didn't mind "Death in its Medico-legal Relations" or even "Lunacy Certificates", "Toxicology".
In fact, they were extremely interesting lectures but
this . . . and those pictures.'

'Not a patch on the real thing, my dear,' said
Elspeth as she carefully held Ferelith's hair away
from the rim of the toilet bowl. 'Why are you taking
this class?'

'I want to be an advocate.'

'Then, face up to it. Try to think of the poor person who was on the receiving end of the violence. Our job, yours and mine, is to at least try to make it better for them, or to at the very least get them some justice. I would imagine advocates only ever get to see the pictures, if that's any consolation. It's the poor police on the beat and the doctor who get the glorious technicolour. My name's Elspeth, by the way, Elspeth Baxter.'

'Ferelith Gallagher.'

'Come on, a walk through the meadows to the Union and a nice hot cup of sweet tea – doctor's orders.'

Ferelith stood up rather shakily. 'I'm sorry about this. It's years since I vomited. I do seem to do it rather suddenly and well.'

'I rather enjoyed it, especially the doctor's orders bit. I've never actually said that to anyone before.'

They laughed together and went out into the courtyard and Elspeth, a naturally gregarious and affectionate person, put her arm into Ferelith's as they fought together against the wind. It was a completely new experience for Ferelith to have a female friend. She had never had a close friend at school in Glasgow mainly because her institution-alized home life had made after-school friendships difficult. Blair, Simon, Pietro, and Dominic, were all men and she was fond of each of them in a different way, but having a woman as a friend was a completely different and special relationship. From Elspeth she learned to laugh. She met her for coffee as often as possible that term and, to her great joy, was invited home with her for Christmas. It was a revelation to find herself, for the first time, in a large happy family circle.

'It's true, Elspeth,' she said as they took the train

back to Edinburgh in the middle of January. 'You
really don't know you're missing something until
you find it.'

'Feel free to borrow any one of our lot at any
time. That's one negative side of being part of a
large family, even a very loving and happy one –
there is absolutely no privacy. The first time I was
ever alone was when I went up the first year: I didn't
know how to handle it, used to talk to myself for
company, but then I began to relish it. When I marry
I plan to have only two kids. What about you?'

It was too early. She could not tell everything, not
yet. 'I don't think I want to marry,' she said lightly.
'I'm wedded to the Law.'

'I hope he's good in bed,' said Elspeth. 'You'll
change your mind, you know. We modern women
are learning to expect everything out of life as a
right. You wanted to take our Flora's baby back
with you didn't you?'

'For one mad moment. He was an awfully sweet
baby.'

'They all are when they're full and dry.'

Ferelith could not imagine having such conversations with anyone else and treasured her growing
friendship with Elspeth and the warmth and cont-
inuing welcome of her family. The term, however,
was very full and, apart from occasional concerts
and snatched meetings for coffee, she saw little of
Elspeth or Simon until after the March exams. She
did well and attributed her success, at least to Mr
Lord, as a result of the bouquet of flowers that he
had sent her from the firm.

At the Christmas of 1937, when she was halfway
through her law course, she realized that she had not
heard in some time from Pietro. She sent a Christmas
card to his family but there was no reply. Was it the

situation in Europe or just the fact that it was years since they had seen one another? It had seemed as if the friendship was meant to last but perhaps it was natural that a relationship would fade and die if it was not nourished.

'Maybe I'll hear of him at Covent Garden one day and I can go round to the stage door and say, Remember me? I worked for your family in 1935.'

'He's not a Jew, is he?' asked Elspeth.

'No, Roman Catholic.'

'Don't think our friend Hitler cares much for you lot either,' added Simon, 'and he certainly doesn't like boys like me.'

'Do you think . . . ?' began Ferelith but then stopped because she could hardly bear to hear the words she had been about to say voiced out loud.

'Of course there's going to be a war,' said Simon. 'If not this year, then next year but there's certainly going to be a war. Hurry up and qualify, Elspeth my pet. Your first patients may well be half the male students at this university.'

'Oh, don't joke, Simon. War doesn't bear thinking about.'

'Start thinking, sweetness, and praying.'

7

EARLY IN DECEMBER of 1937 Dominic came to Edinburgh to take Ferelith to dinner and a recital of Verdi and Puccini duets. The programme had originally been German *lieder* but it was obvious that the organisers felt that no one in Edinburgh, no one anywhere outside Germany, wanted to hear German songs. The tenor had a German-sounding name and a notice appeared in the newspapers a few days before the recital announcing that J.K. had left Germany in 1914 as a small boy because his parents hated the then regime and that he had been naturalized in 1927 and was a most loyal subject of King George VI. Many notices of the same kind, written by grocers and restaurateurs, were appearing daily in newspapers up and down the land.

'How long are we going to be able to listen to Beethoven or Mozart? Or, for God's sake, Verdi? Surely that will become subversive too.'

'I think it's only German music, Dominic, and really only Wagner since Hitler likes him so much.'

'Because he's anti-Semitic and Hitler is anti-everything decent and is going to involve us all in a war.'

Ferelith looked at him sharply. War. Even Pietro had spoken of war as if it were the natural culmination of all that was going on in Europe. 'There mustn't be a war, Dominic. We must talk to one another.'

He hugged her spontaneously and planted a delicate kiss on her forehead and again she wondered, as she had wondered so often before, if he was another like Simon.

'What a little innocent,' he said lightly. 'Peace through negotiation.'

He saw her back to her flat. 'Not quite the same ambience as the Convent, my sweet,' he said, 'but better for you.'

'I feel guilty that I haven't gone back to see them. There were some poor souls there, Dominic.'

'You can't nurse everybody,' he said matter-of-factly. 'What about the Settlement? I hope you're managing to go there.'

'Still doing my one evening. Maggie married Sturrock, you know. She had to, as is politely said, but he's even worse than her father.'

'Physical abuse?'

'All kinds, I would think, but she believes it's coming to her, her fault or something. Her father, by virtue of the fact that he was her father, had the right to thump her and now Sturrock does, especially since she was – well, what she calls easy. I am giving all manner of legal advice.'

'And you not even qualified. Shame on you. I miss the Settlement, you know, and the people. It's strange but it's the one place I feel really at home. I'm useful and I'm liked and I don't have to think if what I am doing is right or wrong – I just know. When we're qualified, Ferelith, let's work for the downtrodden, the refugees . . . so many of us Scots are the children of people who struggled . . . and the Maggies. Let's help the Maggies.'

He kissed her, something he had never done before. 'I must come through and see you more often, Ferelith, and you must come to Glasgow. The trains are so convenient and I do miss you.

Letters aren't quite the same as a cup of coffee and a blether in the Union.'

'After Christmas. I'll make you a New Year resolution. See Dominic more in 1938.'

She never saw him alive again. On the 10th of December in a snowstorm, the Edinburgh to Glasgow express hit the Dundee to Glasgow express at Castlecary near Glasgow. One hundred and seventy-nine people were injured and thirty-five passengers were killed, among them Dominic Regent.

It was the worst thing that had happened to Ferelith since her annulment and she travelled through to Glasgow to Dominic's funeral at the Roman Catholic Cathedral. At the graveside Dominic's father clung to her and it was obvious that he could not come to terms with the tragedy that had hit his family.

'He was such a good boy,' he said over and over again. 'Such a good boy.'

The voice was guttural, heavily accented. Ferelith thought immediately of Pietro.

'They're Italians,' she said to herself. 'Why did I never suspect? Dominic was so proud of being a Scot. His father must have been an immigrant. Goodness, it wouldn't have mattered to me. I didn't even know what I was until . . .' But she did not want to think about that again.

Now, at his son's funeral, Ferelith could do nothing but leave Mr Regent surrounded by family and friends. Dominic's oldest sister, Mary di Rollo, took Ferelith back to the station.

'Such a waste,' she said. 'My father hoped Dominic would marry you, you know, and he came close to loving you. I think going through to see you was the beginning of his campaign to at last make up his mind about what he was and what he wanted.'

'What he was?'

'He was such a beautiful baby. My mother died giving birth to him. Maybe it would have been different, well, of course it would have been different if she had lived. He was talking lately about the priesthood. That was probably what he was fighting? An inclination towards a vocation and a fear of it at the same time. Did he tell you?'

'No.'

'Don't lose touch, Ferelith. There's a bed for you in Glasgow any time you want to come through. We Italians have huge extended families, you know, and you're part of the di Rollo's if you want to be, or if you ever need us.'

'If he hadn't come through . . .' Ferelith began.

'Don't do that,' Mary said harshly. 'You make yourself unnecessarily important in the scheme of things and we can all do without extra burdens. He could have been hit by a tram in Sauchiehall Street; he could have fallen down the stairs at his flat. He was never at rest, since he was a tiny baby, rush, rush, rush everywhere.' She looked up the platform and grabbed Ferelith's arm. 'Quick, there's your train. You're not afraid?'

'No. I'm too numb.'

Mary smiled. 'You did love him.'

'Oh, yes, I loved him.' She would not say that it was sisterly love and not the special love between a man and a woman but Mary seemed pleased and she smiled.

'Come and see us. Make a New Year resolution. My Mauro's Nono makes the best pasta. You'd sell your soul.'

'I'll come . . . to see you, not just for grandfather's pasta. I never knew Dominic had an Italian background. Did he tell you I worked in Italy for a summer? I even speak a little Italian and I certainly eat like an Italian and I have other Italian friends, from Rome. I'm worried about them.'

'Yes. We all have family over there and we worry and we pray. Don't stay away, Ferelith. Come back.'

Ferelith promised again and she sat in the train back to Edinburgh thinking of Dominic whom she would never see again and Pietro whom she might not. She would not make a New Year's resolution to visit the di Rollos . . . Resolutions to love people and to see them and to let them know that they were important should be made all the time – not just at the beginning of the year, along with the resolution not to eat so much chocolate.

Christmas was a gloomy affair, no matter how Mr Lord and his family tried to make it merry. One joy was in the form of a Christmas card from Pietro saying that all his family were well and that he hoped 1938 would be better for everyone. It was not better for Anthony Eden who resigned from the Government on the 21st of February because he was angry over the policies of appeasement towards Italy and its annexation of Abyssinia. No wonder Pietro's card had been so terse. He was unhappy with it too and he was an Italian.

In May Ferelith went back to Glasgow to Mary di Rollo's rambling house in Hillhead, not just to see the family but to watch the King and Queen open the Empire Exhibition. Dominic's death and war in Europe seemed so far away from the glittering crowds and the fun of the huge family party, not attended by old Mr Regent.

'I watch him die a little bit every day, Ferelith. I tell him a new baby is coming and if this one's a boy I say it will be another Dominic for him and he smiles at me and says "that's nice". It *will* be another

Dominic: he was conceived the night of Dominic's funeral. Four kids are enough, I told Mauro, even for an Italian, but it happened, and who'll notice in this family?'

Ferelith laughed. 'Everyone will notice. You and your sister have seven girls between you. A boy will be noticed, believe me.'

Mary laughed. 'Oh, you're good for me, Ferelith. I can see why Dominic liked you.'

Ferelith returned to Edinburgh for her last few weeks as a law student, having promised to become the new baby's godmother. Scottish, Italian and a sprinkling of Irish: that should make a happy combination, she thought.

Ferelith Gallagher M.A. added a Bachelor of Laws degree to her name and title in the summer of 1938. With other students she had waited nervously for the results of the June examinations and was among those delighted to be told that in the opinion of the Department of Law at the University of Edinburgh, she knew enough about Scots law, international law, mercantile law, forensic medicine, private law, conveyancing, civil law and a hundred and one other laws, to be admitted to the select body of Scottish lawyers. But Ferelith, of course, was not finished with education. She had her precious LL.B. At the same time as she had studied for her degree she had done her three years in Mr Lord's firm and her 'master' had granted her a discharge which stated that she had *properly and faithfully served him during the period of her indenture*.

Now she had to do some serious thinking about the way ahead.

If she still intended to become an advocate she had to take her year away from formal education. This was a requirement of the regulations of the

Faculty of Advocates and was irreverently known
as the 'year of idleness'. In England it was termed
devilling but in Scotland the system of having an
aspirant admitted as a pupil to a junior counsel
could not work because advocates worked, not from
Chambers, but from their homes. The year was for
study and in the past was often spent abroad visiting
the famous seats of learning in the Netherlands.
Ferelith could not do this: for one thing, she had
already lived in France for a year and did not feel
that a year spent sightseeing would be productive,
and secondly she was now *on her own* and therefore,
penniless.

If she found an advocate willing to allow her to
attach herself informally to him, to, perhaps, look
up authorities, digest papers, even, if she was bold
enough, formulate opinions, she still had to eat
and pay rent. Simon wanted her to go with him
to Glasgow. He fully intended to be one of her
instructing solicitors when she was called to the Bar.
He felt that although advocates lived and worked in
Edinburgh and travelled through to Glasgow once
or twice a week to plead cases, she herself, as the
first female advocate in Glasgow, could make a very
nice living once she was started. He felt strongly that
she should begin to make herself known in the circle
where she would eventually practise.

'Strike out, Ferelith. You're breaking new ground
all the time. There is only one woman advocate in
the country – Margaret Kydd. You be the second
one and the first one in Glasgow. It's a wonderful
opportunity. Dad has all the contacts: his firm is the
biggest in the city and you'll be proud to *belong* to
Glasgow. Solicitors in Glasgow will be glad to have
an advocate there all week instead of at the other
end of a railway line.'

She considered it carefully. She could see more
of Dominic's family, especially her godchild whose
advent she awaited with a strange mixture of pleasure and pain, and Simon who had been accepted
into his father's firm. But first she had to be accepted
somewhere and she had to be able to live. Simon
had no need to worry about finance and did not
even realize that for her, the year, or even two
years, when fees would not be coming in but when
books and wigs and gown and rooms and more
would all have to be financed, presumably from
the pot at the end of the rainbow. This presented
something of a nightmare. She could, too, see more
of her beloved Sister Anthony, but just before her
graduation the old nun wrote to tell her that she
was being transferred to their house near London.

London, I believe, is a very exciting city and
should definitely be visited by brilliant lady lawyers. You know you are always sure of a clean
bed and a decent meal and you can't beat the
price . . .

When would she find time to get to London? It
went on the list which included opera in Paris and
a second visit to the Eternal City.

'I have to find a junior advocate who'll let me
follow him around, Simon, and I'll have to do some
part-time work too.'

'What about Mr Lord?'

'Not fair to ask him. He isn't an advocate, and he
doesn't need another solicitor. I'll go around with
my begging bowl.'

She did and was not surprised to find a certain
hostility among senior male colleagues. Law had
been a strictly male playing field for so long that

many solicitors, advocates, eminent and not so eminent but, unfortunately, still important law lords, faced the future of a life surrounded by competent female practitioners, with something approaching horror.

'Not while I live and breathe,' said more than one when the twenty odd applicants from Edinburgh University applied for training or places.

'Old stick in the muds,' said Simon, safe in his promise of a junior partnership. 'Don't fret, Ferelith, something will turn up and in a few years you'll have such a splendid reputation that all the old fogeys will be on their knees before you.'

If I don't starve to death first, Ferelith thought to herself but she could not say anything to Simon.

'I think I want, eventually, to move back to Glasgow because I feel as if I belong: I mean I spent most of my childhood there and see my future there. Apart from Elspeth who plans to go back to Dumfries to practise medicine, everyone I care about lives in Glasgow.'

'Then that's settled.'

'No. I must stay in Edinburgh for one more year. I shall send applications to everyone . . .'

'Including the Lord Advocate?' Simon interrupted.

'*Ca va sans dire,*' she teased. 'Of course, Philistine. I think he's watching the post for my letter.'

She did not, as it happened, have to send one letter of application because, one afternoon just before the end of term and completely out of the blue, a visitor arrived at Mr Lord's offices who had been encouraged to watch Ferelith's progress by a fellow advocate and who was now prepared to give her a helping hand.

'But for goodness sake, Oliver, let her think the idea was all yours because she's as prickly as a hedgehog and would just get her dander up. No free lunches for the Ferelith Gallaghers of this world: wants to do everything for herself and hasn't faced the fact that for any aspiring advocate with no family backing, it's impossible.'

'Miss Gallagher,' said Mr Oliver Belanger, 'I have a bit of a problem and I am hoping that you can see your way to helping ease the situation.'

Mr Belanger K.C. was a practising advocate with a large and lucrative practice. He was also a man with strong political views and very definite political aims. He intended, in fact, to stand for Parliament.

'As a general rule, Miss Gallagher, I would have no time to have you shadow me. Over the past twenty years I have allowed enough beardless young wonders under my wings to more than repay any debt I might have to the advocates who set my own feet on the proper path. Now, however, I feel that if I had a depute, not legally you understand, just someone like yourself, with excellent academic qualifications, to do . . . well, shall we call it the dirty work, the day to day work, the reading, the piles of note making . . . Sheriffs and senior law lords like to see me in court, Miss Gallagher, because I do them the courtesy of always being well prepared. Have you any idea of how many hours of work that entails? We are talking of a way of life here, a commitment that would not suit everyone. We are talking twenty-four hours a day every day, including Sunday if I need information on precedents . . . if I need facts, references, opinions. For a year, while I prepare my parliamentary campaign I would like someone whom I could trust implicitly to help prepare my cases. We would meet every morning to discuss what was to be done and then we would meet every evening when I was in Edinburgh to discuss what has been done. I should expect you to come to court with me to listen to me plead, in other words, Miss Gallagher, to be as familiar with my cases as I am myself. My practice is large and varied and you would learn a great deal and because I am buying you body and soul, Miss Gallagher, I should expect to pay you a living wage.'

He stopped for breath and she looked at him squarely. He could have and indeed must have had a dozen requests for a place from the top of the graduating class. 'Why me, Mr Belanger?'

He smiled. 'Perhaps because you graduated with distinction. Perhaps because we both speak excellent French. Perhaps, Miss Gallagher, because I see the way the wind is blowing.'

And with that enigmatic remark she had to be satisfied. She would have loved to have been able to ask him if he meant only that it was obvious that women were going to take their rightful place at the Bar. He could not have meant – oh, what a stupid and conceited thought, Ferelith Gallagher – that she was being watched over by a very senior member of the Scottish Bar. He could not possibly have meant that.

'If you think I can be of use, Mr Belanger . . .' she began.

'If you are not, my dear,' he said in tones that assured her that he meant exactly what he said, 'I will throw you out.'

Ferelith accepted the offer nervously but with gratitude. She could never have hoped to be associated with him, believing this successful advocate to be unapproachable, but in July, shortly after she graduated, she began a year's work at his lovely home in Heriot Row in the New Town of Edinburgh. He insisted that she join him for breakfast which

saved him, he said, time. It also saved her money
for which she was grateful. He discussed the case
or cases with her, and then she left to sit in the
Advocates' Library reading and making notes. She
loved this place with its hundreds of years of
history. It was the main library in the country
with an unparalleled collection of books that the
Faculty of Advocates, at considerable private and
personal hardship, maintained for the free use of
anyone who wanted to consult a text. For years the
Faculty had been trying to have the Government
take over the expense of the library which was
one of a handful of libraries entitled to receive a
free copy of every book printed and entered at the
Stationers' Hall. Alexander Grant, the President of
the biscuit company, McVitie's, had given a free
donation of £100,000 to Lord Macmillan, who was
one of those instrumental in trying to establish a
National Library of Scotland from the nucleus of the
Advocates' Library and then had doubled his gift for
the building of a suitable repository. All his life this
great benefactor had bemoaned the lack of leisure to
indulge in the enjoyment of books and, very sadly,
never lived to see his dream of a National Library
fulfilled.

'We're almost there, Sir Alexander,' whispered
Ferelith every time she entered the law library.

An expense that she had not accounted for was
transportation. It was unthinkable for an advocate
to travel by tram or bus and he – the Faculty had
not foreseen women when it made the guidelines –
could travel by train only if he went first class; otherwise he might conceivably mix with the proletariat
and what? Be contaminated, hear words unsuitable
for his gentlemanly ears? Unthinkable. As a student
Ferelith had often travelled in the third-class section

of any train. Those days were over. Mr Belanger had, of course, his own transportation or he hired a taxi. When she could get away with it, Ferelith walked and remembered often her first lovely learning days in Edinburgh when she had walked miles each day to save a few pence. Now she walked to save her reputation. The idiosyncratic Miss Gallagher who believed in a healthy mind in a healthy body.

Two or three days a week she sat in Court listening to Mr Belanger argue, often from notes that she herself had prepared for him, and several times a week she attended consultations in his luxuriously furnished office. Almost every evening she worked in his study and his housekeeper prepared a supper for her which she, at first, attempted to refuse.

'His nibs says as how a labourer is worthy of his hire, Miss Gallagher. He says as how you're thinner than when you started working for him and he doesn't want to grind you into the dirt. He works like a dog hisself, you know, and he sometimes forgets as others are made of flesh and blood.'

Mr Belanger gave a Christmas party to which Ferelith was invited.

'Do you have a beau, Miss Gallagher, or have I worked you so hard that a social life is a thing of the past?'

'I enjoy my work, Mr Belanger,' said Ferelith diplomatically.

'Good. Now your only job at the party is to enjoy yourself, but I should be grateful if you would help Nancy decorate the tree. I like hundreds of candles.'

The tree was the tallest tree Ferelith had ever seen. It stood in the drawing room, a room she very rarely entered, and she could quite see how Mrs Dimmock would need help.

'This room is too pretty for tawdry paper deco-
rations, Miss Gallagher,' she said, 'although Mr
Belanger is like a child over Christmas and would
have streamers everywhere. I like greenery myself
and will ask you to go to the greengrocer's for
me. We'll put streamers, as will keep him happy,
in his study, but in here . . . nothing as is not in
good taste.'

It was a delightful way for Ferelith to spend a
day and she wondered where Mrs Dimmock had
developed her taste, for when everything was ready
for the party the house looked, to Ferelith, like a
wonderland.

'What his nibs needs is a wife and kids to enjoy
all this,' the housekeeper said archly and Ferelith
blushed. She had never thought of Mr Belanger as
a man. He was her employer, her teacher, and he
had always treated her with the most professional
courtesy, just as she had treated him. Poor Mrs
Dimmock, determined to seek and find romance
everywhere and anywhere.

Ferelith smiled to herself as she hurried away. Probably Mrs Dimmock, her undoubted talents greatly
underused if not undervalued by her employer, saw
every professional woman who came into his orbit as
a possible romantic liaison.

The first guests began to arrive and were welcomed with silver cups of hot, mulled wine. Ferelith
wandered among the public rooms, rather in awe of
her surroundings, and reflected that she had never
seen so many important people under one roof at
any one time.

The bell rang again just before eleven when Mrs
Dimmock was busy with the late supper and the
butler was refilling the punchbowl.

'I'll go,' she said to no one in particular and

opened the door to a tall thin man who was vaguely familiar.

She was disconcerted to find herself kissed heartily and she stepped back in surprise to see his laughing face looking up at a bunch of mistletoe under which she had been standing.

'A happy Christmas to you, Miss Gallagher,' said Lord Angus Webster. 'Did I frighten you? I'm sorry but if you must stand under the kissing bough looking absolutely delectable, what is a poor over-worked lawyer to do? Absolutely the most enjoyable experience I have had in some time. I heard my clerk tell a caller today, "Oh, don't disturb his Lordship: he's doing lewd and libidinous." You are still, Miss Gallagher, standing under the mistletoe.'

Ferelith almost jumped backwards and he laughed. 'You took me by surprise,' she said.

'And you me. Just think. Gallantry would have forced me to treat Mrs Dimmock in exactly the same way. That is why Oliver, the crafty beggar, always hangs the wretched thing right over the door.'

'Let me take your coat, Lord Webster.'

He refused and hung his heavy coat in the cloak-room himself. 'And how are you enjoying beastying for Oliver?'

'Oh, it's wonderful. I'm learning so much.'

'Good. I shall look forward to meeting you in Court soon and remember, you will have an advantage over many a beginning advocate. You will see me up there on the Bench looking so preposterous in my antediluvian wig and you will say, "The last time I saw that man, he kissed me, and he enjoyed it," and I did, Miss Ferelith Gallagher, I did.'

Before Ferelith could think of an answer Mr

Belanger bore down on them and led his friend away. Ferelith stood in the hall for a moment and put her hand against her lips.

'And so did I, Lord Angus Webster,' she said.

8

BETWEEN JANUARY AND June of 1939 Miss Gallagher shadowed Oliver Belanger on several cases that were heard by the Right Honourable Lord Webster of Dalmarnock.

At the first one, when she looked up to find his rather alarming gaze fixed on her she had found herself blushing like a witless girl instead of behaving like a sophisticated and well-educated woman. She had been unable to look up at all after that and had spent the rest of the afternoon scribbling furious notes.

Later she and Oliver had met Lord Webster in the Great Hall and, like Scottish advocates since time immemorial, had walked up and down, hands behind their backs, gowns billowing around them.

'You remember Miss Gallagher, Angus?' said Oliver as they began their perambulation.

'Indeed,' agreed Lord Webster remembering with great delight the last time he had seen and spoken to Miss Gallagher. 'How are you, Miss Gallagher? I thought you handled yourself very well in there.'

That enigmatic remark had left Ferelith blushing more furiously than ever and she was grateful that advocates did not look at one another as they paced the Hall but instead seemed to examine the floor searching, perhaps, for signs of the progress of the past's brilliant minds. She had to stop this immature nonsense. Not for the first time she relived the Christmas party. She had jumped from under the mistletoe as if she feared that Mr Belanger's late-coming guest might kiss her again: he had had, for an establishment figure of such eminence and reputation, quite a gleam of mischief in his eyes. She had blamed his fall from grace on the festive season. She must not let a simple kiss and a few sweet Christmas moments colour her professional association with him.

Perhaps it was because he himself always behaved towards her – after that one lapse – with impeccable propriety, that after that first case she was able to dismiss her nervousness and just enjoy listening to him work. He was, she decided, absolutely perfect: kind, gentle, wise, humorous but also quite ruthless in his pursuit of justice. He had some tolerance for petty criminals but none at all for the hardened felon.

He spoke to her once or twice out of Court and when that happened she found herself tingling with happiness. She would, she decided, miss him most when she left Edinburgh for she had come to the conclusion that she had to do so. Each morning she looked out of the tall windows of Oliver Belanger's town house and saw Edinburgh and all its glories. She walked up from the New Town to Princes Street and crossed over at the Art Galleries. Then with Princes Street Gardens laid out below her and the imposing presence of the Castle to her right, she walked up the Mound into Edinburgh's past. One morning in May she stopped at the Heart of Midlothian outside St Giles's Cathedral. After looking around furtively to make sure a pillar of the Law did not see her she had spat right into the Heart and whispered the old charm: 'I have to leave: I cannot afford to stay. My heart is here and I will, I must come back.'

The decision to abandon her plans or at least to set

them aside for a while had not been easily reached. So often during her studies she had felt that life was treating her too easily. The Religious Order had paid her expenses to the end of her formal education. Then Mr Belanger had sought her out, an unheard-of action. It had been too easy, too pat. Even men were having difficulty in getting work in Edinburgh where there was very much an old-school-tie feeling about the legal profession. She knew of at least one brilliant west-coast student, also, as it happened, a Catholic, who was having a frustrating time trying to establish himself in a club where everyone knew everyone else and where advocates were often sons or nephews of advocates or judges. He had had to borrow his wig and gown from a friendly classmate and lived in terror that he and the other young man – who, obviously had the prior claim – might have to appear in Court at the same time. Ferelith was not so badly off and had managed to buy a second-hand gown and wig which fitted fairly well.

For the first six months of 1939 she had worried and wondered about her future. Once her year of devilling was up, she could not stay on with Mr Belanger and there was absolutely no way that she could afford the type of residence that was expected of the Edinburgh Advocate. She had fought with her conscience and she had finally won. She would not be beholden to anyone: she, Ferelith Gallagher, was now twenty-five years old and must take full charge of her own life. She had rehearsed her speech in the security of her rooms but it had not come out quite so well when she was face to face with her mentor. His reaction had surprised her.

'My dear girl, you can't do that. You must stay in Edinburgh. I'll see to it that you get instructions and you can do some free legal work which will get your name known to solicitors.'

Ferelith had looked around his beautiful breakfast room, a room that spoke of inherited wealth, and she had shaken her head in disappointment and despair. She could not, would not, tell him that if she did only free work she would starve to death and if she became his protégée she would lose her self-respect. He seemed to have known what she was thinking for he argued with her.

'If I could keep you on a retainer, an unprecedented step in Scottish legal circles, sensible but unprecedented, I would do so, but I have enough influence to get you some work. Oh don't bristle. That's how the system works, Ferelith. I can help you get started. There are too many instructing solicitors out there who will ignore you simply because you are a woman. I'll call in a few favours and then once you have established yourself, you will be on your own. You must go to the Bar. Lord . . . everyone says you have a future.'

What had he been going to say? Lord Webster? No, that was too bizarre. Lord Webster was very kind every time they met but he was a kind man, everyone said so.

'I have decided to work as a solicitor, Mr Belanger, in Glasgow. I can get adequate accommodation on the outskirts and Charles Smythe is part of the biggest firm in the city. It'll be wonderful experience. In a year or two I will come back to the Bar.'

'I shall hold you to that promise, young lady. You must remember, Ferelith, that you are the pathfinder. Don't forget your duty, not just to those who have taught you and watched over you, but to those hundreds of women who will read of your work and wish to emulate you.'

The pathfinder. There were just too many tangles in the way. She went to Glasgow and stayed with Mary di Rollo while she looked for digs. These were found, to everyone's horror, in Clydebank.

'You can't live there, Ferelith. Those are slums.'

'Mrs Thomson is as clean as Sister Anthony Joseph. The office is solid, Mary, and that's where clients will see me, and remember for me this is just a stepping stone but I must do it, or lose my self-respect.'

And she loved her work. She saw Simon, who was in the same building, every day, and she had Sunday dinner with the di Rollos. She worked hard and had the satisfaction of watching her Bar fund grow. One afternoon she had worked steadily on the reams of papers that dealt with the last will and testament of one Sydney Smallwood when the door of her office opened . . .

'Miss Gallagher.'

Ferelith recognized the voice and, for some absurd nonsensical reason her heart started to pound, and she found it difficult to look up from the brief she was studying.

'Lord Webster,' she said at last. 'May I help you? Are you looking for Mr Smythe? He is, unfortunately, in Edinburgh today.'

'Yes, I know. I had dinner with him last night and I told him I was on my way here to try to get you back where you belong. All fair and above board.'

She could hardly believe she had heard him correctly.

'Get me back . . .?'

He looked around as if for a chair and she blushed and showed him to the comfortable chair kept for special clients.

'Yes,' he said as he sat down. 'I helped educate you, Miss Gallagher, and therefore have a proprietory interest. I don't like to fail just as you don't. If you are not at the Bar after all these years of expensive education then the Bar and the legal system are losers.'

'I'm very flattered, Lord Webster, but I have strong and compelling and deeply personal reasons for not being called to the Bar.'

He dismissed her reasons with a wave of an immaculately manicured hand. 'You are not the only poor person who has made it, Miss Gallagher. I know at least one senior judge who started out with less than two halfpennies to rub together. I'm angry that I was in London when you decided to run away . . .'

'I did not run away,' Ferelith, as angry as she had ever been, interrupted. 'I made a very difficult but perfectly rational decision and I have no intention of telling you or anyone else my reasons.'

'The status quo is the reason, Ferelith,' he said in a calm voice that effectively took the wind from her sails, 'but things will change and you can change them and I want to help. Will you at least talk to me?'

She looked at him and part of her brain told her that she was dreaming and that this conversation had to be a figment of her imagination. She could not possibly be arguing with the next Lord Advocate, not in Court but in her office. At her audacity there should be a thunderclap which would effectively silence her impertinence.

'Why?' she asked, looking at him candidly. 'I'm sorry. It's a tremendous compliment, your interest in my legal career, but why? There are many, many struggling advocates in Edinburgh.'

'There is only one Ferelith Gallagher and she is not in Edinburgh where she should be . . .' He leaned over the desk and his index finger poked her papers. 'What's that? A will? You don't want to spend the rest of your life among wills and conveyancing?'

'No, and I won't. I'll return to Edinburgh in a few years . . .'

'Oh, Ferelith, don't be too proud. Allow me to help.'

Ferelith looked at him, taking in the well-cut clothes, the well-groomed greying hair on the lean, sensitive face. Should she take him at face value? His interest was altruistic: he was a crusader for women's rights? He liked her?

'Why on earth should you help me, Lord Webster? Frankly, I can't understand why you even remember my name. Oh, I don't want to be rude and —'

'I remember kissing a girl under the mistletoe. I remember a very lovely face under a rather ill-fitting wig. I remember someone smiling at me in approval when I was lecturing. You look surprised. Surprised that I remember you or surprised that I should confess to having as many nerves as the next man? Not allowed for Law Lords?'

'You always look so . . . well, serene and at ease.' How easy it was to talk to him, not senior law lord and very junior solicitor but man to woman, woman to man.

'Easy when one is hiding under a wig. You'll find that too, if and when you come home.'

Home? Glasgow was home but suddenly she was homesick for the Law Courts of the capital.

'I return to Edinburgh tomorrow, Miss Gallagher, and I don't know when I'll be back. Will you have dinner with me and we'll discuss the future of the woman's place in the Scottish legal system in general and Miss Gallagher's future in particular?'

Dinner with Angus Webster? No, she could not.

She might have to ask herself why he affected her so much. This nervous tension was much more than just because he was so senior and she was a mere parvenue. It was the hardest and yet easiest decision she had so far had to make.

'I can't . . .' she began.

'You can't eat. If you don't want to discuss law we could discuss music, art, books . . .' He stopped for a second and leaned very slightly towards her and then immediately straightened up. 'How very, very lovely you are.'

It was obvious that he had not meant to say that. He blushed furiously and at once it was she who felt older, calmer, more in control.

'I'm very interested in the Glasgow Boys,' she said primly.

'The only Glasgow boys I know are those whom I have sent to jail.' So he had a sense of humour too. Well, she had seen that humour in his court appearances, hadn't she? 'There, Miss Gallagher,' he went on, 'you have a duty to educate me. May I pick you up at seven?'

Clydebank. She thought of the tiny room in a tenement where she lived because it was cheaper than anywhere else. Her salary did not cover high living plus the strict regime that she had set herself of saving and paying back the Convent. Her appearance was important, and she had to spend money on clothes which she hid under a huge wraparound coat that she pulled off and bundled up as soon as she reached the offices on Vincent Street. She was not ashamed of living frugally: in fact she was quite pleased with herself, but suddenly she could not bear the thought of Angus Webster seeing her there.

'Could I meet you somewhere?' she asked. 'I . . . I have so much work to do.'

He smiled. 'Rogano's, on Exchange Place. Do you know it? It's almost just around the corner.'

Rogano's. Quite new but already becoming *the place* to see and be seen.

'No,' said Ferelith, 'but I've heard of it.'

'As an artist *manqué* you will appreciate the Art Deco interior. I, on the other hand, merely enjoy a good meal. I must go and make a reservation. See you at seven.'

She watched the door close behind him and pinched herself. She had just made a date with an institution.

'He thinks I'm lovely. Am I lovely? Oh, God, what am I going to wear? I can't go to dinner at Rogano's in this suit. It will look like a business dinner. It is a business dinner. No, it isn't.'

She buzzed the intercom for Sarah.

'I have to go out, Sarah, just for a half-an-hour or so. Tell Mr Sommerville for me.'

'Forgive me, Reverend Mother,' she said to herself later as she took a tram back along Argyle Street. 'I meant this money for the Convent but I just had to have a pretty blouse. I hope he appreciates it.'

If Lord Webster appreciated the blouse in particular he gave no indication but was a perfect, unfrightening host. In fact, Ferelith felt a little silly that she had made too much of that remark in the office. Better to ignore it, to forget for a moment that she had seen interest, even admiration in his eyes. Meanwhile he was not nearly so ignorant of the Glasgow art world as he had pretended to be, though much of the evening was spent discussing the latest books, *Rebecca* by Daphne du Maurier and *Brighton Rock* by Graham Greene.

'What do you mean, you don't have time to read

novels,' he said as he poured her a second, no a third, glass of the most incredibly delicate white wine. 'You must feed the civilized part of your mind too, Ferelith. You cannot possibly read nothing but legal tomes. You will soon become as dusty and dry as they are. If you think novels are too frivolous try George Santayana's latest, *The Realm of Truth.*'

If I can remember a word of this conversation when I get to the library tomorrow I'll borrow it, Ferelith thought to herself and wondered whether admitting to a taste for the cinema would be a plus or a minus.

'If I have time I like the cinema,' she said desperately. 'I saw *Pygmalion.*'

'Oh, the new Leslie Howard film. I missed that. What about Hitchcock? I believe he has a new film this year.'

'*The Lady Vanishes.*'

'Have you seen it?'

'No.'

'Then perhaps when it comes to Glasgow or Edinburgh we could see it together.' He leaned back in his chair and she had the feeling that he was as surprised by what he had just said as she was herself.

That had to be a date, a real date, not a meeting to discuss law or anything else.

'I'd like that,' she said, a little too relaxed to be on her guard.

He smiled gently. 'Me too,' he said and gestured for the waiter.

At her insistence that he should not escort her home he had put her in a taxi.

'You modern young women,' he said half-laughing, half-serious. 'Not the done thing, you know, and I shall bring my own motor when next I come through and will accept no excuses. You live alone, I take it, no worried mother waiting up?'

'It's only ten-thirty, Angus' – when had he become Angus? – 'and besides, I'm an orphan.'

'You are an amazing young woman, Ferelith Gallagher. I salute you,' he said, and as the taxi pulled her away she watched him standing, his hat in his hand, looking after her.

Much later that same evening Ferelith was startled by a strange noise and looked at her watch. It was already two in the morning. She looked at the fireplace to see if the dull thud had been a log falling but the embers in the grate were simply sighing. She listened intently and was just about to throw another log on the fire when she heard a scrabbling at the door.

She stood up, went to the fireplace and picked up one of the heavy andirons. What she thought she might have to do with it, she did not consider. Its cold weight made her feel better and she shuffled to the door with it.

'Who's there?' she asked, her mouth against the wood.

'Sweetness,' she heard very faintly.

She put down the andiron and, with hands that were beginning to shake, struggled with the key and the bolt and opened the door. Simon, his face and hair covered in blood, almost fell into the room.

'I'm so sorry, sweetness,' he breathed, 'couldn't go home, couldn't think.'

She was on her knees on the floor beside him. 'I'll phone for an ambulance, Simon, and the police.'

With a surprisingly strong hand he pulled her back. 'No, please, my father . . . just help me clean myself up. Brandy? Whisky?'

'Oh, God, I don't have anything like that. I'll make tea.'

He almost snorted. 'Yes, tea, and a wet cloth and a towel, please.' Even in his state he remembered his carefully-taught manners.

'You must let me go, Simon, and I'll look at your head first and then make some tea. Here, lie on this.'

'I'm so sorry, sweetness, but I think I'm going to be sick.'

And he was.

Ferelith ran to the sink for a wet cloth and wiped his face. Then she covered the vomit with a towel while she rinsed the cloth and bathed his face again. He had been badly beaten but she was relieved to see that there seemed to be no really serious wound: even the head injury, from which he had lost so much blood, did not appear to be too deep.

'Simon, I do think you should see a doctor,' she said later when he was drinking hot sweet tea, his thin hands clasped around the bowl of the cup for warmth, for stability?

He looked up at her, his eyes shadowed with pain. 'Have you any idea what this would do to my father? I can't go to hospital, Ferelith. I want to stay here until the bruising dies down. May I? Here on the settee? You could go to my flat if you're worried about your reputation.'

He had obviously forgotten in his distress that the settee was her bed but she did not remind him. 'No, my dear friend, I am not worried about my reputation but I am worried about you.'

'If you can tell my father that I have a shocking cold he won't come near me for a few days. Then I will tell him that I fell down the stairs when I got drunk.'

'But you never get drunk: your father knows that.'

'He will be thrilled to believe that I got drunk, Ferelith. He's not blind, you know, or stupid. He is desperately seeking signs of what he sees as a real man in his only son. I can't bear disappointing him again and again. Maybe that's what I was doing tonight, trying to find out for sure, but I can't be what he wants and I can't be what I thought I was either. I'm a nothing, sweetness, an absolute nothing.'

She put her arms around him and he sighed and relaxed and eventually fell asleep. She sat there holding him until the early signs of dawn began to struggle through the smoke-grimed windows.

'I don't understand, Simon,' she whispered into his hair, 'and I don't think you do either. I wish I knew who had done this to you.'

She looked down at him again. He was, according to the world, one of the winners. He had everything – looks, education, position, family. He could not be put into the same list as one of her first clients, Maggie Sturrock – oh, God, she had not thought about Maggie for such a long time and she had promised Dominic – but he was still a victim. He still needed to be helped and protected. Very carefully she stood up and lowered him on to the sofa. Then she went to the cupboard, took out a blanket and covered him with it.

She set her alarm clock for seven and curled up in the armchair for two hours sleep. Simon was still asleep when she woke and before she went out to the communal lavatory to wash, she checked that his breathing was peaceful and regular. His bruising, in the cruel morning light, was horrifying.

'We have to get you out of this slum dwelling,

Ferelith my sweet,' he tried to tease her later through lips that were swollen and painful. 'I ache from head to toe and I thought, Ah, while Ferelith is out earning our daily bread I will soak in a nice hot tub. Where do you bathe?'

'At the public baths or in a bucket in front of the fire.'

'How quaint. I looked around and realized that my bed was *the* bed. Where did you sleep?'

'I was fine, Simon. I'll scramble some eggs. Will you manage that?'

'Sounds divine, and my pa?'

'Wants you to drink hot water, lemon juice, honey, and whisky.'

'What a frightfully good idea. Can I ask you to go to my flat for some stuff and then when it's dark I'll go home, Ferelith, if you'll help me.'

There was no point in arguing with him about reporting his beating to the police, no point in begging him to go a doctor. Several times during the day she had found herself on the point of telephoning the police surgeon but she kept hearing Simon's anguished voice pleading for his father's serenity. She could so easily imagine the headlines.

TOP LAWYER'S SON IN VICE BRAWL
GLASGOW SOLICITOR BEATEN UP IN VICE DEN

If he had been in a vice den. Where had it happened? Why had it happened? What other life did Simon live, Simon who loved paintings and music and everything that was lovely? She would not now or ever ask him anything but she would try, to the best of her ability, to help him, and that started with scrambling him some eggs. After that she went across town to his flat and got him clean clothes, washing things, a bottle of brandy, and a bottle of whisky. She had honey and lemon juice in her kitchen, if he really wanted the hot drink his father had recommended as a cure for his non-existent cold.

'I will never forget your kindness, sweetness,' he said later as she was leaving his flat having seen him safely installed.

She tried to speak lightly. 'What are friends for?'

'It will never happen again, Ferelith, and I'll never speak of it.'

'It's finished, over.'

'It will be when you new carpet comes. Oh, don't fuss: I know you cleaned up beautifully but I'll never be able to look at your carpet again and it was quite hideous anyway, wasn't it?'

Ferelith, who had quite liked the carpet, agreed. 'It would remind us.'

It was several weeks before Simon was well enough or mentally strong enough to return to her apartment and then only to show her brochures for a new development at the West End.

'You can't live here, Ferelith. When the war comes, it's going to be more and more difficult to travel and there'll be unsalubrious characters in plenty around. Far better that you stay closer to the offices.'

'I can't afford the rent on a place like this, Simon.'

'Uncle Charles has paid it for one year: it's to be a "now Ferelith is a fully qualified solicitor and can be worked even harder" present. Please don't argue. He knows, you see, and he's grateful for anything that spares my mother.'

'I didn't help you for gain, Simon.'

'He'd spend the same money on a watch or a

brooch or something for you. He's about the only solicitor who has made any money in the last few years but you're getting qualified just in time for the upsurge in legal business. Accept graciously. You can buy a few bits of fairly good furniture at auction and then just add a bit here and there as you begin to get your financial head above water.'

Ferelith accepted. Living in town actually saved her money. For a year she would have no rent to pay, thanks to Mr Smythe's generosity, and because it was near the offices, transportation costs and time spent travelling were cut substantially. At the back of her mind too was the hope that maybe, just maybe, Angus Webster had meant it when he had said they would go to a film together.

But he never telephoned. And then it was September 1939.

In Rome on Friday the 1st of September Mussolini declared to an interested world that Italy would remain neutral in any forthcoming confrontations. Pietro Angelosanti left the Conservatory where he was studying voice and conducting and disappeared.

In London on Sunday the 3rd of September Britain declared war on Germany. After the King's evening broadcast Ferelith Gallagher switched on her gramophone and turned up the volume. Beethoven's *Fidelio* streamed down Byres Road and earned her angry telephone calls from two of her neighbours.

'It's not because it's German, Miss Gallagher, it's because it's too loud. I'm trying to get my baby to sleep.'

'I know, Mrs Burns, and I'm sorry. It was thought-less to play it so loud but I just wanted to defy Hitler somehow.'

'You won't do that by keeping my baby awake,' said Mrs Burns angrily and slammed down the receiver.

Simon, for one, was relieved that war had act-ually come.

'I know it's going to be terrible, Ferelith, maybe more horrible than anything we could ever imagine, but we've crept along for years trying to pretend that if we didn't look, it would all go away. My father fought in the Trenches, so did Uncle Charles and so did the Honourable Lord Webster . . .'

'He can't have,' she interrupted. 'He's not nearly so old as your father.'

Simon laughed. 'So he is ringing your bells, sweetness, you wicked thing you.'

'Stop it, Simon. I hate you when you're vulgar.'

'I'm vulgar only when I'm scared,' he began but she had rushed from the room and slammed the door behind her.

The letter was lying on her desk. She could not believe it. She recognized the writing, of course, even though it was years since she had seen it. Ferelith dropped the letter from suddenly nerveless fingers.

Blair. Six years and here was a letter, or some sort of communication, from him. Memories, so bitter, so painful, so beautiful, so unbearably tender, flooded back.

'Oh dear God, when will you let me be rid of him?'

She picked up the letter, slit it open carefully with the silver letter-opener Simon had given her for Christmas, and read . . .

Dear Ferelith,

I won't ask how you are because I know. I have always known.

This morning I decided two things. One is that I can no longer live here in luxury while my friends, my tenants, go off to . . . what? Shall I be clever and say, 'do their bit'? I shall wait a few days in hope and then I will enlist in the Air Force.

And why do I wait, Ferelith? Why don't I rush immediately to take the modern equivalent of the King's shilling? It's you. I would like to see you before I go. I love you still: I think I always will love you and time, if I am granted any, will tell whether it is the love of a brother or a lover. From what I have heard, I believe that shooting himself was the only shabby thing our father ever did, if that makes you feel any better. Perhaps it doesn't. Perhaps you say like my mother that fathering you was a pretty shabby thing to do but I cannot sit in judgement. May I see you just once before I go, not to whine or beg, just to see you and to know that you are all right?

I have made my will. You, my closest relative, are my sole heir. It would be poetic justice, would it not, if you were to inherit my shoes, much too big for your little feet.

On Saturday I will be in Glasgow at Rogano's . . . I believe they do a fair meal. Meet me, please.

Blair Winterton

Winterton. So he has taken his father's name back again. Our father's name. God. I don't want his estate. I want nothing. I'm the result of one of the shabby things he did in his uncheckered life, am I? Ferelith Gallagher burst into tears and when she had stopped she telephoned Simon and read him the letter.

'Go, sweetness. How can you resist such a *cri de coeur*? Sounds rather nice, your big brother. Well he would, wouldn't he? He's your brother.'

'I wanted him as a husband.'

'And why not? Stop replaying the old record, Ferelith. You have not committed a mortal sin.'

Was that what she thought? Was it?

'He has no right to storm back into my life like this.'

'He's a victim too, my sweet.'

A victim. Of course he was a victim. That's what Sister Anthony had said all those years ago.

'Go and see him and lay the ghosts, Ferelith. Then maybe you'll be able to decide whether it's lust or daughterly affection you have for old Angus.'

At once she was angry. 'He's not old.'

'It's lust then,' he said and hung up.

On Saturday she was at the restaurant.

She was greeted by the maître d'. 'Good afternoon, madame. Are you lunching alone? I have a very nice table.'

'No, I'm meeting a . . . friend. Mr Winterton?'

'Ah yes. Mr Winterton is already here. We have not had the pleasure of his company . . .' Ferelith could hear him talking as he walked along beside her between the potted palms and the tables but she could not distinguish the words. She made no effort to make them out. Her whole energy was focused on this meeting.

'Ferelith.'

'Hello, Blair.'

The years had not treated him as well as they should have done. His hair was receding and his eyes were dull and looked as if shadowed by pain.

His skin was weather-beaten, a farmer's complexion, the skin of a man who spent a great deal of time out of doors. Well, of course, he was a landowner after all.

'You look wonderful,' he said as she sat down. 'I am so unbelievably proud of you. I know I shouldn't feel the right to . . .'

'Please, Blair. I don't know why I am here. What I did want to say, and I could have written it, should have written it, is that I cannot bear to be mentioned in your will. The idea makes my flesh creep. It's a macabre thought, to contemplate inheriting the estate of a man who shot himself rather than face my birth.'

'I love you,' he said simply and the wine waiter hovering at his tweed elbow saved her from having to say anything. 'I looked while I was waiting,' he explained. 'Shall I order some claret and we'll drink it with fish and defy the establishment?'

She smiled and he muttered to the waiter and she sat back and felt herself begin to breathe naturally. It was not so frightening: it was Blair, a little older, a little bruised but still Blair.

'Why Winterton?' she asked eventually.

'I'm his son. I can't enter his head, Ferelith, but I won't judge him.' He was quiet for a moment as if he was seeing something she could not see or hearing something she did not hear. 'I've lived with my mother for a long time,' he finished eloquently.

'Why join up, really? Isn't there a more useful role for a farmer?'

'I'm twenty-six and I'm not a farmer. I'm nothing useful at all. I lost heart and failed all my exams at the varsity and there was even less need to struggle without you to impress or to bully me into working. I do nothing but ride and fish and shoot. Managers run the estate. My mother wouldn't even leave me that much dignity, but at least I had the guts to take back my identity.'

She had met his mother once. She could remember how formidable she had been. Blair must have found that defiant act very difficult.

He seemed to read her mind or to have heard a question that she would never ask. 'She was furious, of course. It was the embarrassment, not just to her but to his family.'

'Then you do have other relatives?'

He looked surprised. 'Of course I must have, but my estate doesn't belong to the Winterton side: it was my maternal grandfather's.'

'As a lawyer let me give you some free advice. Make peace with the Wintertons and, if you are going to join up, and probably you won't have any choice in a month or two, make another will. I don't want anything from your family, Blair. I don't want to hurt you any more but I have managed well enough without your . . . our family. The Catholic Church, especially a very determined old nun, helped me and so if you want to please me, send them a donation, but don't burden me with this, please.'

He stared into the depths of his glass and eventually smiled as if he had seen something in the reddish-violet liquid that pleased him.

'Let's have a good lunch and I'll meet you here again as soon as this nonsense in Europe is sorted out and we'll talk again.'

She smiled. 'That's more positive, and now let me tell you, Mr Winterton, that I've developed extremely expensive tastes.'

Nearly two hours later, feeling very content and just a shade light-headed, she walked in front of

Blair out of the restaurant. Her way was barred by a tall, stooping figure.

'Miss Gallagher, how very nice to see you.'

It was Angus Webster. For some reason Ferelith blushed. It was a Saturday. She had every right to have a good lunch with a personable young man.

'Lord Webster. Nice to meet you again too.' Oh, she was being too friendly: she should not have had that third glass of wine. 'This is Blair Winterton, my . . .' Had she been about to say, brother? No, she would not admit the relationship. It was an accident, nothing more. 'My friend,' she ended weakly and the two men shook hands.

'Well, you have moved into higher circles, Ferelith,' said Blair as they waited for the taxi he had ordered for her. 'Webster is definitely the right kind of legal brain to cultivate.'

'That was a nasty thing to say. I'm not cultivating him.'

'Just as well. No doubt he thinks that, at the very least, I'm important and, at the very worst, that I'm an immoral liaison.'

Ferelith looked distressed.

'Gosh, he is important to you, isn't he?'

'Oh, I don't know.'

'If you can't bring yourself to say, "my brother", just introduce me as Blair Winterton.'

'I don't intend to introduce you as anyone at all,' she said angrily.

He laughed and taking her hands turned her around lightly to face him. He looked into her face and it was Blair, the old Blair, the man she had had no right to love.

'You won't have a chance, Ferelith. I'm a soldier off to war, remember.'

The spring day seemed suddenly to grow cold and she shivered.

'I'll write,' he said as he ushered her into the taxi, 'and please answer – just friendly letters between friends.'

She said nothing because if she had tried to she would have started to cry. As the taxi pulled away she looked back and saw him still standing there, so alone, on the pavement.

'Oh, God, keep him safe,' she prayed and then, emotionally exhausted, she lay back against the nicotine-smelling seat and began to cry.

9

'IT'S MADNESS, FERELITH, sheer madness. You must help.' Dominic's sister Mary, now calling herself Maria was desperate. 'He came from Aulla nearly forty years ago. He's as Scottish as you are.'

For months the country had been in the grip of fear. Men and women who had known one another for years and had eaten and played and talked and worked together in friendship now watched one another furtively, looking for signs of they knew not what. 'Alien' was the swear word. Men who had lived ten, twenty, thirty, years as Britons, who had changed their names from German or, as in the case of Mary's father, from Italian, now found themselves classed as aliens.

'Dominic would have been an alien. Dominic Regent, born Domenico Regente. If it wasn't so tragic, it would be funny, Ferelith. There won't be a fish and chip shop open if they round up all the Italians who own them. London won't have a decent West End restaurant. It's insane. We must join together to fight the common enemies, Hitler and Mussolini, not people we went to school with.'

'Mr Smythe is working on it, Mary.'

'Maria. I'm Italian, Italian.' She broke down and burst into tears and Ferelith bent over to comfort her. Her father, Dominic's father, had had to register as an alien. He had to report to his local police station every day. If that indignity was not enough, there was now talk of interning aliens. Some, with no doubt many among them who were subversive,

had already been interned for their protection as
well as the safety of the realm. But to intern an
elderly man who had spent most of his life working
hard, paying taxes, improving his community, was
surely an obscenity.

'The Lord Advocate is asking for Scots aliens to
be released, Maria. The Regional Commissioner for
Scotland is working day and night on these cases.
All I can say is please be patient.'

'Are you going to give me that crap about the
wheels of justice grinding slow?' snarled Maria,
'because if you are, don't bother. My father has been
half-dead since Dominic's death. To be interned,
away from me and the children, will kill him.'

She stood up, pushing off Ferelith's comforting
hand.

'I told him we could depend on you but I see we
can't.' She swept out slamming the door behind
her, and Ferelith, feeling more than slightly sick,
sat down and looked at the empty chair where the
vibrant dark-haired young mother had sat just a few
minutes before.

'She didn't mean that last bit,' said Simon who
had come in just in time to see the door slam.

'Oh, I know but they've been so good to me and
now the first time they ask me for help . . .'

'You chose the job, sweetness, and this is just
the first time you're going to, well I won't say fail
because you have no chance to fight, but you're not
going to win. If the Lord Advocate can't do it, a
barely qualified advocate who isn't even at the Bar
isn't going to fare any better.'

'It's so ludicrous, so stupid, so . . . unjust.'

'Maybe internment won't be too dreadful. It's not
prison: it's somewhere to be safe.' Simon wondered
if even he believed what he was saying.

Ferelith was angry. 'Won't be too dreadful, for him, away from a baby grandson who is his soul reason for living.'

Simon looked at her and wanted to comfort her and, as usual when he felt inadequate, he joked. 'Have you heard about this local defence thing? I'd better join. I'll look sweet in uniform, don't you think?'

'What local defence?'

'Our esteemed Secretary of State for War, Anthony Eden, has asked for local defence volunteers. He wants about a quarter of a million men between fifteen and sixty to well, patrol, and look out for fires and lights at windows and all manner of things . . .'

Simon's joining of what came to be called the Home Guard was knocked into the shade later that month by the evacuation of the French town of Dunkirk. For two weeks, a few hundred warships, and several hundred small boats of every description, helped by the ceaseless vigilance of the Royal Air Force, took two thousand Belgian soldiers, one hundred and ten thousand French soldiers and two hundred and twenty-five thousand British soldiers off the beaches of France and ferried them to safety in Britain. It was an unimaginable feat of heroism and filled the hearts and minds of the world with praise and thanksgiving.

Funny things happened too. Simon went off to the weekly meeting of the Home Guard. His platoon was an odd assembly of men, of all ages, all types, solicitors, bankers, bakers, shopkeepers. In charge was a fresh-faced former public-schoolboy with the ink scarcely dry on his commissioning papers. He took his job very seriously.

'Gentlemen,' he said, 'it is likely that the enemy

is about to land. Scotland is faced with invasion. It
is up to us to do our bit for king and country.'

Simon tried to stand to attention: he tried to be like
the others who appeared to be listening attentively.
Instead he found himself wondering if their leader
had shaved yet. There was such a delicate bloom to
the young cheeks.

'I have come up with a plan which will give us a
little time . . .' The boy soldier blushed and Simon
knew that he had been about to say 'until the real
army gets here'.

'It's no more than a delaying tactic but I think it
will work.'

The boy stopped and looked at the, in most
cases, much older eyes of the men in front of
him. He sighed. He wanted to be somewhere else,
somewhere where he might do great things, be
noticed, make a difference to the course of the
war.

'I assure you that this will work, give us the time
we'll need. When you hear that the invasion has
started I want you all to go into your butler's
pantry' – he blushed again at this faux pas – 'or
your kitchen and take all the soup plates out and
turn them upside down on to the roads. I appreciate
that you may find this' – and he glared at Simon –
'quite ludicrous but if you look you will see that
upturned soup plates resemble landmines.'

Simon had to bite his tongue to stop his wicked
sense of humour from asking if his mother's Spode
would be better than her Minton or did it matter?
He could hardly wait to share it with Ferelith. But
Ferelith had no time for Simon's juvenile sense of
humour.

Maria di Rollo had telephoned Ferelith during
the evacuation of Dunkirk. 'They have interned him,

an old man whose only crime is that he was born in Italy.'

What could she say to the sobbing person on the other end of the telephone. 'I'm sorry' sounded so inadequate, and it was, but it was all the words she knew.

'It'll take time, Maria, but once the mass hysteria is over, commonsense will prevail. I promise you we'll get him out. I'll petition the Lord Advocate. I know a law lord . . . slightly. I'll get in touch with him.'

She had given Maria her scraps of hope and she was left to wonder why she had mentioned her law lord. It would take time to release the detainees who should not have been detained. Many of them, like Vincent Regent, or Vincenzo Regente as he now insisted on being called, were quite wealthy and knew many members of the legal establishment. That would not help. War. They were at war. Things that would have taken a telephone call, a wink, a quick handshake in peacetime waited for the mills of justice.

Still, she had promised to do everything she could and, she had to admit it, she wanted to contact Angus. He had half-promised to take her to the pictures. He had meant it when he said it, she knew that as she knew the sun came up every morning. Was he shy of her? When he was alone did he think about the age difference? More likely a wealthy, sophisticated and busy man had no time to think of anything but his job.

'Face it, Ferelith,' she said to herself. 'That dinner meant too much to you and meant nothing to him. But this call is work, it's to do with the Law.'

'Lord Webster, please.'

She sat gripping the receiver, her stomach churning with nerves and embarrassment. It's work, she told herself over and over.

'May I ask who is calling?' The voice was educated, well modulated, of indeterminate age.

'Ferelith Gallagher.'

'One moment, please.'

Her knuckles were white. She tried to relax.

'Miss Gallagher?' It was the same woman, his secretary. 'Lord Webster is engaged all day, but if you are going to be in your office he will try to ring you back sometime this afternoon.'

Disappointment dropped in her stomach like a stone.

'Yes, I'll be here. I'm rather busy.'

Why had she said that? Because she was not going to move from the office in case he called but she did not want him to know that.

'I am busy. I am busy,' she told herself and proved it. The telephone rang three times during the afternoon but Sarah did not announce Lord Webster. Finally at a quarter-past seven, Ferelith decided to go home and to get something to eat. She had had nothing but Sarah's stewed tea and a digestive biscuit all day. The telephone rang in her office as she turned out the light.

'Ferelith,' said that unforgettable voice in relief. 'I just knew that I would find you still at your desk. It was nice of you to call and I'm sorry I couldn't speak to you.'

He thought it was a personal call, that she had got tired of waiting. She was glad that the light was out to hide her embarrassment, if only from herself.

'It's the internment policy, Lord Webster,' she said stiffly. 'I have a client, a friend really . . .'

She told him the story, at first haltingly but as her

embarrassment faded she became more articulate. He listened attentively.

'I'm afraid government policy is very clear and the first priority is the safety of the realm. Nineteen thousand Italian fish-and-chip shop owners or West End restaurateurs have been interned and will be deported . . .'

'He's an old man, a good tax-paying businessman who built up a thriving business that employed several hundred Scots. He's not a threat to the King's peace.'

'I'm quite sure that applies to many of them. Ferelith, I will do what I can. I will certainly get his documentation but every lawyer in the country is flooding us with these requests. If I investigate and find myself in total agreement with you, and I'm sure I shall, I will do everything I can to expedite his return to his family.'

She could ask no more. He could not wave a magic wand and it would be childish to expect him to do so.

'Thank you sir.'

'Sir, because this is a business conversation? May we have a personal conversation now? I thought we were beginning to be friends. Are we friends, Ferelith?'

'Sometimes I thought we were and then I remember that I am a very junior solicitor and that you are . . . you.'

'I think only that I am a man and that you are a woman and that when we're together I'm not the man I thought I was, but become the man I hoped to be. Does that make sense or am I moving too quickly?'

'Yes.' It was all she could say because forces were at work in her that had blazed brightly once and which she had damped down and tried to smother.

'I wish you would come and work in Edinburgh. Then we could see one another and we could go so slowly, wherever it is that we are going.'

'I can't leave Mr Smythe.'

'I know and I can't get to Glasgow, not because I don't want to, but because of the pressure of work. Have you seen that film with a nice young man yet?'

'No.'

'I'm glad. I'll ring and let you know about your client.'

On the 1st of July the *Arandora Star* sailed into exile from Liverpool with a cargo of aliens, mainly German and Italian nationals or of German or Italian descent. Off the north-west of Ireland, a country of awesome beauty that Vincenzo Regente had particularly liked, the ship was torpedoed by a German submarine, and it sank with an incredible loss of life: nearly two hundred with German surnames, nearly five hundred Italians. Mr Regent died in the cold waters of the Atlantic while his baby grandson staggered across the drawing room carpet of his parents' lovely Glasgow home, and perhaps wondered why such an amazing feat of creativity was not met with the acclaim that young Dominic, now called Domenico, felt it merited.

And Ferelith Gallagher closed the door of her office and sat at her desk and cried. There had been one terse phone call. Yes, it would seem that Vincenzo Regente's only crime was that he had not become naturalized. Lord Webster would take his case up with the Home Secretary. There was a second call.

'He went down with the *Arandora Star*. I am so sorry, Ferelith.'

'I'm sure you did everything you could,' she said quietly.

He was silent and she could hear the hummming down the wires between Edinburgh and Glasgow.

'This isn't the time,' he said. 'I'll call later.'

But Christmas of 1940 came and went and the receptionist did not announce Lord Webster; and then it was early 1941 and the telephone finally rang.

What a nuisance. She had waited for months to hear from him, and now that he was indeed asking her to see a film with him, she was right in the middle of the most important work that she had yet been given. The feeling of abject disappointment was surprisingly intense.

'I can't,' she said. 'I just can't see that I have the right to take the time.'

He could hear the disappointment in her voice: it mirrored the regret he felt.

'If we ever do manage to woo you away from Charles, you'll be well worth it,' he tried to say lightly. 'May I ring you in a week or two?'

Total honesty at all times, in all relationships. She could hear Sister Anthony's voice.

'I should like that very much,' Ferelith said.

'Good, me too,' he said. 'I shall ring soon.'

She put the receiver down but still held her hand caressingly on the receiver. What a lovely voice he had, warm and gentle but strong and . . . Ferelith Gallagher, you sound just like the poorest of women's magazines. Strong and gentle. What a cliché. Get to work.

She picked up her pen, shook her head to rid it of all lingering thoughts of Angus Webster, and got to work, steadily, conscientiously.

Hours later, she had just made up her mind to leave the office so as to catch a late tram when the telephone rang again.

'Ferelith?'

She recognized the voice at once and her heart began its emotional seesawing.

'Ferelith. Oh, thank God you are still there. I hoped and prayed that I would catch you.'

'Blair, we said when the war was over.' It was almost two years since she had spoken to him: she had almost forgotten him.

'I'm going off tomorrow. I have to see you, just one more time.'

'Oh Blair, what is the point of this?'

'I want to be able to think of you as my sister . . .'

'Your father's second greatest mistake,' she interrupted bitterly. How that still rankled.

'Please. If we can be friends as we were in those early days. Do you remember? Walking up and down the Royal Mile: strolling in Princes St Gardens while it was growing, this love we . . . I still have.'

'Blair. It would be better that we did not think of one another at all, put that whole sorry episode behind us.'

'It wasn't a sorry episode and I regret only the way it turned out. Please, Ferelith. I have stayed away doing all the sensible things I should have done. I've dated pretty Waacs and Wrens and anybody else who could help me stay sane in the hell of the last two years, but I can't go out to it again without seeing you. You're my sister, for God's sake. We share the same blood.'

She had never before thought of it like that: the same blood. She could never get rid of him because he was a part of her. He was her brother and he was going off somewhere . . . destination unknown.

'I can see you for a quick cup of coffee, no more. I have important work to do tomorrow.'

'I'm at Central Station. We could have coffee in the bar.'

Damn, damn, damn: another complication she did not need when she was trying to keep her mind clear. All that was missing now was an air raid. Please God, please God, get me to the station and back to Hillhead in one piece.

Funny that she had not thought of a uniform. The bar was full of them, blue ones, olive ones, khaki ones. It was full of cigarette smoke too, desperate laughter and quiet, strained voices. She peered through the tobacco-induced peasouper, looking for expensively cut but well-aged tweed. Blair, in the uniform of an Air Force officer, was at the bar and she pushed her way through to him without seeing the tall, distinguished man with a briefcase and an overnight bag who balanced a whisky glass and a sandwich.

She could not deny her love for him. It swelled in her and she smiled at him in real affection. He bent and kissed her cheek, a brother's kiss, light as a feather.

For a moment she leaned against him and felt the pent-up feelings drain out of her. She felt relief and a quality she could only describe as peace.

'A drink, little sister? Whisky?'

'I'm developing a taste for white wine.'

'Shouldn't think they'd have a decent wine.'

'I really don't want anything to drink, Blair. Can't we sit down somewhere for a few minutes?'

'The floor?'

They laughed.

'We would have done that years ago,' she said.

'I'm not only a gentleman but an officer now,' he said with mock seriousness. 'Must keep my dignity.'

'You haven't lost your sense of humour.'

'I lost everything else that counts,' he said matter of factly but so, so sadly.

'Blair, I am prepared to think about you, to deal with you, to build up a relationship with you . . . a brother and sister relationship.'

'I'll settle for that. Just don't cut me out of your life, Ferelith.'

'I won't do that. You are very important to me too.'

'You two going to gaze into each other's eyes all night or are you going to order a drink? If not, give someone else the bar space.'

'I must go anyway, Blair. I have so much work to do.'

He pulled her to him and held her hard against his greatcoat. She put her arms around his neck and nestled for a moment against him. Then she broke away.

'I have to go. Write to me. You know my address?'

She turned quickly and struggled through the press of people to the door. There were tears in her eyes and she did not recognize the man who, with sadness etched on his face, opened the door for her.

'Thank you,' she said with a sob.

'Good night, Miss Gallagher,' said Lord Webster of Dalmarnock and closed the door quietly behind her.

Outside she stopped, the voice finally having penetrated the core of misery. It was Angus Webster. Oh, God. She had told him that she was too busy to see him and then she had immediately gone, it would seem, to meet someone else, someone whom he had met two years before. She thought of what Blair had said then. 'You make me sound important. At the very least, an immoral liaison.'

She groaned aloud. Why was life so difficult? Did it ever get easier? It seemed that no matter how sophisticated her outer shell became the inside was still this seething mass of doubts. Why had she not told Angus two years ago that Blair was her half-brother? Now he thought she had lied to him. Well, if you think that, my dear Lord Webster of Dalmarnock, I really don't care.

But he never called to invite her to see a film. Still she found herself hoping that on one occasion Sarah would answer the telephone, turn to her archly and say, 'It's his Lordship. No doubt a very serious legal question. I'll leave you alone to answer it.'

She waited in vain.

She had her first letter from Blair, a letter that was too destroyed by censors to be enjoyed. She did not know where he was, but gathered that he was not in Britain, was on almost constant alert, and had flown several sorties. He gave her an address which told her nothing, but to which she replied telling him as much as she thought he would find amusing about her work. How, although it was at times terribly stressful because she was now being asked to instruct a practising advocate on criminal cases, it could also be very funny.

Not that there was anything funny about the Reid case. Billy Reid had deliberately stalked the man whom the police, no matter how they tried, could not convict of raping Reid's fifteen-year-old daughter. One night he had waited outside the pub where his intended victim, Tom Kay, spent most of his waking hours and when Kay had emerged in an alcoholic haze, Billy Reid had proceeded to kick him into unconsciousness. It had taken three inebriated chums of Kay, plus a perfectly sober large barman to get him off his punching bag while there was still some life in it. It certainly looked as if the rapist, if so he was, would be unlikely to repeat his crime for some time to come, if at all. Billy Reid had not run away. He had waited quite calmly beside the unconscious Kay until someone had run to the nearest unvandalized phonebox and put in an emergency call.

Charles Smythe convinced Billy that the young female solicitor in his office was really the member of the firm best able to find him a good advocate.

'The thing is, Mrs,' Billy said to Ferelith, 'they polis didnae really care whether my wean got raped or no. Wan of them said she was asking for it, the way she dresses and the build she his on her. Well, whit am saying is a lassie of fifteen disnae ken whit she's asking fer and she should be able to, well, be a wee bit, ye ken. They're saying she had experience: ah didnae ken that, but gettin shugged by a sixteen-year-old boyfriend is no the same thing as gettin raped by a man older than her faither and wi a build on him lik a bull. An if yer law says different then ah don't gie a fuck fer yer law.'

'The last of the vigilantes,' said Simon when Ferelith discussed the case with him.

'He really thinks he should get off and possibly with a commendation for gallantry.'

'I can't help a sneaking feeling of admiration.'

'Simon, Tom Kay may be the dregs of humanity and he may well have raped that girl, but it is possible that he will never walk again, never mind any other activity. I'm desperately sorry for Sheila:

she certainly was not treated with the sympathy and understanding she should have received, but, sweet Jesus, imagine the chaos if each of us was to take the law into our own hands or, worse, to totally disregard the law. Where would we be then? We are better than animals, even Tom Kay, even, God forgive him, Billy Reid. Sheila has not been fairly treated, not by the man who raped her, or, God forgive us all, by the law, but we have to work to change the law, not to cut it down and throw it away.'

'Don't you wish you yourself were defending Billy?'

'Oh yes, partly because I think I might just feel as he does had I been in the same position, but I have the education and the training to help me discipline my instincts, something the Billy Reids of this world have never learned. Nigel Watson will probably try to get him off. I would fight the case from the standpoint of "Guilty as hell, but driven to it in a moment of passion". I only wish the moment had not gone on so long,' she finished drily.

'And if Kay dies?'

'Then I will probably be instructing my first case where our client is, as the book says, "hanged by the neck until he is dead". Charming thought. I shall leave you to think about it.'

He left and Ferelith looked at the door which he had closed quite firmly behind him. Yes, the solicitor could go away: she would now ring Nigel to see if he was willing to hear about the case. Then there would be a trip into Edinburgh for consultations and then she would more or less fade into the background. Someone else would do the job that every fibre of her being told her she could do as well if not better.

Damn it, damn it, why should an advocate have

to live in a specific area of a specific city? she thought. Why shouldn't I be allowed to defend Billy Reid right from this office in Glasgow? I may be right up to date but my profession is still stuck in the Middle Ages. It still thinks that advocates are gentlemen who don't have to concern themselves with anything so tawdry as earning enough money to pay their bills. She thought of Lord Webster's gown. She had seen it several times when she had been a student and it had been months before she had realised that it was slightly different from the gowns of men like Mr Belanger. Lord Webster's gown appeared to be the usual full gown of the Scottish advocate but there was a small flap sewn onto one of the sleeves. This showed the Scottish bar that this advocate had, in fact, appeared in a Scottish case in the great London Law Courts. All English barristers wore flaps on their sleeves, a leftover from the days when money for a defence was never openly discussed between gentlemen but the little pocket was there so that the client might surreptitiously insert a generous donation.

'Some day, somehow, I will be an advocate,' Ferelith promised herself as she asked the operator to connect her with Nigel Watson in his correct upper-middle-class home in the New Town of Edinburgh.

On Thursday, the 13th of March 1941 Ferelith was in her flat for once. Sometimes she wondered why she bothered to pay for electricity and heating – she was never there. Suddenly the sirens went off, a strange, screaming, wailing noise. Gas masks had been issued in 1938 and her gas mask, which bumped against her legs causing bruises every time she was forced to carry it, was at the door of the

flat with her bag containing her ration book, a few
photographs, her birth certificate, her degrees, her
passport, and the treasured little gold brooch that
Dominic had given her when she had graduated.
She turned off the lamp, picked up the bag, and
left the flat. She should go to the shelter.

Outside the noise was even worse and the con-
fusion was frightening. She could already hear fire
bells and police horns. Her hope that it might have
been no more than ARP practice melted. Great
swords of light were arching across the sky and she
stood transfixed by the strange, frightening beauty
of the grey metal of the planes caught in a sudden
beam. She could hear what she assumed to be the
ack-ack battery at Duntochar. In the Clyde a war-
ship was firing back. On the devastated Clydeside,
stricken gas mains erupted and fires exploded into
life. Singer's timber yard and the Toker Distillery
were very flammable and, in a few terrifying minutes, the entire area was transformed into a raging
inferno of fire and annihilation. German bombers
were using these fires as flight paths to wreak ever
more destruction.

They'll destroy the whole city, everything. There's
no chance of survival. The thoughts were very clear
and she was very cold but very very calm. She found
herself turning away from the shelter and walking
on and on, farther and farther westwards. She did
not know how far she walked or how long. Then
there was a huge whoosh right in front of her and
she found herself sucked into a vortex and still her
mind remained calm.

'I would have expected to be blown out, not
sucked in,' she announced quite clearly but there
was no one alive to hear. She had lost her bag . . . her
birth certificate . . . Dominic's brooch. She had lost

her contact with Dominic and then she remembered
Domenico's toothy, slobbery grin and she laughed
and cried at the same time. She could never lose him.
She picked herself up from the very edge of a bomb
crater and screamed as she looked into the shattered
window of a car with its dead driver grotesquely
staring at her as if he objected to the condition in
which he found both himself and the road. And the
road was a mess. Tram rails were corkscrewed like
the most bizarre exhibits from the most avant garde
art group. Ferelith caught what was left of her coat
on broken steel and yelped a bit with the pain as it
also scraped her legs.

'My God.' Her legs. What had happened to them?
They were covered in dirt and blood and yet until
now she had felt nothing. She stumbled on, still
unsure of where she was going but glad only that
her limbs functioned.

'Is there any part of Glasgow left standing?'
Ferelith looked through red-rimmed eyes but all
she could see was the glow of fires all over the city.
'It's the end of the world. I can't believe we can go
on from here. Doesn't the Bible say it will be a fire
. . . It's today and I'm too tired to care.'

She was standing in the middle of what had been
a street, looking at what had been the orphanage in
which she grew up. There was a huge crater in the
ground. Part of her mind tried to remind her that
the Mother Vicar General had moved the orphans
and most of the community to Ireland at the start
of the Blitz. Sister Anthony is safe. Sister Glenn is
safe. I have lost only a few possessions, nothing
that counts. She looked down at her feet. They
were bloodied now like her legs and she saw to
her surprise that somehow she had lost her shoes.

The wind changed and the smoke drifted away

and Ferelith began to laugh and then to cry. Her castle, her ruined castle, that had withstood everything man and the elements had thrown at it for almost one thousand years, still stood there defiantly at the end of what had been the driveway.

'Up yours, Adolf,' she shouted.

She turned and hobbled away from what had once been her home, the place where she had dreamed her first dreams. 'I'm leaving you the way I came to you,' she said. 'No shoes, no clothes, nothing, but I'm like that castle – indestructible.'

She wondered if tram conductors would let her on without money. 'Stupid worry, Ferelith. Are there any trams? Dear God, am I the only person in Glasgow left alive?'

An ambulance, its siren screaming, raced past her and answered her question and she decided to head for the offices, if she was not too disorientated. She limped on and did not see the car that screamed to a halt beside her.

'Ferelith, dear God, I've been looking for you all night and I've used about all my petrol.'

'Simon.' She fell into his arms with heartfelt thankfulness and he lifted her up and carried her to the car.

'Thank God you're a light weight,' he said. 'I never saw myself as Clark Gable.'

'Your father?'

'Fine. He wants me to bring you there.' He looked at her in puzzlement. 'You do know your building got one of the last raspberries from Jerry: not too bad but you can't go back there tonight . . . this morning. He has plenty of room. You can't stay with me. Look there's a thermos of tea with lots of sugar, and there's a blanket. Wrap yourself up.'

'What brought you out to the Convent?' she said.

'I knew you were too tough to kill and so I went to all the places you might be. None of them are there and I thought: wounded rabbits run home.'

'I'm not a wounded rabbit.'

He took his hand off the wheel and pressed her knee. It was the first intimate gesture he had ever made towards her. 'No, sweetness,' he said, 'you are a lion.'

10

SIMON ENLISTED IN the Royal Scots Fusiliers.

'Damn it, Ferelith, Bevin has just announced the registration of a hundred thousand women. All the young unmarried women, twenty and twenty-one-year-olds and he's even asking married women who can do war work locally to volunteer. He's promising an expansion in nursery facilities, day and night. God knows what I'm capable of doing. I'm hardly keen on the sight of blood, as you well know, but they'll find something for me to do that's useful.'

'You'll look quite pretty in a kilt,' teased Ferelith to stop herself from clutching him hysterically and begging him not to go.

'We're in trews actually,' he said grandly. 'Probably better: I'm a wee thing skinny for a kilt,' he finished in a dreadful parody of a Highland accent.

'What does your father say?'

Simon struck a pose. 'Damn proud, my boy, damn proud,' Simon quoted. 'His cook discovered a *thing* called a rissole yesterday, by the way. Eightpence the pound. Dad's going to eat them while I'm away as an offering to Mars in exchange for the life of his son and heir.'

'A rissole?' asked Ferelith as if her life depended on the answer. 'What's that?'

'It's some kind of sausage without meat, all veggies. He'll loathe them,' he said and stood up to go.

'Oh, Simon, Simon, please, can't you list yourself as a conscientious objector? Even the BBC is going to hire them.'

'Ah but, sweetness, a conscientious objector knows to what he has a conscientious objection. I'm not in that category and especially not after this shelling. I object strongly to the strong exploiting the weak. I object to the systematic destruction of beautiful buildings and paintings and yes, I object very strongly to useless blood shedding, especially my own, but I just can't take any more and the fact that we are killing women and children in Germany doesn't really fill me with enthusiasm, but maybe if I can do something to help stop this . . . this lunacy . . . You know I realized the other day why I went into law and it's not because my father wanted it or because there was an easy place into which I could slot myself. It's because I believe in reason, in reasoned argument. It's the only way for civilized people to behave. Maybe if I was to go and see Hitler and put the case to him *reasonably*. I say Hitler, old chap, you really must see reason. It's so obvious to the rest of us. Trouble is, sweetness, no matter how well couched the argument, if you're arguing with someone who refuses to see the other fellow's position or who is unable to see it then you're up the Clyde without a paddle. The only other thing, Ferelith, is my flat. I would be so grateful if you would stay in it and look after Traviata, my cat, for me. You can't stay with Maria for ever and God knows when your own flat will be fixed. If I leave my place empty it'll be vandalized or squatted in, or whatever. I've told Dad and the dragon lady: she'll be wickedly excited at the thought of you lying in my bed waiting for me to return. I must go. I'll send you an address as soon as I get one and you must

write regularly. I shall pretend to the other chaps
that you are my pin-up, and you are, my sweet,
you are.'

He dropped his keys on the desk, hugged her
quickly and was gone. She waited without moving
until the sound of his hurrying feet had died away
before turning off the lamp by her desk. She moved
to the window and pulled the edge of the blind
back a millimetre but she could see nothing. He
had disappeared into the fog.

First Blair. Now Simon.

Work, as always, was the antidote and there was
plenty of work. On the night of the first blitz of
Clydebank, the night in which her own flat had
been damaged, she had asked Simon to take her,
not to his father's home but to Maria and Mauro.
Mauro, with a frightened Maria behind him, had
answered the doorbell, a golf club clutched in his
hand. Maria had taken one look over her husband's
massive shoulders, seen the grimy blood-stained
girl and had pushed Mauro aside and rushed to
Ferelith.

'Wine,' she had ordered her husband, 'then a hot
bath and sleep. Food too. You too, Simon.' She had
stopped and looked closely at him. 'Why are you
still immaculate?'

'I didn't get blitzed,' explained Simon meekly but
she had not waited for an answer to her question.

Hours later he had wakened up on the sofa of the
di Rollo's sitting room to find a small boy using his
handmade shoes as cars and to be told by Maria
that Ferelith was well, was still asleep, and would
remain with them.

'I have plenty of clothes for her,' she had laughed.
'I get fatter with each baby but I never throw
anything out because I kid myself, one day I'll

be a sylph again. She will be the best-dressed,
bombed-out refugee in Glasgow.'

And so Ferelith had stayed on and for the first time
in her life, if she didn't count her one lovely holiday
all those years ago with Elspeth Baxter's people,
found herself living as a member of a family and
she loved it. She drove into Glasgow every morning
with Mauro and then went home with a briefcase
full of papers, but before she could deal with them
she had Domenico to bathe or Alicia to help with her
homework, or she had to listen to Gaia, who was in
love. There were huge Italian meals to help cook
and to eat, but she was pushed away while Mauro
and Maria washed the dishes because, 'Ferelith is a
career woman: she has real work to do, not dishes
to wash like any peasant.' And no matter how much
Ferelith protested that she would be perfectly happy
to wash dishes, she found herself alone in her room,
her briefcase open on the table, while she listened
to the muted sounds of love and laughter from the
kitchen.

Yes, better for the di Rollo's and for Ferelith herself
that she take up Simon's offer of his flat.

Ferelith heard about Blair in a letter from one
Jamie Winterton, who was, he said, both her cousin
and Blair's. The letter put the phone call she had
received earlier that morning completely out of
her head.

I'm so sorry to have to tell you that the injuries
are quite horrific and it is unlikely that Blair will
survive. He came to see me before he went off
this last time and told me the whole story and,
of course, each of you has the family's sincerest
sympathy. Blair listed me as his nearest relative
because he did not want you to receive the

telegram that I have just received, but he did
ask me to let you know if he was killed. I felt
that you would want to know about this mess
too. I will stay here in London as long as need be
and if you would like to come, we can find a bed
for you. My wife joins me in this invitation.

Lord Winterton, Jamie, finished by giving her the
telephone number of the house in London where
he was staying while Blair was being treated in
hospital. She could not telephone until the morning
and she spent the night packing and praying. She
had to go to him. How like him not to want to
bother her – as he would see it – with injuries. A
clean death was all right but no complications, no
pity. She was at her office as soon as the blackout
was lifted and asked the operator for the number.

Lord Winterton was at the hospital but his wife
spoke to Ferelith.

'He was shot down, my dear. Blair managed to
limp back to their field and they crashlanded. Blair,
and Graham Smith the navigator survived, but only
just. It looks really bad.'

'I want to see him.'

'Of course. We're bunking at a friend's flat and
you're most welcome. I'll stay for a few more days
but I must get back to my children. God knows why
we're worried about propriety at a time like this. If
you let me know what time your train gets in I'll
try to arrange to meet you. You don't mind a bus,
do you?'

A bus. Ferelith laughed. How like the British
aristocracy to worry about inconveniencing guests.

Two days later, after a journey that she did not look
forward to repeating, she found herself in London.

There was a Naafi canteen open and she went in. The thought of a cup of hot, sweet tea drew her irresistibly. She managed to get to the counter and to count out the few coppers asked for the tea and then tried to find somewhere to sit to drink it. She intended then to find her way to Jane Winterton's without bothering her hostess.

The appearance of the tall young man who approached her gave her a start. Blair. It was Blair, uninjured, unhurt.

'Lord Winterton?' she asked shakily.

'Jamie,' he said, 'and you must be Ferelith. I've been trotting back and forth from the hospital just in case your train arrived before the end of the war.' He smiled at her with Blair's smile and handed her the canteen cup and saucer she had put down on the bare table. 'Come on, there's a good girl, finish your tea – you look dead on your feet – and I'll either take you home for a nice hot bath or we'll go to the hospital.'

'The hospital, please.'

'Of course. Now, I'll try to ring Jane so she'll save hot water for you and then we'll buzz along. There's no change today I'm afraid, but at least he's no worse.'

Where had he managed to find a car and one with petrol? It was joy to sink back against the cushions – she had stood from Glasgow to York and then taken turns sitting from York to London – and to relax. As they turned in to St Thomas's she realized with a further sinking of her spirits that she had never been in a hospital before and she hoped that she would cope. Everything was forgotten, however, as soon as she entered the corridors and smelled that strange hospital smell of carbolic.

Jamie led her unerringly to the ward where Blair

and too many other hurt and battered bodies lay as testament to man's savagery. She would not have recognized him. She had known him intimately but under the swathes of bandages he looked hardly different from any of the others.

The nurse who was standing by his side checking the monitoring equipment looked up at their arrival and smiled with pleasure. Lord Winterton was obviously a favourite.

'Hello, Nurse,' he smiled in return. 'I've brought Squadron Leader Winterton's sister, Miss Gallagher.'

'The cage?' Ferelith's voice when she did force it out of her mouth was a squeak.

'I'm sorry,' Jamie whispered. 'I should have told you about his legs. If he lives, he'll never walk again.'

Grief almost suffocated her. Blair who loved to ride, to walk his land, never to walk again.

She put out her hand to touch him, to hold him. Where was there skin uncovered by bandages?

'He's been badly burned, Miss Gallagher,' said the nurse in a soft Irish voice, 'but I sometimes hold this hand here and I like to think he feels my presence.'

Ferelith went to the other side of the bed and the nurse relinquished her place. Blair's left hand lay quietly on the starched white sheet.

'Hold him, Miss Gallagher,' ordered the nurse. 'Sure maybe he knows you're here. Sometimes faith and love do more than medicine.'

Ferelith sat down and held Blair's hand and watched the nurse move away to the next bed.

'She's a marvel that girl,' said Jamie. 'If I hadn't Janie I'd steal her away from all this. She seems to be on duty every time I come. I'm sure she does more than her share.'

'Probably all of them are doing that, Jamie. I'll

stay for a while. I'm not tired now. Why don't you go home to Jane and I'll find my way there later.'

'If you're sure. I'll come back to fetch you though: I'll want to visit him again.'

He left, but fifteen minutes later was back with a mug of hot, black tea and a roll spread with some kind of fish paste. 'Sorry, it's all the canteen could find,' he said, and left again.

Nothing had ever tasted so good.

She ate the sandwich and drank the tea and looked at Blair, at the bandages that covered everything but his left hand, at the tubes and machines.

'A victim too.' And now he was a victim or a casualty of this war.

'I wish I could make it up to you,' she whispered. 'I wish I could make it all better.'

She was sound asleep, her head resting on his hand when the doctor came. He apologized for waking her.

'Sorry, Mrs Winterton,' he said.

She looked at him in surprise. Mrs Winterton. She had been Mrs Winterton for such a short time. Then she realized that the tired doctor had merely assumed that she was Blair's wife. Probably most of the women who sat by the beds were wives or mothers or sweethearts.

'I'm Ferelith Gallagher, his sister,' she said.

'You'll have to leave for a while, Mrs Gallagher,' he said dispassionately and pulled the curtains around the bed.

'Why don't you pop down to the café,' said a nurse. 'We'll be a while and there might just be some soup or some nice meat-paste sandwiches.'

'I'll just wait here, if you don't mind.'

The nurse shrugged and disappeared behind the curtains and Ferelith walked slowly up and down the ward. What were they doing to him? Was there any change? Would he live?

It seemed an age before the curtains were opened again. Nothing looked different but one nurse had a large bag of soiled dressings. She smiled at Ferelith.

'He's quite a fighter,' she said.

'There's nothing you can do here, Mrs Gallagher,' said the doctor. 'We have done all we can. It's now up to your brother and his God. Go home and come back tomorrow. If he gets through the night he has a chance.'

'I'll stay.'

He shrugged much in the same way as the nurse had done and moved on to his next patient and Ferelith resumed her vigil.

'Hello, I'm Jane,' said a voice beside her.

Ferelith smiled tiredly and held out her hand to the elegant and immaculate young woman who stood beside her.

'Oh, poor lamb, you're exhausted,' said Lady Winterton, giving her a quick hug. 'How is he?'

'They say if he comes through the night he has a chance. Jane, I'm sorry if you came especially for me but I have to stay.'

'I thought you might say that. I couldn't bring the hot bath but I have a little picnic for you.' She reached into her capacious handbag and drew out some newspaper parcels. 'There's some tough old pheasant: the sauce made it edible but I hate cold sauce, don't you? The claret in this beaker is fearfully good and we only decanted it because you were coming so you must have your share. This salady thing is something we ate in the States. My dear, it's the most divine way of eating boring old cabbage, and there's a wodge of cheese and some oatcakes. Nurse Thomson will bring you some cocoa later when she's having some. Jamie thinks she fancies him, the silly man, but it's Blair. He was conscious when he came in and he grabbed her hand and said, "Don't leave me." I think she's afraid he'll give up if she's not there and who knows? There now, you're quite exhausted listening to me and so I'll toodle off. Tomorrow I must go home to my babes but I'll see you before I go. You won't mind staying in the flat with Jamie? He's the soul of honour and besides my grandmother is doing voluntary nursing, would you believe, and she'll pop in and out all the time. *Au revoir.*' She kissed Ferelith and turned to leave, and Ferelith, already sipping the glorious wine, watched her stop and chat to other invalids who were conscious and alone. When she did reach the doors she turned and waved.

'Ray of sunshine that,' said a nurse, 'but I don't need to tell you that.'

'She is lovely, isn't she,' said Ferelith and opened her parcel of 'tough old pheasant'.

Perhaps it was the wine but the pheasant, the cabbage salad, the cheese and biscuits were delicious and gave her an almost immediate feeling of wellbeing.

'That's the wine,' she told herself and settled down beside Blair, holding his hand and talking to him until her mouth was dry and her throat ached. Nurse Thomson, the nurse she had met when she first came in, brought her some hot cocoa. The nurse too sat for a moment and Ferelith sympathized with the fatigue so obvious in her face and body.

'You really shouldn't do more than your shift, Nurse,' she said. 'You'll be no good to any of them if you collapse with exhaustion.'

'I'm a professional, Mrs Gallagher: I don't do any more than my hours unless I'm caught up in an emergency, and God knows there have been enough of those lately.'

'I'm sorry. I had no right to speak at all. It's just that Jamie . . . Lord Winterton said that you always seemed to be here.'

'He looks like him, doesn't he? I've been trying to make a face for him and thought he must have had that same pleasant face.'

'Must have had . . .' Oh God, was Blair to be disfigured as well as crippled? The nurse saw her look of horror.

'I'm sorry. You hadn't realized. He was terribly badly burned. We'll be taking those bandages off to let air in to aid in healing. Then we'll see how bad it is going to be. Certainly some scarring but his eyes are fine. Once the awful swelling goes down the doctors say he'll see perfectly.'

'Jane did tell me. I just didn't take it in.'

'No, you don't, do you,' said the girl sadly and was silent for a minute remembering her own experiences.

'He came in just after . . . just after I lost my husband and my little girl,' she said. 'Jim had leave. He hadn't seen Fiona for a year. "I'll fetch her from the baby sitter," he said, and got there just in time to start digging her out of the rubble of the house. They told him to wait for the fire brigade but he scrabbled with his hands, calling her name. A wall fell in on him. They brought them out together. He had been almost on top of her. I buried them together too. In Daddy's arms for eternity. And then I came back to work and he came. "Don't leave me," he said and I want badly to be here when he comes round.'

'When he comes round? The doctor . . .'

The nurse laughed and stood up. 'Doctors? What

do they know? Haven't I lit a candle every day since he came in?'

'He isn't a Catholic.'

'It's only people who care about labels, Mrs Gallagher. Now I must get back to work. It's been a lovely break.'

She picked up Ferelith's empty mug and walked off down the ward.

'Nurse Thomson.' Ferelith's joyous cry stopped her. 'He moved. His hand moved. I'm sure of it.'

The heartbroken girl of a few minutes before was gone. Nurse Thomson was the consummate professional. She hurried back to Blair, bent over him for a few minutes and then straightened up. 'I'll get Doctor Ellison,' she said.

Dr Ellison was a woman in her early thirties, tall, slender, and attractive. She was also extremely efficient and once more Ferelith found herself on the wrong side of the curtains waiting with baited breath for the professionals to do their jobs. It seemed hours. Other personnel came back and forth, some wheeling trolleys in, others wheeling trolleys out. Each and every one passed Ferelith as if she did not exist.

At last the curtains were pulled back.

'Are you the next of kin?' asked Dr Ellison.

Ferelith's heart plummeted with fear and she felt herself grow cold and begin to tremble. 'I'm his half-sister. Lord Winterton, his cousin, is officially listed as next-of-kin.'

'Then I'd get in touch with him. We're going to operate. He's putting up such a fight, we think he's strong enough for us to go in and give him a hand.'

Ferelith looked at her watch, although she knew perfectly well that neither Jane nor Jamie Winterton would object to being telephoned in the middle of the night. 'I'll ring now,' she said but Ellison had already forgotten her.

The Wintertons joined her nearly two hours later but Blair was still in surgery.

'Did you think we weren't coming?' asked Jane. 'We ended up parking the car – I hope it'll be there in the morning – and walking the last few miles. The streets are abysmal.'

'Don't chatter, Janie. Have you heard anything, Ferelith?'

'No, just that he seemed to have decided to breathe for himself and so they thought they could operate to help relieve some of the pressure.'

'That's wonderful news. Now we wait and pray, I suppose.'

They waited until the early light of dawn began to filter through the blackout curtains of the waiting room. Sometime later a porter came and lifted the blinds altogether but still there was no word from the operating theatre.

'I would kill for a cup of tea,' said Jane just as the door of the operating room opened and Dr Ellison, looking so different in a grey suit with a pink blouse, came out.

'You can see him, just two of you, for one minute.' She smiled and suddenly she was a human being sharing their joy. 'My husband always said the Scots were as tough as old boots.'

Ferelith and Jamie went into the special recovery room, where those patients still too seriously ill to be returned to a large ward were being monitored on an individual basis. The cage was still in place over Blair's legs but there were fewer tubes disappearing into various parts of his poor shattered body.

Nurse Thomson was there. 'It's still touch and go,' she said, 'but he's breathing on his own.'

'When do you expect him to regain consciousness, Nurse?' asked Jamie.

'That's what we're waiting for, Lord Winterton. He seems to know I'm here because there's faint pressure – that's what you felt, Mrs Gallagher, isn't it? – but he's heavily sedated. I really think you should persuade Mrs Gallagher to get some proper rest in a real bed.'

'I'd like to stay.'

Jamie put his arms around her and gently pushed her from the room. 'Head of the family,' he said. 'I'm ordering you to rest.'

Ferelith went with him willingly. Until he had put his arms around her she had not known just how exhausted she was. Even the relief of seeing Blair without the breathing apparatus had added to her fatigue. She contributed nothing to the next several hours, had no real knowledge of how she got from the hospital to the luxurious flat where they were staying. She half-felt Janie and an elderly woman, whom she later found out to be Jane's grandmother, undress her and get her into a bed with crisp clean white sheets and then she slept and slept. She slept without moving for eighteen and a half hours and woke feeling happy and relaxed and unbelievably refreshed. She lay for a moment wondering where she was and how she had got into the most enormous, most beautiful four-poster bed. Then she remembered and jumped up. Blair. She was in London with Blair's cousin and Blair was going to be all right. She just knew he was. Perhaps it was Dr Ellison and her cool skill or Nurse Thomson's candles or a mixture of the two.

'Good morning, you must be absolutely famished.' It was the elderly lady she vaguely remembered and Ferelith rushed to take the tray that she was carrying.

'I'm tougher than I look, my dear. I'm Merry Price, Janie's granny. The poor darling has had to get back to her children. She does hope either that you can get down to Surrey before you go back to Glasgow or that she'll be back in town before you leave. Eat up, eat up, you must be famished.'

'I don't believe that's a boiled egg,' said Ferelith looking at the exquisitely-appointed tray.

'No, it isn't. It's an hallucination,' laughed Mrs Price, 'and so I shall tell any inspectors who call. Enjoy it, my dear. When you're finished, have a lovely hot bath and then join me downstairs. I'm going into the hospital myself this afternoon and you can come with me. Jamie carried straight on from the station after he'd put Jane on the train. He'll be back in an hour or so with the latest news.'

How old was she? Ferelith wondered as she sat down to enjoy the egg that supposedly wasn't there, the toast soldiers, and the delicious pot of coffee. She had to be in her seventies and yet, here she was doing voluntary war work. What indomitable spirit. Later Ferelith was to find out that in 1916 Mrs Price had been left a widow with two daughters – the older of whom, Jane's mother, had just married – and a huge estate to run. She had not buckled under the weight of grief but had decided to get on with the job that had to be done and she was, over thirty years later, still doing it.

Much later she drove Ferelith in an ambulance to the hospital.

'Do you know I have never really had a driving lesson.'

As Ferelith hung on for dear life she felt that she could well believe it, but she smiled with closed teeth and tightened her grip on the seat.

Jamie was at Blair's bedside and he greeted his grandmother-in-law with real affection.

'She's quite remarkable,' he told Ferelith when the old lady had gone off to do her shift. 'She bullies people into getting well: she says that they become so fed up with her that they get well in sheer self-defence.'

'Perhaps she'll bully Blair for us,' said Ferelith softly as she looked down at the bandaged body. 'Do you know, Jamie, that I'm finally coming to terms with the fact that he is my brother. I would have loved to have had a brother, any relative at all, growing up.'

'Now you have lots of us,' said Jamie and proceeded to tell her all about his own two quite remarkable children, his sisters and their husbands and children, and Jane's younger sister who was not yet married but was cutting a path strewn with broken hearts through Society. 'She also does hours of ghastly work with Granny, something I won't let Janie do, and so we forgive her everything and try to comfort her rejected swains as best we can.'

They stayed in the hospital until desperate hunger drove them to try to find something to eat. Blair had not yet moved and Nurse Thomson was back on duty.

'I'll ring you at your flat, Lord Winterton,' she promised, 'if there's the slightest change.'

Ferelith and Jamie hurried out of the hospital. 'If we're lucky, we'll get home before Granny, who does everything beautifully except cooking.'

Ferelith laughed and tucked her hand into his arm to keep up with him as he playfully raced across the almost empty parking lot. They almost bumped into several men who were coming in the hospital gates as they were leaving. The men all raised their hats to one another as they avoided the collision and Ferelith's laugh caught in her throat.

'Why, Mr Belanger,' she said, 'how unexpected to see you in London.'

'Ferelith, but why are you not in Glasgow? Angus Webster, I'm sure told me that you had an engagement. We must fly. It's these interminable War Aid commissions.'

He raised his hat again and before she could introduce him to Jamie, had rushed off after the others.

'An old friend?'

'Yes. No. In a way.' Ferelith was nonplussed. 'I shadowed him at the Scottish Bar. He's a very good friend of . . . a friend.'

Jamie tucked her arm back into his. 'London is just a big village,' he said consolingly. 'I always meet everyone I know here – and usually when I don't want to.'

11

JAMIE DIPLOMATICALLY SAID no more about the encounter as they fought their way home through London's blitzed streets. Ferelith felt that he deserved some kind of explanation but first she gave herself time to marshal her thoughts. She was distressed to realize that she had remembered nothing and nobody after Jamie had written with the news of Blair. She had been looking forward with a singing heart to a hastily-arranged dinner engagement with Angus Webster. 'I'm deputizing for Cameron in a lewd and libidinous,' he had said. 'Can you possibly dine with me at such short notice?' And although he would definitely have understood if she had telephoned and explained or even left a message at the Court, she had rushed off without a thought of anyone.

Her mind had been so full of Blair that until she had met Oliver Belanger she had forgotten everyone and everything else. Mr Belanger had been surprised and would, no doubt, tell Angus that he had seen her in London. Would he say that she had been arm in arm with a very attractive man? No, and he probably would not even mention the encounter. Angus had every right to be furious and hurt. Still, the important thing, the only point that really mattered at this precise moment in the great scheme of things, was that Blair was going to get well. She could explain to Lord Webster: she could tell him everything and if he refused to accept her apology then he would be the loser. She said this to herself very bravely but a teeny-weeny feeling inside told her that she too would be a loser if he did not retain his confidence in her integrity.

Jamie had some sausages and some powdered eggs. He also had a bottle of very good champagne.

'Rather decadent, champagne and sausages, or will this become the *in* thing to have for a post-bombing supper?' He was joking as Jane would have done, sensing that Ferelith was still rather ill at ease in his company as well as being distressed by her meeting.

'I'm afraid I've rather blotted my copybook with Lord Webster of Dalmarnock,' she said. 'I had a date with him and I forgot completely. Very flattering to him. Mr Belanger is perhaps his closest friend and I wouldn't like Angus, Lord Webster, to get the wrong idea.'

'I'm your cousin, Ferelith, and Blair is your brother. Your friend will understand and besides, it's unlikely that your Mr Belanger will mention that he met you. Good friends don't do that sort of thing.'

'It might slip out if Angus is worried.' Would he be worried? Only if she meant something to him and why should she? And here Ferelith found herself telling someone she barely knew what she had been unable to formulate for Maria or Elspeth or even Simon, who knew her better than anyone. 'I quite like Angus, and we have seen one another once or twice and I had agreed to a real . . . date I suppose and then your letter came and all I could think of was Blair. I phoned my office and got them to deal with all business for me, and with Simon's cat too. People are becoming so used to handling one another's tragedies but I completely forgot Angus and then to bump into dear old Oliver . . .'

'He'll understand,' said Jamie handing her a glass of champagne and wondering who Simon was and why his cat was a tragedy, if indeed it was. 'And your Mr Belanger will be discreet. I caught only a quick glimpse but I saw a kind face.'

'It doesn't matter. It's just that one hates being rude,' explained Ferelith gulping the champagne as if it was water.

'Of course,' agreed Jamie and refilled her glass. 'You go and sit down. Put your feet up for a minute and I'll see if I can remember what Nanny told me to do with powdered egg. Supper will be an adventure.'

Mrs Price arrived back just as they were about to eat. They were looking at the mixture that Jamie persisted in calling an omelette and which Ferelith, after three glasses of champagne, called something quite unladylike, and wondering if they were either brave enough or hungry enough to eat.

'No, no darlings, don't eat,' she said. 'We're going out for real food. I met an old beau this afternoon: he's something frightfully grand at the War Office and he asked me to dinner and I told him that I had my grandson-in-law and his cousin here and he said 'bring them too'.

'I can't, Mrs Price,' said Ferelith. 'It sounds wonderful but I would like to go back to see Blair and if he is doing well I will really have to start thinking about going back to Glasgow. Other people are doing my work for me, you see.'

'Heavens, the conscience of the Scottish Calvinist. But you must of course do what is right for you, my dear.'

Jamie elected to eat his sausage omelette too and to drive Ferelith back to the hospital. 'After all, Granny, there is meat in a sausage . . .'

'I wouldn't count on that, darling boy,' laughed the elderly Mrs Price, who had too much experience of the recipes for sausages through two world wars.

'And we can't afford to waste food,' went on Jamie. 'But you go out with your old flame and behave yourself.'

'Absolutely not. Don't wait up. Use my car, if you like. There's just enough petrol to get you to and from the hospital.'

Ferelith was delighted to avail herself of this offer. One day, she thought, one day she would be able to do something in return for all the nice things these lovely people were doing for her. She tried to express some of this as Jamie drove her back to the hospital. He looked at her in total surprise.

'But Ferelith, you're family,' he said as if that explained everything.

Family. She had never been part of a family. The Sisters at the Convent had tried to make the orphaned or abandoned children feel that they were part of a family. Each was a viable and important member of God's family and that was nice, especially when the world was very dark and troubled, but a family, a real family, that was different. And now these amazing people, Jamie and the lovely Jane and eccentric Mrs Price, were saying that she was a part of this family. But she was the illegitimate daughter of Jamie's uncle, his second biggest mistake. Would she have been acceptable if Sister Anthony had not fought for her right to advanced education, if Sister Anthony had not had some pull with an old school friend who just happened to be the Bishop? Did Jane and Jamie even think of these things? Were they even important at a time like this?

You must learn to accept, Ferelith, she told herself

and thought of Simon whom surely she loved more than any other human being but not with the kind of love that she had once had for Blair. Her love of Simon was surely a maternal love. She wanted to protect him, to shield him, but thinking of their relationship she realized that he had always been strong, that perhaps she had needed him as much as he had needed her. Have we used one another, Simon? she asked him across the miles, and is that necessarily wrong?

Blair opened his eyes that night as Ferelith sat holding his unbandaged hand and Jamie sat dozing into his coat collar.

'Blair,' said Ferelith very softly as if she could not believe it. 'Blair.'

He looked at her for a full moment, trying to focus his eyes, and then he seemed to smile very gently and closed his eyes again. She was terrified and gripped his hand hard.

'Blair,' she almost called his name and Jamie sat up with a start. 'He opened his eyes, just for a second, but I'm . . .'

Jamie, affected by Ferelith's obvious fear, stood up, came close to the bed, and leaned over his cousin.

'Dear God, Ferelith, you scared me,' he said. 'He's sleeping. You must have imagined it.'

'Imagined what?' It was Nurse Thomson.

'He looked at me,' Ferelith almost sobbed. 'He opened his eyes and smiled, I'm sure that he smiled.'

The nurse bent over her patient and then straightened up. She turned and smiled at Blair's family. 'His breathing has changed,' she said. 'He's breathing very easily now. I'm sure he'll be more alert later.'

The relief was palpable. Jamie felt it too. His

uncle's suicide had separated him from this member of his family for too many years and he had been horrified that he would lose Blair just a few years after having found him again. Now his horrifically and permanently injured cousin was being restored to him and with him this other cousin whom he accepted at face value, never having given any thought to the unfortunate accident of her birth.

'Aren't you glad we had champagne with our sausage omelette?'

'I shall never drink anything but, with sausage omelettes,' she said.

'Let's make a pact,' he said. 'Champagne and sausage omelettes at all times of crisis.'

'Sounds wonderful,' said Nurse Thomson whom they had not noticed return to her patient's bedside.

'Especially the champagne,' joked Jamie.

'Oh no, your lordship,' she said seriously. 'Especially the sausages. Real British bangers. My mother has these awful rissoles. They look like a sausage and you can't wait for your teeth to sink in but then you taste the vegetables. Ghastly.'

Ferelith thought of Simon's father eating his rissoles happily as he waited for news of his son. She had to get back to Scotland, to work. But she could not leave until she knew that Blair was out of danger, that he would live.

She stayed in London for eight days and refused Lady Winterton's offer to meet the rest of the family in Surrey. Life's decisions were awfully difficult. She would like to know the Winterton children; she would like to stay at Blair's side until he was ready to leave hospital. But at the same time, she had to be in Glasgow to look after her growing career, to care for Simon's ghastly cat, to touch base with his lonely father and his rissoles and, yes, she had to admit it, to try to mend her fences with Angus Webster.

The day she left was also the day that Jamie returned to his regiment. It had never occurred to her to wonder why a young able-bodied man was not in uniform; but he had been recuperating from an injury himself when Blair had first been shot down and had had his leave extended on compassionate grounds. Now he felt that it was time to 'get back to work' as he called it. Blair would stay in London until he was completely out of danger and then he would be transferred to a hospital in Scotland.

'I'll visit as often as I can,' Ferelith promised the now conscious Blair. 'I'll come back down to London and you'll be tired of seeing me when you come home.'

He merely smiled, since talking was still an almost insurmountable strain.

'Does he have any idea of the extent of his injuries?' Ferelith asked Jamie the night before she left.

'He thought he had no legs at all but apart from knowing that they're still there he's not really assimilating much. He has taken it for granted that you and I are here together. In a day or two he'll wonder.'

'I wish we could move him to Scotland now.'

'He'd never survive the journey. Don't worry, Ferelith, he's in excellent hands here.'

They looked together at Nurse Thomson who was by Blair's bed as often as duty allowed.

'He has established a rapport with her. He won't really begin to fret for visitors for quite a while.'

Again they were silent, thinking of the many operations that Blair still had to undergo.

'I wish I could be here all the time.'

'I know,' said Jamie, 'but it's much more important to be with him when he really knows what's
going on. We, you, have got him through the
worst . . .'

'Oh, not me, Jamie, all of us and especially, I think,
Nurse Thomson, and her part in his recovery will
remain constant. And there will be lots of visits from
the amazing Mrs Price.'

And so Ferelith consoled herself on the nightmare
return journey to Scotland with thinking of her
newly-met family and she looked forward with
delight to meeting them all again soon.

First she had to speak to Lord Webster and this
seemed to be very difficult to arrange. He was
not in Edinburgh. No one knew where he was
and Ferelith found herself asking Miss McBride,
his secretary, if his lordship had possibly gone to
London on business.

She was to wish she had not.

'I am not at liberty to discuss his lordship's whereabouts with anyone, Miss Gallagher,' said Angus's
very firm secretary. 'His lordship usually lets his
particular friends know where he is himself.'

And that's put my gas at a peep, thought Ferelith
to herself, in the old language of the children of a
Glasgow orphanage. Miss McBride has me down
as a not particular friend and I suppose that is
exactly what I am, a not particular friend of Angus
Webster.

'You will tell him that I phoned,' she said and then
hung up. She had the feeling that Miss McBride had
enjoyed dismissing her. Should I write but what if
the dragon-like Miss McBride opens his personal
mail when he is out of town? I couldn't bear to
have her witness my apology.

She decided to swallow her pride when Angus had not contacted her after three months. It's too late to apologize now. I should have done it at once. It's never too late to apologize. If you have done something wrong you must make an effort to set things straight. So she argued with herself. She wrote several times and tore the letters up and then one afternoon the telephone rang in her office and the Gorgon, as she had taken to calling Miss McBride, was on the other end.

'I have Lord Webster for you, Miss Gallagher, if you are free.'

She felt like a schoolgirl about to come face to face with the hero of the school football team. Why? It was an absolutely ridiculous reaction.

'Yes, of course,' she said as easily as she could manage and hoped that when Angus came on the telephone her voice would not sound quite so strangled.

'Could we meet?' he asked without even saying hello. 'I feel I owe you an apology and they're better handled face to face.'

'Yes, of course . . . we can meet, I mean. You don't owe me an apology. It's the other way round and I've been trying to pluck up, no, to handle it the right way.'

'Are you free for dinner? There are one or two places that can still manage to do a decent plate, not pre-war standards but better than Spam, I think.'

'I'd like that.'

'Shall we say Rogano's or would you like to try somewhere else?'

'No, that would be fine.'

'Can you possibly meet me at eight? I have so much work while I'm in Glasgow but I'll see you home. You're at Simon's flat?'

'Yes.'

'Very sensible. See you at eight.'

She had to get home. She would boil a kettle and wash her hair. If she practically sat on the gas fire her hair would be dry in half-an-hour. The black dress, supposedly very flattering to red hair and green eyes, that she had bought for the date she had not kept, would be perfect. If she pinned her hair back with the tortoiseshell comb Simon had given her for her last birthday and wore her very last pair of nylons she would look all right. A memory from the past came mocking her. She was in the Convent deciding to become an advocate. She was going to be brilliant, stunning, and sophisticated or words to that effect. She used to worry about being beautiful, she remembered. Well, she was quite bright and she was sophisticated, at least on the outside. 'Two out of three isn't bad,' she said just as she had said it all those years ago.

War had done away with so many pretensions. One no longer thought of the right time to arrive for a party, if there was a party, Getting across the city at whatever time trams were running was of paramount importance. The tram drivers were threatening to stop their trams after eight if they were not allowed to use more lights, saying reasonably enough that it was dangerous to drive the huge machines if the driver could not see hazards on the lines. That German planes could see the lights too was obvious.

'Six o' one, half a dozen o' the other,' said the tram drivers. 'If we put on the lights the Jerries'll see us. If we drive in the dark we'll crash or run over things.'

'Please don't strike tonight,' Ferelith begged and decided to make her way to the restaurant as soon as

her hair was dry. Better to wander around or hide in
the ladies than to be late or not to get there at all.

She arrived at seven-thirty and went straight
to the ladies room. Angus, who had also been
faced with a similar dilemma, saw her and smiled.
Impossible to follow her and so he decided to hide
behind his evening paper until she emerged.

When she did he pretended that he had only just
spotted her, although he had spent a delightful
thirty-five minutes deciding that her hair was less
red and more golden than he had remembered, and
that her legs were longer and that she was quite the
nicest thing he had seen in some time.

'Let's get everything straight before we go into
dinner, Ferelith,' he said when he had taken her
coat and given it to an attendant to hang up. 'We'll
have a drink of something . . . there was only rum
the last time I was in, very interesting stuff . . . and
then we'll have whatever they offer.'

'Lord Webster, Angus, please, I have to apologize. I forgot all about you. That sounds dreadful
but —'

'I know, my dear, but it puts me perfectly in my
place and I deserved the set-down. The fault is mine.
I should have realized that only something terribly
important would make you just not turn up. You
see, it's just that . . . and at my age I should know
better but I couldn't . . . God this is difficult. I find,
Miss Ferelith Gallagher, that you have become very
important to me. I used to tell myself that my interest was purely academic: that I hated to see the waste
of a fine mind, but it's more. And then, you see, you
are so much younger and I feel I have no right, have
no chance but if we could be friends . . .'

'Oh Angus,' said Ferelith. 'I don't want to be
friends.' Heavens, what was she saying? Logical

thinking, Ferelith, reason. 'I mean I do, of course I do, but I don't think of you as older and I do think of you . . . rather a lot.'

When had he taken possession of her hand? He looked at it as if he wanted to remember every vein, every line. The barman coughed.

'You don't have champagne, I suppose?' asked Angus and the waiter went off to try to do the impossible.

'It's terribly complicated, Angus. I don't know where to start.'

'Your cousin, Lord Winterton, wrote to me, a short little letter and just to say that he had told you that your brother, the young man I saw you with here, had been terribly injured.'

'It's much more complicated than that,' said Ferelith. 'Blair is not my brother, not the way you mean. He is my half-brother. I am his illegitimate half-sister.' There, she had said it.

'Poor you.'

'No . . . Oh I suppose yes, but I never thought of life as having dealt me a hard hand until I met Blair. You see we didn't know about one another. We met at Edinburgh University. We were married, Angus, for all of three and a half weeks. I spent one night with him, slept with my own brother.' She looked at him as she said the words and saw distaste on his finely-featured face. She had expected it. She would leave. She picked up her gloves and he covered her hands again with his and she felt his warmth and sympathy and felt the tension drain away.

'Poor you,' he said again. 'How could your parents have allowed it to happen?'

'Our father shot himself when he realized that I was on the way. My mother lived only a few hours after my birth and Blair's mother tried to cover up

the blot on the family honour. She even changed
her name and Blair's back to her maiden name, told
him his grandfather wanted his family name to be
carried on. Blair didn't know he was a Winterton
until after our horrible débâcle and he promptly
had his name changed back again. I was given my
mother's name because only one old nanny in India
really knew anything about me and, of course, she's
been dead for years and my dreadful secret really
died with her, but Mrs Crawford, Blair's mother,
knew something, and she had me investigated when
Blair and I became friends. She did the same with
all the riffraff he met at school and university,' she
said lightly, trying to show that it didn't really hurt
although it did, terribly.

'Has it never occurred to you that you look alike?
I noticed it when I saw you with Blair Winterton.
The hair is different but the green eyes and the fine
features are similar.'

Ferelith did not answer the question. 'I don't think
Jamie – Lord Winterton – has really figured out my
place in things.'

'His letter proves that he doesn't really care
about such things. He likes you and he obviously
loves Blair.'

'He's a nice man and his wife is a dear and she has
this wonderful granny who flies around London in a
dreadful old ambulance bullying wounded soldiers
into getting better. You can easily imagine her
saying things like, "Eat up all this mush and you'll
grow big and strong."'

'We had better go into the dining room and eat
up all our dinner too.'

Ferelith could never remember what they had
eaten. It could have been old carpet. She was conscious only of her happiness that Angus was there

and that he was the most interesting man she had ever met. He was kind and gentle and clever and sophisticated and he made her feel sophisticated too.

He had a car and he took her home. She knew that with every fibre of her being she wanted to invite him into Simon's flat.

He stopped at the door and turned her to face him.

'I thought I would ask you to make me a nightcap but I daren't. If you say no my heart will break and if you say yes I won't be able to control myself and I feel so so strongly that control is needed. I think something very wonderful is happening and I want it to grow slowly so that its roots will be deep and strong, so that it won't break with the winds that life will throw at it. Do you feel anything like that?'

With tears of pure happiness in her eyes she looked at him and nodded slowly. He put his arms down by his side and leaned forward and kissed her very lightly on her mouth. She had closed her eyes and she felt his lips, soft and undemanding like the weight of the petals of a rose and just as perfect. When she opened her eyes he had gone.

She drifted upstairs like the selfsame petals and spoke nicely to Traviata, who smirked as if to say that she could not be got round so easily. A woman with a philistine's taste in music was no substitute for a man who knew his Wagner and who fed his cat on fresh chicken. Traviata refused to make allowances for the shortages caused by war and would continue to blame Ferelith for her uninteresting diet. Ferelith ignored her and went to Simon's desk and sat down to write letters, to Simon, to Jamie, to Blair, and to Angus Webster.

She did not post the last one: it was too early.

12

ANGUS ASKED FERELITH to marry him on Christmas Eve, 1942. She wished desperately that he had not chosen such a lovely happy night. She did not want to spoil Christmas for either of them.

'I can't,' she said.

'May I ask why? It seems to me, Ferelith, that we love one another very much. Is it because I am so much older?'

'Oh Angus, how can you think such a thing? I have never, since I was a student, considered your age.'

'Then why, my darling? I do love you so. Are you afraid that I don't? Am I perhaps not passionate enough?' He took her roughly in his arms and kissed her eyes, her lips, and then he buried his face in her hair. She could feel him trembling and the passion in her rose to meet his. He pushed her away. 'Oh, Ferelith, if I were to give way to my passions.'

'I love you Angus and, if you will wait, I will marry you one day.'

'One day,' he burst out. 'Ferelith, I am forty-seven years old, nearly twenty years older than you. I want a wife and children and . . . Is that it? Is it your career? Oh, darling, I would never stand in your way and, I know you want to be independent and to make a success of the Law on your own but if you marry me, you can come to Edinburgh immediately and go to the Bar.'

'I know and I don't want to marry you to have you finance my career. Oh Angus please, there are so many thoughts going around in my head. Blair.

Simon and Jamie, still out there somewhere. I feel I have no right to be so happy while they are living in danger and fear . . .'

'They would not . . .'

'Oh please don't say that,' she begged. 'I have to be quite honest, Angus. I want you but I have worked so hard. I owe it to Sister Anthony and Reverend Mother and the Bishop who allowed the use of funds even though I was a mere female. I owe it to them to be the best I can be. I want to get to the Bar. I have saved and saved these past few years and I'm almost ready, but there's Simon and Traviata and besides, I want to take silk.' There it was out. She had said it. The dreams were still there.

She could not tell what he was thinking. His face was calm, the eyes cold and distant. 'There are no women K.C.s.'

'Isn't it about time there were?'

He thought carefully. He always would try to see both sides. 'Yes,' he said finally.

'You want me to marry you and you want children. How could I possibly combine the two? Each job would require all my energy.'

'I will never force you to have a child. I will never ask you. I will never mention the attractiveness of all our friends' children. I will never look in prams parked outside restaurants or shops.'

She put her arms around his neck and leaned against him.

'Oh, not fair, Ferelith,' he said.

'I would like to sleep with you, Angus.'

He pushed her from him almost roughly. 'I have spent my life telling undisciplined males that if they want to do so they can control their desires. I love you, Ferelith, and I want you, all of you, but I want it all and that means marriage.'

'And I can't marry you just yet.'

'When? When you have become the first female King's Council, or will I have to wait until you become Lord Advocate, or why not Lord Chancellor? Will you stagger up the aisle with senile old me then?'

Ferelith took refuge in tears and Angus stamped out slamming the door behind him.

Traviata came over and insinuated herself on to her lap.

'Oh God, Traviata, what have I done? I love him. Why did I drive him away? I don't want to spend the rest of my life with someone else's cat.'

At that the cat stood up, stretched and stalked proudly from her lap. She had merely been offering a little comfort. Her heart, if she had one, belonged to Simon, if it belonged to anyone.

Ferelith laughed through her tears: rejected by a man and now by a cat. Was there any more humiliation in store? She had hoped, really hoped, that Angus would stay with her for Christmas and she had therefore refused Maria's offer of an Italian family Christmas. Was it too late to change her mind?

'We are on our way to Midnight Mass,' said Maria when she answered the telephone. 'Meet us there, bring your toothbrush and prepare to be awakened as soon as you have fallen asleep.'

'I'm feeling absolutely miserable, Maria, even the cat hates me.'

'Then you should definitely be with us. You won't have time to feel sorry for yourself. It's all systems go in a big family on Christmas Day and even worse if they're Italians.'

She knew she should not have telephoned as soon as she had hung up. It was futile to hope that watching the joy of Maria and Mauro and their large family would make her feel better. It would only make her realize what she had thrown away and for what? Was she doomed to spend the rest of her life with law books and a cat? She thought of Pietro. He had believed that her dream of high office was somehow unfeminine. Poor Pietro. Where was he now? Was he even alive? Again there had been no correspondence from him or his family. She thought of Blair, still in hospital but oh so much better. He said he had accepted that he would never walk again.

'Of course I'll be able to ride, Ferelith. Americans control their horses through the reins: legs are better but since mine don't function I'll work something out.'

She pictured some of the powerful animals he had owned before the war. He could never control them. She hoped he would not try.

Now her tears were for Blair and his lost dreams. Was he replacing old dreams with new ones?

My dreams are the same as they always were, Blair, she sent the thought through the air to him. A happy marriage, a career. Only the man has changed. Do I always demand too much of life? Am I greedy to want everything?

There was a beautifully-wrapped gift from Jane under the tiny tree she had decorated with red bows and a few white candles. A little angel she had bought in Rome sat lopsidedly among the top branches. She cried for Jane alone with her children and worrying about her husband *somewhere out there*.

Where do tears come from? Where is the bottomless well?

'Oh, pull yourself together, Ferelith, go to the

di Rollo's and be happy if it kills you,' she said to herself.

And she thought, and almost prayed, that it just might. The love in the di Rollo family was almost tangible: the way they spoke to one another, the way Mauro and Maria touched one another as they passed, doing the million and one things that needed to be done in a large family, the way the older girls rallied around to help their mother and their elderly aunts prepare the gargantuan meal, the gratitude everyone showed for even the humblest of presents. This is family, thought Ferelith, and no matter how they try to make me part of it I'm still on the outside looking in.

The doorbell rang as Aunt Sophie was serving the soup and when Mauro returned from answering it, he pulled with him a very embarrassed and dishevelled looking senior law lord. No need for talk, no need for explanations. Ferelith ran to him and Mauro pushed them back into the hall for a few minutes of privacy.

'And don't let the soup get cold,' he ordered, very much the paterfamilias.

'I'm sorry,' said Ferelith and Angus together.

'I should have . . .' they began again and stopped and looked at one another and then Angus bent his head and kissed Ferelith Gallagher as she had not been kissed for a very long time. She felt all her doubts melt away at his touch.

She could feel the words *I'll marry you tomorrow* forming on her tongue but before she had a chance to utter them he was speaking against her hair. 'I love you, Ferelith, but I respect your hard work, your grit, your determination. I won't change my mind about wanting to marry you, about loving you, but I won't ask you again until you let me know that you are ready and if I have to wait until I'm senile then I'll wait.'

'Aunt Katia says the pasta is getting soft,' said Alicia from the dining-room door. 'Mummy has set a place for your friend, Aunt Ferelith.'

Ferelith was never able to decide whether she welcomed or resented the interruption. The rest of the day was pure joy, with Angus joining in as soon as Mauro and Maria could be made to relax and forget that he was a lord. The children, especially Domenico, who fell asleep on his new friend's lap, had no problem dealing with Ferelith's friend. Had not Alicia caught them kissing in the hall?

'Where did you spend last night?' Ferelith asked him as they washed the dishes together in blissful companionship.

'In my car, in terror that either a policeman or a reporter would find me and think me a vagrant. Can you imagine "Senior Law Lord found asleep in car". Ferelith, it isn't that I'm a law lord? You're not afraid of a nepotism thing?'

'An unsubstantiated and totally unjust accusation of nepotism? No. I honestly haven't thought of that. Maybe when they make you Lord Advocate, I'll worry a little.'

'We must see you a K.C. before that but it will take some time, darling. A man would expect to wait at least ten years.'

'Women have been waiting hundreds and so I warn you, Lord Webster of Dalmarnock, that at least one of them will be beating on your door before ten years is up.'

Ignoring his soapy hands, he put his arms around her and kissed her long and hard. 'I am tempted to say something provocative about which door I hope

to find you beating on but if I do one of those delightful girls is bound to come in and hear me and rush
off to tell everyone about Aunt Ferelith's sex-mad
friend. Now, let's finish the dishes because I must
get back to Edinburgh. I usually spend Christmas
with my sister and her family and although she
is absolutely thrilled at the idea that I might be
spending Christmas in the arms of a goddess, I
would like to get back to wish them joy. You could
come with me and meet them, officially presented
as it were.'

Memories of her official meeting with Blair's
mother came unbidden into her head.

'I'm not ready.'

He kissed her again. 'Blast this war. I won't be
back in Glasgow for some time. I'm doing a bit of
work in London as you know and so if you don't
hear, don't worry. I'll be thinking of you every
minute of the day.'

'When you're not thinking of work.'

'Every minute of every night then.'

'Me too.'

'Think of me at midnight on New Year's Eve
and I'll think of you. Say I love you, Angus, and
wherever I am, I'll hear it.'

'You say, I love you, Ferelith.'

There was an explosion of laughter, a smothered
'Soppy' from the door, the sounds of running feet,
furious Italian scolding from Maria and then silence.
They looked at one another ruefully and then leaned
together for a few minutes. Ferelith could feel his
heart beating.

'I'll tell them to behave next time you come or we
won't have them as bridesmaids.'

'Bridesmaids?' His face was joyful.

'Yes, and a solemn little page boy.'

'He'll still be little or is it the one who is on the way?'

'Men aren't supposed to notice such things.'

'I notice everything when I'm with you.' He noticed that she had not answered his question but he said nothing and, instead, dried his hands, rolled down his sleeves, and reached for his cufflinks. 'I brought my mother's engagement ring . . . ?'

She shook her head gently.

'I never give up,' he said lightly. 'You should have seen me on the rugby field, bloodied and battered but unbowed.'

He said his goodbyes to Maria and Mauro, and Ferelith stood alone in the dark on the doorstep and watched him drive away. There were no streetlights and the houses were dark and shuttered. Inside though, surely in almost every one, parties were going on, tired children were being put to bed, exhausted parents were cleaning up the detritus of Christmas revelries.

'A few more years, Angus,' she whispered as the dark bulk of his car turned the corner and disappeared out of her vision, out of her life, 'to get somewhere on my own. Is that too much to ask?'

In the New Year Ferelith went to London again, to visit Blair, and to see Angus who was doing *something* in a government office. She took Angus to meet Blair at the hospital and while they were there Jane too came to visit. It was a family reunion of a sort and reminded Angus that the woman he loved had not as yet met any member of his own family.

'I hope Nurse Thomson plucks up courage before Blair goes back to Scotland,' he said later that evening as they had supper after seeing the heart-throb, Lesley Howard, in *Pimpernel Smith*. Finally they had managed to see a film together.

Ferelith looked at him, her fork halfway to her mouth. 'What are you talking about?' Then her face was flooded with joy as the realization of what he had been saying struck her. 'Oh, you don't mean . . .?'

'Of course I do. She loves him. I know enough about being in love with someone to tell.'

'But enough to spend her life with him, the way he is?'

'If he hadn't been your brother and this had happened, wouldn't you have stayed with him?'

'Of course, but that would be an easy decision. I knew him when he was . . .'

'He's still the same, I believe.'

'Yes, even stronger as a person, but he was such a fine athlete and he loved his horses, great huge brutes with rolling eyes and tossing heads.'

'I can see you share the family love of horseflesh,' he said laughing.

'I do, but only if they are in one field and I am outside it. But, Angus, if it's true, if she loves him as he is and wants to spend her life with him, what can we do to help?'

'Help the romance along, you mean? Nothing, darling, it's disastrous to interfere. They must work it out for themselves. She has two months to make him realize that she, the woman and not the nurse, is indispensable to him.'

When, a few days after her return to Scotland, a tearful Ferelith telephoned his hotel, Angus thought that something had happened to Simon or to Jamie.

'No, I feel stupid, but it's Leslie Howard. The Germans shot down the civilian plane he was in: somehow I felt he was very special to us. I just loved him in *Gone With the Wind* and *Pimpernel Smith*, our film.'

'I don't believe I am hearing this from a rational,

intellectual woman who is preparing to take the legal world by storm.'

'It's not allowable to mourn for someone if I put K.C. after my name?'

'Of course it is, but Ferelith you didn't know him. Are you shedding tears for everyone killed in this war?'

'Yes, I am. Do you know that Goebbels has just declared Berlin a Jew-free city? Do you know what that means? And I am also very angry with landlords who don't repair their properties and illegally evict people who complain and oh, I wish . . .'

He held his breath but she stopped her declaration, if she had been going to make it.

'. . . I wish this war was over and that you were back in Edinburgh and Jamie was back with Jane and the children and that Simon was here because then I could come to Edinburgh . . .'

She stopped and she could almost hear him wanting to ask the question that he had promised not to ask.

'Germany can't hold out much longer,' he said instead.

But it could and it did. Mussolini and Hitler met again in Northern Italy to discuss the worsening situation and, in a daylight raid, five hundred American bombers rained tons of bombs on the Italian capital, destroying railyards and airfields but avoiding the historical buildings. Later martial law was declared in an attempt to prevent civil war. In the same month, the anti-Fascist Marshal Pietro Badoglio asked the Allies for peace terms to celebrate Mussolini's downfall, and the Fascist party was abolished. But still Hitler refused to bow to what the rest of the world was beginning to see as inevitable.

In Glasgow Ferelith worked as hard as she could in an attempt to stop thinking of how much she missed Angus and how much she wished she had agreed to marry him.

'How could I keep up this pace if I had to consider a husband?' she asked herself, 'and if I had a child?'

Ruthlessly she abolished such thoughts. Angus loved her and she loved him. Marriage would come in time. First there was Blair to worry about.

Nurse Thomson resigned from the hospital and travelled with Squadron Leader Winterton as his private nurse back to his home in Fife. Jane and her two children travelled with them. Jamie would be happier if his family was far from the dangers of bombing. It seemed a perfect opportunity for the parts of the family to get to know one another. Ferelith promised to make the long trek to Fife as often as she could and in the meantime she taxed Jane with keeping her informed of the progress of the love affair.

'She'll have to ask him,' Jane whispered into the telephone one cold winter evening. 'He is Winterton all over: the soul of honour.' Luckily she could not see how an illegitimate and unwanted Winterton took that remark. 'He gazes after her if she so much as crosses the room, and he asks the children constantly about her whereabouts. They're turning into perfect little spies. They'll say: "She's talking to the gardeners about raising chickens, Uncle Blair, to help the war effort." Or: "She's asking the keepers about raising trout in the duck pond." And even: "She's having a bath." How much they saw of that activity I really do not want to know. But when she is in the room with him he behaves as if he hadn't even known she was gone.'

'He's in love,' said Ferelith, 'and you have no idea how happy that makes me,' and to Jane's consternation, she burst into tears.

Wisely Jane said nothing but made soothing murmurs. The embarrassed Ferelith hung up and went to moan about the Court of Appeal ruling that savings from housekeeping money belong to the husband.

'It's appalling,' she told all her fellow solicitors who would listen to her. 'With supposedly extinct dodos on the Bench, women need women advocates more than ever.'

She discussed the Appeal court ruling with Charles Smythe. 'You can't possibly agree, Charles,' she argued. 'If a woman scrimps and saves to put a few pence aside for her rainy day, surely it belongs to her and should be spent just as she wants it to be spent.'

'A man, in this case, the breadwinner and provider of the houshold finance, could quite justifiably argue that he must have given her too much housekeeping in the first place.'

'But if she feeds the family well and still has a shilling or two left over then surely she is entitled to keep it?'

'If she feeds the family well on his income and has money over, then obviously he gave her too much in the first place.'

Ferelith almost literally gritted her teeth. She was appalled at how the most rational and logical of thinkers could suddenly find herself wanting to clout someone who could not be made to agree with her. She breathed deeply and continued, 'Not if she has worked really hard to learn new ways of economizing and making a little go a long way.'

'The difficulty would not arise in a happy home

in the first place, Ferelith. A man doesn't pay his wife a wage.'

'Then he damn well should,' snapped Ferelith and flounced out while his shout of 'You should be arguing at the Bar' followed her down the corridor.

He was right, of course. She would only be really happy when she could do the work she had been trained to do. And to be supremely happy she would be married to Angus too. Why, why, why, was it virtually impossible for a woman to have everything? Men seemed to do it quite easily. Where was it written – Thou shalt not have a man and a career?

She took some comfort from looking at her growing bank balance. Soon, please God, the war would be over and she could leave the luxury of Simon's flat and the dubious comfort of Traviata for whatever she could find in Edinburgh.

She phoned Angus. 'I need you,' was all she said.

'As soon as I can, darling. Just wait for me. I'll come as soon as I break the back of this work that somehow keeps coming.'

'We'll eat here. I'll make something with pasta. I learned a few delicious things while I was in Italy.'

'Italian food. My favourite. I'll bring the wine. Just wait for me. That's as definite as I can be. One evening soon I will knock on your door.'

'And Simon's dragon lady will think lascivious thoughts.'

'So will I, my darling,' he said and hung up.

She worked and she waited and she kept the ingredients for her easiest but tastiest sauce in the flat so that she could make dinner the moment he arrived. She thought of how lovely it would be to be in Edinburgh and to see him, to talk to him, every day. Soon. There was almost enough money in the savings bank to ensure a dignified existence until she could secure cases and then they would marry and, and . . . She pushed away the enticing thoughts and scolded herself for her romantic fantasies. Ferelith Gallagher K.C. or Mrs, no Lady Webster? Both, please God, both, but when I am ready.

And then one evening he was there and she opened the door and forgot all her good intentions – and so did he. He kissed her and they stood for a minute just inside the door while he whispered words that meant everything and nothing, sweet words, loving words, and then he laughed and moved away from her, set the bottle of wine down on the table in the hall and reached for her again. She went into his arms and – did one push and did the other guide? – but they went into the bedroom and not into the little living room where the tiny dining table was set for two. They fell together on to the bed and before he entered her she had a feeling of *déjà vu* – I have been here before but this time it's right, it's complete – and she surrendered to him as he surrendered to her and together they cried out in exquisite joy.

Hours later she woke to find him sound asleep beside her, his arm across her breasts, and she turned and gazed into his face. She had never before seen him asleep and she followed his jaw line with the tip of a finger and smoothed the lines on his forehead and her heart ached with love for the whole man, this wonderful man who had given her himself. He felt her touch and his eyes opened and he smiled, not in surprise but in delight that he was where he had always dreamed of being, and he began to kiss her, and again she responded passionately.

At last they lay back exhausted, fulfilled, but in each other's arms.

'Ferelith,' he asked after they had lain there contentedly for some time, 'did you make dinner? I'm perfectly happy to lie here with you for the rest of my life but I'm absolutely starving.'

She snuggled even closer to him, enjoying this companionable closeness almost as much as she enjoyed the passionate intimacy of the hours before. But she laughed, got up and pulled on her dressing gown and went to the kitchen. The smells of garlic and onion and tomatoes soon brought him in after her. He opened the wine, poured it and toasted her, and then stood with his arms around her while she stirred the sauce.

'What are you making?' he asked. 'That smell is tantalizing.'

'It's the poor Scot's equivalent of an Italian sauce. One onion and one carrot, twopence. A powdered egg omelette plus sauce and *Mama Mia*.'

'This is perfect,' he said, his lips against her hair. 'I can handle anything with you to come home to . . . marriage will be so wonderful . . .'

She turned and looked at him. 'Angus, it will be wonderful but I won't always be at home.'

'I know. I meant only that when you are at home it will be wonderful. Shall I ring my sister or do you want to let Blair know first?'

Ferelith turned back to the burning onions and turned the flames down under the pot. She felt as cold as she had felt happy a moment before. 'Tell him what?'

She felt him stiffening behind her but his arms

stayed around her waist. She could feel their warmth on her skin.

'Ferelith, you are going to marry me now, aren't you?' He dropped his hands and she felt alone, confused.

'No, Angus, not now. We made a bargain . . .'

'But after . . . Ferelith, I am a very disciplined man. I never meant . . . damn, what a trite thing to say but it's true. I never meant, or did I? Did I come, hoping to seduce you?'

'For God's sake, Angus, you didn't seduce me. If anything we seduced each other. It hasn't changed anything except perhaps to show us how well suited we are, how wonderful that side of our marriage will be. This is the middle of the twentieth century: you don't have to marry me to save my honour.'

'Am I supposed to congratulate you on your modern thinking, Ferelith? I'm an old fogey, I suppose, but I happen to believe in old-fashioned virtues like abstinence. I can't say that I wish we hadn't made love . . .' He looked at her and she could not doubt his sincerity. 'I have never had so much pleasure or happiness in my life . . . but it's not the way I operate. I want to marry you.'

She looked at him. Why had it all gone wrong? They had shared some magic. Why couldn't he accept that? Lovemaking before marriage wasn't really in her life script either but it had happened and . . . was it wrong? A few minutes ago he had been strong and virile and in command and now he was beset with guilt. Surely it wasn't wrong. They loved one another: they were going to marry. It could not be wrong to give each other such happiness.

'I told you before about how severe I am with rapists,' he began.

'For God's sake you didn't rape me. Perhaps it was the other way round. All right we pre-empted marriage by a few months. We're not loose people, Angus. I haven't been with anyone since Blair. I love you . . .'

'Not enough to marry me, Ferelith.' He turned and went back to the bedroom and she left the sauce and hurried after him. He was pulling his clothes on and he turned from her to hide his body.

'I'm going and I won't be back.'

What could she say? What could she do? Give in? Say, as she had almost said on the previous Christmas Day, *I'll marry you tomorrow*? Let him finance her career?

'I'll leave you to let yourself out,' she said stonily and walked like an old woman into the kitchen where she stood, stirring the sauce that could not cook because she had turned off the burner, while tears of desolation followed one another down her cheeks.

Simon's cat leapt from the counter-top where she had been sitting and rubbed against her ankles in a gesture of comfort.

'We're in the soup together Traviata,' she said. 'Two fallen women with no prospect of getting out of the mess we got ourselves into.'

Traviata smirked. She, at least, had the hope that Simon would return to her.

Christmas of 1943 was miserable for Ferelith. She spent the holiday season alone with Traviata. She had lied to Maria and had said that she was going to spend Christmas with Elspeth Baxter now happily married to another general practitioner and living in Ayr. She ate a cheese sandwich for Christmas dinner, having no heart at all to cook for herself or Traviata, who turned her nose up at the fish heads begged for from the local fish man, and whined to be let out.

She apologized mentally, not to the cat, but to Simon who trusted her to look after his pet in the style to which he had accustomed the animal.

'Blair has sent me a pheasant, Simon,' she whispered across the miles, 'and I'll cook it and give her some tomorrow. I just can't bear the thought of "Tis the Season" and Ho, Ho, Ho.'

On New Year's Eve she sat before the fire and listened to music, Beethoven's *Fidelio*. Leonora had stayed faithful to her love and eventually had managed to be reunited with him.

'Please, please, please,' Ferelith whispered but to whom she did not know, and then just as her clock struck twelve she whispered *I love you* across the miles to Angus and fell asleep weeping and hoping that he was thinking of her too.

Worldly success can cost too much. Had her pride cost her everything she really wanted? She argued with herself constantly. Why is it wrong to want a home and a family and a useful career at the same time, a career for which her academic and dramatic ability and not the name of her husband was responsible?

13

IT WAS GOING to be a good year. The war was nearly over, or was it? All the signs in London were that peace was just around the corner. People began to look forward to normal life, to doing things like going to the theatre. The Old Vic company which had been bombed out of its theatre in Waterloo Road reopened at the New Theatre in the West End. Ralph Richardson and Laurence Olivier starred in *Peer Gynt* and *Richard III* respectively and, true to Old Vic tradition, took small roles in one another's plays. John Gielgud, another splendid young actor, played Hamlet and a fellow called Donald Wolfit acted the finest King Lear that several of the critics covering first nights had ever seen. A note of sadness in that otherwise reawakening year was the death of Sir Henry Wood, founder of the Promenade Concerts.

Pre-fabricated houses that could be erected in a few hours by a few workmen were designed for demobolized servicemen and bombed-out families. The prefabs, which sprang up like mushrooms after rain, were to stand for a few years until 'proper' rebuilding of Britain could proceed.

But the war refused to end.

The Benedictine Monastery at Monte Cassino, from where Hermann Goering had stolen millions of pounds' worth of art treasures, was finally taken and thus the way was cleared for the Allied advance on Rome. A few weeks later Rome itself fell to the Allies. Ferelith felt some solace at the news of the relief of the Eternal City and sat down once more to write to Pietro. Maybe now there would be some communication from him. She could not believe that it had simply been a case of out of sight out of mind.

In August 1944 she went through to Fife to see Blair. She had not told Nurse Thomson that she was coming and decided to take a taxi from the station. A game of cricket was being played on the great lawn that swept up to the house. A sturdy little boy wielding an enormous bat was obviously the batsman. The fielder was a pretty young woman in a spotted dress, whom Ferelith at first did not recognize, and the crowd consisted of a solemn little girl and two dollies. The bowler who was making more noise than everyone else put together was in a wheelchair.

'Stop, stop,' screamed Ferelith to the startled driver.

He screeched to a halt. She paid him, threw her overnight bag down on the edge of the driveway, and sped across the lawn.

'Blair, oh Blair,' she sobbed while the tears rushed unchecked down her cheeks.

The bowler saw her and held out his arms and she ran into them.

'Hello, little sister,' he said. 'Good heavens, my bowling's not that bad: good enough for young Jeremy here.'

It was not the first time that Ferelith had met Jamie's two children and she soon walked up to the house with them to see Jane while Nurse Thomson, the young girl in the spotted dress, pushed the wheelchair along beside them. The change in everybody was evident. In the few months since she had seen them the children had grown as all children do and were almost unrecognizable. Nurse Thomson, obviously familiarly now known as Emma, was plumper and softer, her face rosy and unstrained, but the most incredible difference was in Blair himself.

'I'll make a horseman of this young man before his daddy comes home,' he said, watching Jeremy playing with toy soldiers at his feet, and Jeremy looked up, smiled at his cousin, and toppled Napoleon.

'You should see them, Ferelith,' said Jane. 'Blair sits in the middle of the paddock holding the lunging rein, poor Emma whirls him around like a dervish, and Jeremy trots around on his pony.'

'Daddy will be pleased when he comes home, Auntie Ferelith,' said Jeremy, 'and Uncle Blair is going to start Constanza just as soon as Mummy agrees.'

'Now.' Constanza removed her thumb from her mouth long enough to express her opinion.

'You look so wonderful, Blair. Nurse, I mean Emma, you have done wonders with him.'

Emma smiled. 'He did it himself.'

'So I did,' agreed Blair. 'At home with almost all of my favourite people waiting on me hand and foot, it would have been uncivil not to get well and strong.'

'What do the doctors say?'

He looked straight at her but she could not read the enigmatic look. 'I'm as good as I'll ever be,' he said lightly. 'Some bits, including the legs, will never work again, but the bits in working order are superb,' he finished with an evil, leering laugh at Jeremy. 'Feel my muscles.'

Jeremy got up with the air of someone who had done this often before but who was prepared to humor the patient. Obligingly he felt the biceps held out for his inspection. 'Very good,' he said. 'Bigger than yesterday.'

'Bowling does that,' Blair informed Ferelith, 'and beating horrid little boys.'

Ferelith watched the two of them together, and then caught the look of anguish on Emma Thomson's face and the one of compassion for both of them on Jane's.

'Could he, well, I mean . . .' She and Jane were alone after dinner in the great bedroom that Blair had deemed suitable for his cousin's wife. The children were in bed and Emma was getting Blair ready for the night

'Father a child? I don't know. That information is a little too intimate for me but surely marriage isn't just about sex and children. I would love to have Jamie here to know he's safe. Just to hold him would be so wonderful. I know I've had it all and it's easy for me to pass judgements but I do think that marriage would be good for both of them. She lost everything in this senseless war too: it would be nice if they could salvage a little happiness.' She turned away and began brushing her hair vigorously. She kept her face away from Ferelith but she could see her reflection in the mirror. 'What about you, Ferelith? Don't you ever long to throw away your unused barrister's wig and jump into bed with some nice young man?'

'No, I want more than anything to wear that wig, and yes, I want to jump into bed with, not a nice young man but a very nice older man. He loves me still . . . oh, I blew it, Jane, and I can't bring myself to talk about it, even to you, but I do love him. I said no when he first asked me and he's never going to ask me again. I have to ask him and I'm afraid.'

'Of rejection?'

'No, in a way I'm afraid of the power I seem to have over him and I believe he still loves me, I know he does, but I'm afraid that having come so far but not quite far enough . . . Blast. It's stupidly melodramatic and complicated but I suppose I'm a little afraid of . . . losing my identity, I suppose, being compelled to give up my work before I break all the bounds imposed on it.'

'Would he expect you to give up your career? I suppose being older he's . . .'

'Wonderful and understanding. I love Angus Webster and he wouldn't ask me to give up the Law but I might feel there were things I would have to do as his wife . . .'

'God, you're not afraid of sex are you? It's great fun, but as Charles the Second said, "There's more to marriage than four legs in a bed."'

'I'm not afraid.' She blushed furiously as she remembered her total abandonment to Angus. 'It's the "more" that's in marriage that scares me. I dreamed as a child of having Angus's next job and as an old nun at the orphanage used to say "there's more chance that pigs might fly and we'd have to shoot bacon."'

'What is his next job?' Jane, looking not much older than Constanza in her dressing gown and slippers, curled up in the middle of the bed and prepared herself for a good gossip. 'Come on, I'm family and I won't tell a soul.'

'Lord Advocate.'

'How splendid, I'm terribly impressed, but doesn't someone like that die in harness?'

'Oh, no. He could resign when he's older or if he was offered a different post, with the Government for instance. He's spending a lot of time in London doing hush hush stuff just now, but the higher up the ladder he gets, the less I feel that I want to marry him. It's so complicated. Blair wanted to marry me and I knew quite well that marriage to him would finance my career. Look at the trouble that decision got us both into. I couldn't bear it if people thought I was being given cases or privileges because of patronage.'

Jane, whose entire existence had been guided and controlled by position and patronage, looked at her shrewdly. 'They will anyway, Ferelith, and if you want my advice you will believe that a marriage is made between two people and they are the only two people who count in it, and they must ignore innuendos and raised eyebrows and all the other nonsense that jealousy carries with it. Now, enough about you. What are we going to do about Cousin Blair?'

Ferelith laughed and remembered ruefully that Angus too had thought one should not interfere. 'I thought marriage was between two people.'

'We have to get them married first and then we'll leave them alone.'

But Emma had been more able to take care of her personal life and her future than they had given her credit for, and the next morning a beaming Blair told the family at breakfast that Emma had agreed to become his wife.

'I think he means, that after much arm twisting, he has agreed to become my husband.'

'Gosh, Emma,' said young Jeremy as he moved his meatless sausage round and round his plate looking for a hole into which it might, with luck, disappear for ever, 'you must be strong if you can arm wrestle Uncle Blair.'

'She is indeed, young Jeremy,' said Blair, 'and now we must pray that this damn war ends quickly because Emma wants your daddy to give her away.'

'I have decided to come to Edinburgh. The war will soon be over and Simon will come back to look after Traviata. In the meantime his father says the cat can live with him. She has been there often with Simon and there are enough of his things there for her to recognize. Can we at least see one another occasionally?'

Ferelith had thought constantly about her decision since the night Angus had walked out. She had heard nothing personal from him and had seen him only once when he was on business in Glasgow. They had not spoken: he had nodded to her as he passed, no warmth at all in his stern face. Now she had decided to contact him, to see if there was to be any future for them. She had telephoned his house late at night and if he was surprised he had given nothing away.

Now he spoke to her. 'I can't believe you don't understand how difficult it would be for me to be in the same room with you remembering the last time we were together.'

'Of course I understand. I was there, remember. My feelings were the same. But I have to ask you if we still have a chance.'

'Oh, Ferelith, if it was anyone else I would think you were playing games with an old fool. You know how I feel about you. My God, I dream about having you . . . and I wake up and you're not there. But I can't sustain one of these terribly modern relationships or, if we are to believe what is said of our Victorian parents, these terribly old-fashioned relationships.'

'Could we meet on neutral territory, just to talk about my chances . . . of succeeding at the Bar?'

'On your own?'

She nodded and, even though he could not see her, he seemed to know. 'All right. I was to dine with my sister on Tuesday. I'll come through instead and we'll go out . . . immediately.'

She looked at herself in the mirror as she prepared for bed. She had lost weight she could ill afford to lose. Her skin seemed to have lost its glow and her hair was dull. Being unhappy in love did nothing for one's overall charm. But if he noticed when he arrived he said nothing. She took his coat and hung it up and then they sat on opposite sides of the room and tried to chat. Abruptly Angus stood up.

'Let's go out to dinner before I start eating that very charming lamp shade . . . or you, Miss Gallagher,' he said with a rather heavy attempt at humour. He held her coat for her and could not prevent his hands resting for a moment on her shoulders and at his touch she sighed.

I love this man: I want this man. Don't let me say the wrong thing.

They went to their favourite restaurant where they were welcomed as old and valued customers.

'The war can last only a few months' longer,' said Angus as they drank their after-dinner coffee, or whatever was masquerading under that name. 'Simon will be back soon, and Jamie, and life will get back to normal. Am I foolish to hope that you are going to change your mind about marriage?'

'Dear God, Angus, when I am with you I hear myself saying, "yes, tomorrow", but I can't Angus, not until I've had a little time at the Bar to prove myself.' She laughed drily. 'Once I know I'm good I won't care how much patronage I get.'

He grasped her hand so tightly that it hurt. 'Ferelith, I'm almost fifty. I always wanted children but until you I never met a woman whom I wanted to marry. I'll give up any rights to becoming a father, if you will only come back to Edinburgh with me now. I can get you a flat, a few cases and then you will be on your way.'

'But too many good advocates are in the forces, Angus. They're coming back and they'll want my cases . . .'

'And some of them will get them because they are men, and some because they are better.'

She accepted this. She had little or no experience. 'I have to be fulfilled as an advocate, Angus, and I have to know that I am where I am because of my ability, not because all the good male advocates my age were fighting a war or because everyone knew that my patron was the Lord Advocate. I want to get started and then, when the war is over, to fight for my career on equal terms. I don't want special treatment, just equality.'

'For God's sake, Ferelith, there will always be doubts. We all have them, men too. Are you in danger of becoming over-sensitive about this man versus woman thing?'

She looked at him sadly. 'I hope not, my darling, but if you will just give me a little more time to fight the male establishment on its own ground.'

'A little time? What is a little time? A month, a year, five years?'

'A year,' she said desperately. 'Give me a year.'

He drove her home to Simon's flat and Traviata. He kissed her gently on the lips. It could have been a kiss from little Jeremy so sexless was it.

'If you change your mind, telephone at any time, day or night, but I will never approach you again, Ferelith. I cannot drive from Edinburgh to Glasgow time after time with my heart pounding and then back again and again with my hopes blitzed. Come to Edinburgh and practise but this is goodbye.'

'Goodbye?'

'Yes. No one will be able to hint at nepotism, no one will say, oh she's only got where she is because of her lover, because her lover is bowing out.'

'Angus, no, wait.'

'Everything, Ferelith. I won't have a part-time wife. I've waited too long as it is.'

'You promised that I could still work.'

'You can, but every night or almost every night I want you in my bed which is where you belong. You think about it.'

'You're bullying me.'

'My darling, you have bullied me for years.' He turned and she could hear him running lightly down the stairs.

Mrs McGillivray, Simon's iron lady, had been an interested spectator. 'Well, and what is my Mr Osborne going to think when he comes back?' she said.

Not for the first time in the years she had lived in the flat Ferelith wanted to shout, 'Shut up, you horrid old trout', but she reminded herself that she was a brilliant advocate and trained to stifle her emotions. She stifled them successfully until the door was closed against the old woman's knowing face and then she fled to the safety of the bedroom and cried her eyes out.

Angus was a beast. No, she was. Angus was unreasonable. No, she was.

At last she fell into an exhausted sleep and woke

up next morning with a blinding headache and mascara all over Simon's silk bed cover.

A perfect reason for moving: she would have everything dry-cleaned for his return. She took a few days off and went into Edinburgh to see Oliver Belanger.

'Things are changing, Ferelith. Soon advocates will live anywhere, where there's hot and cold running water and telephone lines, of course. See your solicitors at Parliament House. It's merely a question of letting solicitors know you are here. After all, you are fully qualified. Take some free cases while you're waiting for some fees to come in: that way you will become known and, naturally, if I can help in any way . . .' He laughed as he saw her body tense. 'Touchy, touchy, no more than one would do for a young man, my dear. You really cannot fight the entire system, Ferelith. Save your energy for fighting for your clients rather than against the status quo. You'll get awfully bruised doing your Don Quixote impersonation. You did study Spanish didn't you?'

She nodded.

'Good. Facility with foreign languages, besides Latin, is going to be invaluable after this war. Now, go back to Glasgow when you have found a *pied-à-terre* and tie up all the knots. Let me know when to expect you and I will put the word around.'

She had to be grateful and to realize that she could not manage without someone's help. Being sponsored by Oliver Belanger was somehow more acceptable than being beholden to Angus to whom she wrote at great length to explain what she was doing. He wrote back from London where he was working. It was a letter that could have been written by one's former university professor.

The dying war monster is, like most monsters, even more bitter in defeat and has unleashed a secret weapon on London, a pilotless, jet-propelled aircraft that travels at an unheard of speed of 400 mph and which is capable of carrying a ton of high explosives. We call them doodlebugs. They have a strange horrifying tell-tale engine noise which scares everyone but what is more frightening is when everyone stands, panic stricken, listening for it to stop.

She telephoned. 'Can't you come home? It's safer here.'

'If I was a young strapping fellow, I'd be in Italy, or God help me, in the Far East. Try to think of it that way.'

And Ferelith, who had no one but herself to blame for the fact that she was not with him permanently, had to agree. Eventually though, he did return to Edinburgh where he found Ferelith furiously angry at the constant snide remarks of many solicitors.

'I don't know who told them that we were . . . friends, but I am so angry that many males seem to feel I'm getting some instructions because of you. Have you told any of your colleagues about me?'

'Of course I have. I'm not ashamed of being in love with you, Ferelith.'

Immediately she softened. 'And I'm not ashamed of being in love with you but for anyone to hint that cases come to me because of whom I know . . . it makes me want to scream. And I have had only two sets of instructions. I'm going to be in my dotage before I get anything decent.'

'Apply to become Advocate Depute. You won't make a great deal of money, and I know you want defence work, but do your bit for the Law and get yourself known at the same time. The word "patronage" will stop, believe me.'

'I know, but I saw doing my bit as coming later. I want to help people, to right wrongs, to make a stand for weaker members of society, women, children. Oh, God, I want to scream.'

'Go ahead. I had hoped that you might murmur tender endearments but if you need to scream or throw something, do so.'

She laughed and threw her arms around him. 'I don't care who comes in. I love you Angus Webster because you are, *sans doute*, the world's nicest man.'

He accepted the accolade graciously and then said, 'I had forgotten that you were a linguist.'

'Oliver said something like that a few months ago.'

'He's very Churchillian: foresees a United States of Europe, a European Court, Parliament.'

'Oliver is definitely in his dotage.'

On the 14th of February 1945, St Valentine's Day, the exquisite baroque and rococo architecture of Dresden, its Dutch and Flemish paintings, were all reduced to a pile of smoking rubble by a day and night of relentless bombardment, and in Fife Squadron Leader Blair Winterton married Mrs Emma Thomson. The bride was given away by the groom's cousin, Colonel Lord James Winterton, and was attended by the Honourable Constanza Winterton and Miss Ferelith Gallagher, the well-known advocate. The groom's man was the Honourable Jeremy Winterton. That the groom was in a wheelchair and the father of the bride on crutches was, at the groom's request, not reported in the newspapers.

Ferelith wept with happiness for Blair, for the peace and joy on his face, for the serenity emanating from Emma and with grief for herself.

I want Angus to look at me the way Blair is looking at Emma, she thaught. I want to look at Angus the way Emma is looking at Blair, and all I have to do is to pick up a telephone.

But she did not.

The war in Europe ended finally in May and Ferelith forgot her heartbreak and joined the millions of people all over the country who surged into the streets to welcome peace. At 3 p.m. she listened to the Prime Minister's broadcast. 'Advance Brittania. Long live the King.'

It was wonderful and like every other woman in the crowd she kissed complete strangers and shook hands with any hand that reached for her, but at midnight when the war officially ended she was completely alone wondering where Simon was and if he was even alive. Where was Pietro? Where were countless of others who had probably disappeared from the face of the earth with nothing to show their passing? 'No more, dear God, no more,' she prayed with Christians and Jews, Muslims and Buddhists, with everyone who was sane.

The blackout ended in July and almost a month later Japan surrendered unconditionally. The war, which had lasted almost six solid years, was over. It was time to change her career pattern again. The fighting men would soon be coming home. Advocates would be returning to the Bar. Would they receive preferential treatment? It did not matter. She would fight for her chances. Surely she was now well enough known to become a defending advocate. She decided to telephone Angus.

'I thought you would know, Miss Gallagher, but he has gone to London again. I think we know why, don't we?' she finished archly.

So it had come as she had always known it would. He was to be made Lord Advocate, Senior Law Officer for the whole of Scotland.

He'll be Lord Chancellor one day. I can't be married to the Lord Chancellor. What am I going to do? Ferelith's mind was in a turmoil.

'Shall I ask him to call, Miss Gallagher?'

'No, no thank you. It isn't important.'

The announcement of Angus's advancement was in all the papers the next day and Ferelith resigned from her office as Advocate Depute. She should have stayed in the post for some months but since, as an Advocate Depute, she was actually deputizing for *the* Advocate, in other words, Angus Webster, she was quietly allowed to return to her almost non-existent private practice.

She sent Angus a terse note to congratulate him but she did not telephone his office and he, in turn, did not try to contact her.

'He's too busy,' she consoled herself. 'And my note was hardly flowery. When things settle down . . .'

She defended a man who was accused of injuring his milkman by hitting him in the face with the milk bottle he had just been handed. The milkman said the defendant had been building up to it, never happy with where the bottles were put on the step, always complaining about the noise they made being set down.

'He jist went crazy and hit me wi' them.'

Ferelith was deeply sorry for the milkman who had had his nose broken but she was able to prove that her client had hit his milkman in the course of an epileptic seizure. It had been an involuntary movement, and he was not, therefore, responsible for his actions.

Her next case also involved the subtle difference between what the Law termed 'wicked recklessness to consequences' and 'involuntary action'. Her client, Joe Butcher, was accused of wilfully and maliciously wounding a man who had tried to rob the till in his small garage. Joe had been working on a car at 2 a.m. when he had become aware that someone was creeping up behind him. He had swung round, with the spanner he had been using in his hand and had hit the housebreaker with it, fracturing his jaw. The prosecution claimed that Joe had no right to take the Law into his own hands and that the force behind the blow was excessive and therefore wickedly reckless. Ferelith maintained that Joe, a man wounded in the defence of his country and now working all out at all hours to keep his family fed and his business in the black, had acted by instinct, almost unaware that he had a spanner in his hand, when he had hit out at the person who had set out to rob him of what little money he had earned that day. The jury of fifteen men agreed with her. Joe Butcher was found 'Not Guilty'.

'Yer a star, Mrs,' said Joe as he left the Court. 'Onything needs doin' in yer car, you jist leave it tae me.'

She wanted to share her triumphs with Angus, to tell him that although she had no car, she had her own personal mechanic, but he did not approach her and she could not approach him.

And then one day, Simon turned up at the Court of Session in Edinburgh. He was in uniform and was thinner than ever but he was still the same Simon.

'Hello, sweetness,' he said, 'what a dreadful class of person you are defending. Can't you get a nice corporate swindle where everybody goes to the opera after their day in Court?'

She could not speak. She looked at him, at the lines etched into his face, at the scar – why had he never told them he had been hurt? – running down his cheek.

'Simon,' she breathed, 'oh my dearest Simon,' and she threw her arms around him and hugged him to her as if she would never let him go.

They stood there holding one another, laughing, talking. At last the war was over. Simon was home in one piece. Only Pietro to worry about still. Ferelith hugged Simon, again unaware of the man who had just entered the Great Hall from the courtrooms. Simon saw him as he looked up from Ferelith's shoulder.

It was the Lord Advocate. His face was a picture of anguish and acceptance, and yes, of unbelievable hurt. He moved across the polished floor to the library and left the Hall quickly, the doors swinging furiously and then quite gently behind him.

Simon pushed Ferelith violently from him. She looked at him in stunned surprise.

'Run like hell, Ferelith. That was Angus,' he said.

She looked at the swinging doors. 'Angus?' she questioned again.

'Don't think, just act, for God's sake, Ferelith, for once just do.'

She reached up and touched him very gently on his scarred face and then she turned and ran from the room. She pushed past several eminent men who were not used to being so rudely handled, and by a member of the gentler and weaker sex at that.

'Angus,' she screamed. 'Angus.'

The word fled before her as she ran down the stairs, her leather shoes beating out a tattoo on the marble stairs. The sound was so full of a primeval anguish that at the door, a servant of the crown, who would never normally have been so bold, put out his hand and stopped the way of the Lord Advocate of all Scotland.

'The lady, my Lord,' he said anxiously. 'It's Miss Gallagher.'

Angus made as if to push past him and then he turned, looked up, and saw her resting at a bend in the grand staircase, her hand holding her aching side, her breath coming in short gasps. There was no more room, for either of them, for the sin of pride.

'Angus, oh, Angus my darling, it was Simon.'

She held out her arms and Lord Webster of Dalmarnock, Lord Advocate, ran up the stairs and, to the obvious delight of several advocates, solicitors, policemen, court officials and, no doubt, several petty and not so petty criminals, stopped her explanations with his lips.

'I am so tired, Miss Gallagher,' he said, 'I am so tired of finding you wrapped around various young men,' and then to, the accompaniment of hearty cheers, he kissed her fiercely again.

When she could breathe Ferelith looked up. 'Angus Webster,' she said humbly, 'please will you marry me?'

'With so many witnesses to your discomfiture should I say no, Miss Gallagher,' he said smiling down at her in a way that made her heart behave as it had never ever done, even in the giddy happy days of youth, 'how can I say no?'

There was a second enormous cheer but when the Lord Advocate looked up from kissing his fiancée, every legal head was looking firmly somewhere else.

14

MISS FERELITH GALLAGHER and Lord Webster of
Dalmarnock were married quietly, at least as quietly
as they were allowed to be married, in December 1945. Blair gave his half-sister away and the
bridal couple were surrounded by children of all
ages. Ferelith kept her promise to Maria's daughters, and Constanza Winterton too was a brides-
maid, Domenico was the ring bearer and Jeremy an
extremely officious and efficient usher. The service
was conducted by a Catholic Priest. The couple
stood in the aisle near the front of the small chapel
and not on the altar, because Angus was a Presbyterian and had neither the intention of changing nor
even any inclination to change his allegiance. After
the wedding Lord and Lady Webster went to Italy,
to the eternal city, Rome.

Ferelith wanted to find Pietro or at least to see
how the war had treated the family.

Angus had hoped to see the fabled city of Venice.

'The Venetian Republic has rather an amazing
history. I would quite like to see some of their ideas
transmitted to the Scottish legal system.'

'Like incarcerating someone in a cell below the
water line?' Ferelith teased.

'Have an immediate effect on lost memory. Can't
you just see some of our worthies as the water
rises . . . noo that ye . . . glug, glug, mention it,
yer lordship, glug, glug, I dae kinda remember
breaking intae that hoos, glug, glug.'

Ferelith laughed. 'I can't think that any other man

would contemplate looking for an old male friend of his wife on his honeymoon. You are very special, Angus Webster.'

'I know,' said Angus taking her into his arms, 'and I shall expect to be suitably rewarded.'

They decided to devote the first few days of their honeymoon to discovering one another and then, without calling, they would visit the *pensione*. It had rained almost non-stop since they arrived but the weather had not ruined their enjoyment of the city.

'This would have been miserable in Venice, darling. Don't you agree?'

Ferelith did not wait for an answer but looked out at the rain. A man, extremely handsome and well built walked quickly past the window. He saw as no threat to his masculinity the frilly pink parasol he held over his expensively-cut suit.

'I love Italians, don't you, Angus? I bet he's a judge: he's perfectly secure in his masculinity and so he picks up the only thing that's to hand when he steps out into the rain, possibly from his mistress's frilly little apartment. Can you imagine some of our legal friends with pink umbrellas? I shall buy one for you as a souvenir.'

'I'm not nearly secure enough in my masculinity to carry it. If, on the other hand, instead of going to look up the Angelosantis, we were to stay here in the hotel while you reassured me . . .'

Ferelith frowned at him in mock horror. 'Shame on you, Angus Webster. You have been married for five days and still all you can think of is . . .'

'Cappuccino,' said Angus to save the non-English speaking maid's possible blushes.

After their continental breakfast, which was more than adequate for Angus and not nearly enough for Ferelith, they stepped out, *sans* pink brolly but adequately protected by the big black umbrella, into the rain.

They were on the street that leads to St Peter's and although they had been in Rome for four days they had never yet toured the building.

'Let's see St Peter's first.'

'If you weren't a veritable tiger, Lady Webster . . .' Angus stopped and gazed down into his wife's wide green eyes. 'Dear God, how I love to hear that name. Lady Webster, Ferelith Webster, Mrs Webster.'

'You were saying?' Ferelith knew exactly what was going through his head and she loved it.

'I would say you were procrastinating.'

'No. I just feel that there is all the time in the world. Let's go to St Peter's. I need to buy a souvenir for Sister Anthony . . .'

'We should have brought her with us. Sister Anthony would have loved this . . . Sister Anthony said to look at that.'

They walked up the street and into the massive square that fronts the Vatican. They stood for a few minutes in the rain admiring the grandeur of the buildings and then went in.

'Can't you feel it?' Ferelith whispered.

'What?'

'Peace. Serenity. Holiness. It's tangible.'

'It's very dark.'

'Oh, Angus. Have you no soul? Just think of all the holy people who have worshipped in here for hundreds of years.'

They wandered around admiring the marble statues, the magnificent paintings, the signs that showed where St Paul's or St Patrick's Cathedral would have disappeared into the vastness that is St Peter's. Ferelith went to light candles at an altar, an activity that Angus always found faintly embarrassing, and a moment later Angus saw his wife of five days being exuberantly hugged by a man who had approached from the other side. She was squealing not with fear but with pleasure and was hugging her assailant as vigorously as she was being hugged.

'You did say you loved Italians, Ferelith,' said Angus drily.

She could not speak. Tears of joy were washing down her cheeks and she could not release her hold of the young old man who seemed to be having difficulty in letting go of her too. He recovered first and stood up and held out his hand to Angus.

'Pietro Angelosanti at your service, signor.'

'Angus Webster,' he said while his heart pounded unpleasantly in his breast. 'I am Ferelith's husband.'

'Her husband? *Cara*, you have another husband. Oh, I am so happy for you.'

Ferelith looked up at Angus and took pity on him. 'Let's go outside. We can't talk here. We'll have lunch. Pietro, we were actually on our way to visit your family.'

'*Cara*. They will be overjoyed. I too, I am full of happiness.' He looked at Angus and smiled and his smile was that of a man a thousand years older than Ferelith's husband. 'Signor, you are confuse. Come. My home is near and my parents will be with great happiness to see you. It is a time of great joy for my family.'

They went outside and once more Ferelith and Pietro looked at one another and hugged and laughed and cried.

'Is this Italian or Catholic or what?' asked Angus,

who was feeling slightly jealous. Pietro had known Ferelith before he had known her and well enough to embrace her like a . . . a sister.

'Oh, Angus.' Ferelith threw aside the umbrella and almost danced in the rain. She was dizzy with relief that Pietro was not one more casualty of the war. She was married to Angus and she had found Pietro. She felt that she could touch her own happiness.

'Come, signor,' said Pietro. 'You have captured the bird of paradise. Be generous, for her heart is big enough to have a corner for me and I am no threat. Look, we will go to a trattoria until we have talked and then you must come to drink coffee with my parents.'

He took them to a small restaurant hidden from the street and they ate and drank and talked until late afternoon. At last Ferelith leaned back contentedly.

'We have told you everything about us, Pietro, *mi amico*, but you have told us nothing about your life, and I cannot begin to tell you how much your silence worried me these past few years.'

'Well, we were on the wrong side during this war, *cara*, but I could not write. I was a partisan, in the hills. It would not have been safe.'

'And your parents?'

'All well. Rome was spared, you know. Such a civilized war. "Oh, General, bomb that area but not that area and if you move this battle a few miles you will miss the great wine cellars. Don't mention it. You're welcome."'

'I can't believe it was so cold-blooded.'

'Your wife is still naive, Lord Webster, after two husbands and a legal career, she believes in human goodness.'

'Don't you, Pietro?' Tears had started into Ferelith's eyes. She could not bear to have her day spoiled.

'Of course I do, *cara mia*. And now will you come to visit my family? They will insist you stay for dinner, Angus.' He laughed at Angus's look of horror. 'That is all we do in Italy, signor. Eat and talk and make love . . . and music sometimes.' He turned to Ferelith. 'They speak of you often and with affection.'

Pietro smiled and went on, 'There is to be no debut, *cara*, and no great football career either. The war has changed my plans.'

'You're going to work with your parents? How wonderful. We'll come and stay. You'll love it, Angus.'

'Yes, come, Angus, and stay. I think you are almost an Italian, so much you like the food and the wine . . .'

'And Verdi,' smiled Angus, 'but I think there is more you wish to say if my wife would stop speaking for you.'

'You are definitely the right man for her, Angus. Once I thought it might be me but I will baptize the bambinos, no?'

'I hope so,' smiled Angus while Ferelith looked at Pietro with incredulity.

'Baptize? Oh, how wonderful. You're a priest?'

Pietro shook his head. 'I have been hiding in the hills for five years, Ferelith. After Christmas I start in the seminary and you will come back to Rome for my ordination, but now we must go.'

They went back in time to the hotel where the wounded Ferelith had hidden and where she had begun to feel alive again. Pietro's parents welcomed them enthusiastically, insisted that they stay for dinner, were furious that they had gone somewhere else for lunch and demanded to know why they were not staying in the family hotel. Angus used all the diplomacy that had taken him to his position to placate them. That night Ferelith cried all the way back to their hotel but they were tears of joy, and after she and Angus had made love she wept again and the tears were tears of peace and fulfilment.

'I never knew such a woman for crying,' said Angus. 'What do you do when you're unhappy?'

'Get angry and fight,' said Ferelith and kissed him again.

The next day Angus bought her one of a pair of glass candlesticks – 'so that we will come back for its mate' – and she bought him a frilly pink parasol which they carefully carried back to Edinburgh and put in an umbrella stand in their bedroom.

For the next five years Ferelith devoted her not inconsiderable energies to her marriage and to her work. She was blissfully happy, sometimes so happy in her personal life that she felt something had to go wrong. But nothing did. Angus kept to his promise. He did not mention other people's children and he did not peer into prams parked outside shops. Ferelith wrote often to Pietro and each time she did she remembered his offer to baptize her children and sometimes she felt that it might be nice to have a child.

But she did not. Because there always seemed to be just one more person who needed her help, just one more person who felt rightly or wrongly that 'a man wouldnae understand. They're no made the way we are'.

As well as her growing and lucrative private practice she offered her services to the solicitors who found advocates for those unable to pay. Scotland had had some kind of legal aid for the needy for nearly five centuries. It was a system of which Ferelith and her peers were justifiably proud. Legal aid was not usually available in criminal actions and sometimes Ferelith refused to take cases that she knew she would lose.

One such was the heartbreaking story of Martha McPhaill.

Ferelith read the account of the accident that had befallen the McPhaill children in the *Scotsman*. The children were part of a gang of children who constantly played in a quarry that was being worked by a local builder. There were fences around the quarry but they had not been maintained. Children and often adults bent on some purpose other than play had enlarged the holes in the fences until any small child could climb through into the working area. The huge machines that clawed at the sides of the hill during the working day stood silent and still at night but their very size made them dangerous. The children had been with a gang who had sat on one of the earthmovers that was itself on ground heavily undermined by last century's digging. Their game, their constant rocking and bouncing, had caused the machine to tilt and the already-weakened earth had caved in taking the machine and such children as could not jump off in time with it. The McPhaill children had been swallowed up by the quarry and it had taken the police and the fire brigade hours to find their bodies.

And now Ferelith's nightmare had come true. The mother of the children she did not want to represent sat in her office.

'It was the woman up our close. She said as how we could get some money.'

Ferelith looked at the woman sitting or, to be

accurate, crouching on the edge of the chair as if
she were afraid that her work- and life-stained coat
would sully the perfection of this advocate's office.
An attempt had obviously been made to remove
the worst of the stains and the outline of a hot iron
was visible on the almost threadbare material. The
shoes, which were scuffed and down-at-heel, had
been polished, as had the plastic, masquerading as
leather, handbag.

Ferelith sighed inwardly and her whole being
flooded with sympathy which she immediately ban-
ished. She said nothing and the woman went on.
Ferelith appeared to listen although she had already
heard it so many times before and had carefully
sorted out the gold from the dross. Unfortunately
there was mostly dross.

She could not take this case to court and that, as
Angus had taught her and the other students all
those years ago, was the main part of an advocate's
brief, knowing which cases to try and which to
abandon.

*Much of your work will be in staying out of court, not
rushing pell-mell in to it . . . Knowing what music to
play in particular circumstances is a large part of the
advocate's skill . . . he, or she, has to, shall we say,
appreciate, yes, appreciate the minor susceptibilities of
any given judge.*

But there was no point in taking this case any
further. The Law was quite clear. There was no
fault to find with the quarry owners.

'They shouldnae huv had them machines where
the bairns could get at them,' Mrs McPhaill went on
dejectedly. She had lost horribly two of her children
and she was trying desperately to blame somebody,
to make someone responsible, someone who could
perhaps give her – Mrs Thomson had said – as much

as £1000. 'It wouldnae bring the weans back but it might make the pain a little less for them that were left behind.'

Ferelith rose and her slender elegant figure in its beautifully-cut grey suit seemed to make Mrs McPhaill shrink even farther back into herself. Ferelith saw her withdraw and she sat again on her own side of the desk and folded her ringless hands, with their beautifully-manicured nails, on the blotter in front of her.

'Mrs McPhaill, I have read everything very carefully and I have listened to everyone. The children were trespassing . . .'

'They were weans, jist weans.'

'I know, but they had been warned repeatedly. There were huge notices all over the fences . . .'

She was interrupted again. 'There wis holes in the fences: they shoulda fixed their fences.'

'The Law does not demand that the owners maintain the fences on their own property, Mrs McPhaill. The machines were parked on their own land next to their quarry and there were notices all over the perimeters . . . the outside fences. Because of the heavy amount of trespassing that goes on in that area, the owners had repeatedly telephoned the local police, they had put a notice in the local newspaper . . .'

'My bairns dinnae . . . oh, God, missus, my bairns didnae read the papers.'

She began to sob loudly and horribly with her mouth open. Her nose was running and she did nothing to stop the flow. Ferelith looked around desperately and then handed her her own immaculate white-linen handkerchief with the discreet F embroidered in one corner. Mrs McPhaill snatched it but instead of wiping her eyes or her nose, she stuffed it into her open mouth and went on sobbing, now holding her frail body with both arms and rocking herself backwards and forwards. Ferelith rose and fetched her a glass of water. She steeled herself to remove the soggy linen from the woman's mucous-covered mouth and dropped it into the wastebasket.

'Drink this,' she ordered and Mrs McPhaill did as she was bid, noisily gulping the water and then wiping the back of her hand across her mouth.

'I'm dreadfully sorry, Mrs McPhaill, but there is nothing I can do.'

'Fucking bitch.' The venom with which the words were uttered disconcerted Ferelith and she started back from the hatred in the wild eyes that stared up at her.

'You've nae bairns huv ye?' She looked at Ferelith's hands again and saw no wedding ring. 'Naw, nae men's fancied ye, huv they, and that's why ye sit here in Buckingham fucking Palace telling the likes of me ah cannae get money for a deid bairn, twa deid bairns. Well their faither's outside and he's no much but he'll comfort me fer your wickedness and whas gone tae comfort you, ye stuck-up bitch. Dae ye think ah cannae hear Glasgow under that posh voice? How dare ye tell me ah cannae get money for them. They said you was the best. They didnae tell us ye were a stuck-up bitch. Well, ah can get legal aid for another lawyer as clever as you, maybe wan wi a hert.'

She jumped up, pushed past Ferelith and rushed out of the office.

'I take it Mrs McPhaill was none too pleased?' Simon had come in as noiselessly as Mrs McPhaill had exited noisily.

'Oh don't Simon. I can't bear it. The poor woman

thinks if she goes round and round the offices she'll find someone to take the case.'

'Well, she will, sweetness.'

'But not to win it. Poor woman, not to win it.'

He closed the door swiftly and reached her just as her unsteady legs gave way and she threatened to fall to the floor.

'Ferelith *mon ange*, my reputation should anyone come in and find us in a clinch.'

She laughed as he had known she would and sat up in her chair.

'I think a healing restorative. Come along, be a good girl and Uncle Simon will take you to lunch.'

'I haven't time.' She gestured to the pile of files on her desk.

He moved over and tipped them into the waste-basket on top of the handkerchief and she squawked angrily and rescued them.

'Come and eat a nice big lunch, Ferelith, or I shall bring my work in here and be dubiously sweet all afternoon.'

'I've already had enough to bear today,' she said and reached for her coat. 'I'm going home.'

'Home?' he asked, 'or home home?'

'Home home. I want Angus. I want his sense and his calmness . . . and other things I won't bother you with.'

'Doesn't bother me the teeniest bit, sweetness, but Ferelith, have you counted the number of times you have run home to daddy in the past few months?'

'If you call him that again . . .'

'Ferelith,' he interrupted. 'I would call him that if he was thirty, never mind fifty: it's just a word. The point is, you have to restrict your work.'

'I don't want to cut down.'

'You can't have a marriage where each half of the

couple spends most of its time in a different house,
in a different city, for heaven's sake.'

'But the work I really care about is here.'

'Cases like Mrs McPhaill are everywhere, sweetness. You adore Uncle Charles but you can't abide
smarmy George. I've had an idea. What would
you think about my opening my own offices in
Edinburgh, a kind of expansion of my father's
office, and if anyone needs to make the ghastly
journey from Edinburgh to Glasgow twice or three
times a week, it will be me, with only my poor old
Traviata to worry about?'

'The road will get better.'

'Just think, a hundred years ago we would have
gone on the canal. Progress is slow but sure. In
twenty years we will fly between the coasts but
in the meantime, for the sake of your marriage
and your sanity, restrict your practice. And you'll
be nearer Blair and Emma,' he added as a final
inducement.

'You'd actually move to Edinburgh to be with
me?'

'I spent too many miserable years away from you
already. Besides I want to be godfather to all your
children when you get around to having them,' he
finished lightly and wondered why she stiffened,
but then he had never tried to understand her or
any other woman.

Ferelith now had her own car as well as the
mechanic to go with it, and she drove home to
Edinburgh thinking about Mrs McPhaill and her
hopeless struggle for compensation. How do you
compensate anyone for the loss of a child? That
made her think of Blair and his useless legs. He
had asked for no compensation for his loss: he had
borne it as the price he was prepared to pay to save

democracy. He would have been prepared to pay with his life if that sacrifice had been asked of him. At least he had won Emma who had made her own sacrifices.

And now there was Simon who was prepared to give up his home so that she might be a little more comfortable. And what had he hinted at, perhaps unwittingly or unknowingly: that he might be a godfather to her children?

'Should I tell him that I do not intend to have children? Is that what I intend? I'm still only in my mid-thirties. Plenty of time, and meanwhile there are Mrs McPhaills out there. Almost time for us to hear from Maggie Sturrock again, or Jean or Elsie or . . . or . . . or.'

There was her home. The lights were on in every front room. Ferelith's heart leapt as she saw Angus, dear, kind, loving, gentle Angus standing in the doorway waiting for her.

15

FATHER PIETRO ANGELOSANTI was ordained in 1950, just in time to offer up his first Mass for a swift end to the conflict in Korea. Ferelith and Angus flew to Rome for the ordination, and Angus found the pomp and magnificence of the ceremony, combined with its innate simplicity and veneration, quite breathtaking.

'Perhaps it's the man-made glories of the Church, darling, or the magnificence of the music but I am quite overwhelmed.'

Ferelith thought of that solemn moment when the men presented for ordination had prostrated themselves on the floor before the altar. Their bodies had expressed acceptance of sacrifice but also whole-hearted belief in the existence of God. Their exulta-tion had been almost palpable: they were where they wanted to be after years of inner and outer struggle. She had felt like that to a smaller, but no less real, degree when she had married Angus. Again she felt the stirrings of conscience. Had she obeyed all her marriage vows? These young – yes, and some not so young – priests now being hugged and kissed and photographed by loving families had made solemn, binding vows that morning. Each one intended to keep them.

'It's a great privilege to have been here,' she whispered to Angus. 'It's so easy to believe in God in a setting like this.'

He looked down at her and smiled. 'God is just as present on the Scottish hills, or is that a dreadful

thing for a good Scots Presbyterian to say in this
centre of the Roman Catholic faith?'

She smiled but said nothing. How could she tell
him that the ceremony had left her with a slight
feeling of sadness, not for the priests who were going
to keep their vows against almost insurmountable
odds, but for the ones who would fail in small or
large measure.

I'm getting old, she thought. It's not that I think
that I haven't kept my own unspoken vows.

After two days spent trying to absorb a little of
the glories of the city they flew back to Edinburgh
and Ferelith drowned herself in her work.

She talked to Simon, now happily esconced with
Traviata in a lovely flat near the Dean Bridge, and
asked him to find her cases dealing with injustice
to women. He knew of several, mainly dealing with
evictions.

'It seems that certain landlords have taken advantage of the fact that men were at the Front and their
womenfolk were at home unprotected. Some men
didn't come back at all and not all were casualties
of the war. The marriages were the casualties.
Landlords are still letting houses run down, they're
refusing to carry out proper repairs, they're putting
rents up and they're evicting families who can't pay,'
Simon said.

Ferelith stood up and walked to the windows that
looked out on to the peace and urban tranquillity
outside Simon's flat. The trees were wearing their
glorious autumn colours. She could see the beauty
of the room behind her reflected in the long Georgian
windows. She would fight tooth and nail for this.
Those women who had so much less had no weapons with which to fight.

She turned from the window decisively. 'Let's

take the bastards to Court. We'll swamp the Courts with cases. Judges will become very aware of this problem: they'll get fed up dealing with the same spivs all the time and maybe they'll lock some of them away. At the same time landlords who're a bit iffy will see that we mean business.'

There was no trouble in finding cases. The trouble was that there were not enough hours in the day to deal with them, but Ferelith and Simon worked day and night. Angus, if he worried that his wife was spreading herself too thin, said nothing, but supported her quietly with his love.

And then the threatening phone calls began. The number was unlisted but several times when Ferelith was alone, except for her daily help, in the house, the telephone would ring and she would pick it up expecting to hear the voice of a friend or a colleague and a harsh guttural voice would speak.

'Yer a bit too busy, Miss Gallagher. I suggest you tone down yer attitude a wee bitty or else. Do you understand me, Miss Gallagher, or will I need tae make myself clearer?'

'Who is this?' But the phone was dead and Ferelith would take herself to task for asking such a stupid question. Call yourself an advocate? He is going to tell you his name, isn't he?

She did not tell Angus until the windows were broken.

'I'm not backing off, Angus.'

'I wouldn't expect you to back off but we'll have to take better care of you.'

'Can you keep this out of the papers?'

Angus tried, but naturally, since Ferelith was the wife of the Lord Advocate, threatening phone calls and broken windows engendered a great deal of press coverage. Ferelith had the windows replaced

– twice – and tried to avoid photographers. She had
worked very hard to remain, in her professional life,
plain Ferelith Gallagher. It was very painful to see
luridly headlined pictures of herself walking across
the cobblestones between St Giles's Cathedral and
the Law Courts in all the newspapers.

'So much for anonymity,' she said to Simon.

'It's good in a way, sweetness. Now they know
they're taking on the big guns. A wee lady lawyer
is easy meat: the wife of the Lord Advocate is not.'

'The wee lady lawyer will throw you right out
on your *derrière* if you say anything like that
again.' Ferelith glared at him. She should have
known better.

'Ooh, I just love it when you talk French at me,' he
leered at her, and left the room followed by a very
heavy legal tome.

Angus was not so sanguine as Simon. Ferelith
had been so distressed by her inability to help
Mrs McPhaill receive compensation for the loss
of her children that she had rushed straight into
finding clients she could help. She cared nothing
for the fact that her fight with slum landlords
would bring her into direct battle with organized
crime. Who really owned these slum properties?
Angus had been a lawyer long enough to know
that the names on the title deeds meant little.
He was also quite sure that the people who were
harassing Ferelith had always known that he was
her husband and that the knowledge did not worry
them. They believed themselves to be above the law.
He could not ask Ferelith to restrict her campaign:
he could only worry.

His worst moment came when she was accosted
on the road right outside their house. She had
been working late in the Advocates' Library and

had taken a taxi home. The porch light was on to welcome her and she could even see the low light from Angus's study as she stooped to pick up the briefcase she had put on the ground while she had been paying her fare. The taxi drew away as she gathered up her things and turned to climb the stairs.

There was the sound of running feet and a heavy body cannoned into her, sending her and her briefcase flying, to land with painful abruptness on the stone steps. 'See this, fuckin' bitch: it's a knife,' snarled a low voice and then abruptly she was released.

A policeman had appeared from nowhere and Ferelith's assailant took to his heels and fled.

'Go after him, go after him,' Ferelith yelled as she scrambled around in the dark picking up her papers, but the constable stopped to help her up.

'He's well away, missus.'

'Did you get a good look? Where were you when he attacked me?' Ferelith was dreading the door opening and Angus appearing at the top of the stairs.

'I was checking some basement windows, Lady Webster.'

Later Ferelith, still considerably shaken, had tried to joke with Angus who had, as she had dreaded, heard their voices and came out to investigate. 'Checking basement windows: he was having a fag, more like.'

Angus looked at her white face and her pale shaking hands, now wearing his rings. Even upset and in pain she had put her rings on again as soon as she had been able to get to her bedroom. She was no longer Ferelith Gallagher, the advocate: she was his wife. 'Ferelith . . .' he began.

'Oh, I couldn't bare it if you told me to stop, Angus.'

'I wouldn't dream of it. You are quite right to fight but I reserve the right to worry and to do what any husband would do in the circumstances.'

'Angus Webster. How many husbands can provide a six-foot policeman outside the door? I don't want special treatment.'

'For God's sake, Ferelith. You are my wife. Am I supposed to sit back and not interfere because of your ridiculous notion that you fight all your own battles?'

'It's not ridiculous.'

'Who gave a certain editor an earful because he, so she said, treated the Lord Advocate unkindly?'

'That's different. You're my husband. You're not allowed by your position to fight back.' She saw that he was about to blow unpatchable holes in her defence and so retreated, wisely.

'Anyway, darling, all it needs is for some judge to put one of these rotten landlords behind bars for a considerable period and for more of the legal profession to back me.'

'That would help and that will happen but it's not so simple as that. You are sitting on a hornets' nest, Ferelith, and hornets mean business.'

'What do property owners plagued by hornets do, Angus?'

'Burn them out, I suppose.'

'Exactly. We shall burn them out and we'll start by redoubling our campaign to find out who really owns all these slum properties with creative tax accounting.'

Angus was not the only person worried about Ferelith's activities. His worries were, of course, wholly altruistic. The same could not be said for others in the legal fraternity.

'Women in the Law are bad news,' Matthew Robertson, a junior advocate, complained at a luncheon where several senior advocates were also present. 'And this aggressive woman is bringing the wrong publicity to the office of Lord Advocate,' put in another.

'Move with the times, laddie,' said an older and wiser head. 'Women lawyers are part of the twentieth century whether you like it or not.'

'But even criminals don't accept them,' argued the first young man. 'Did you hear Jimmy Taylor in court today? "Mak shair the lassie gets this doon richt." He thought she was a clerk.'

'Jimmy Taylor is an illiterate oaf and totally unfit to clean her shoes. We should be applauding her work, not setting obstacles in her way. She's a damn fine advocate and has won most of her cases.'

'Cases she gets because of her husband,' a rather disgruntled and unsuccessful member of the Bar complained.

'Really? He sends her riffraff, the dregs of society, child molesters, wife beaters, and now these slum landlords? I would have thought he could guide some nice fat money-earners her way. He should encourage her to keep her hands clean and to work only with the huge corporations who cheat the Government and each other, but who are supposedly model citizens who appear at every benefit and give huge cheques to every conceivable charity.'

Since these were the only clients that several of the lawyers had some were ashamed and others annoyed.

'That was unnecessary. All crime is dirty; we all agree on that.'

'Let's make sure we do and let's make sure that we back our female colleague to the limit. It won't hurt us, you know. Remember that the Lord Advocate thinks the sun rises and sets on her head. Oliver Belanger is also rather fond of her. For a while there it was thought that he too had his eyes on the delectable Miss Gallagher.'

'Wasn't there some scandal in her past, some sexual hanky panky which one can easily believe in with looks like hers – all well hushed up, of course?'

But here the jealous young lawyer had gone too far.

'I wouldn't play with that one, laddie. It could be the end of your career.'

'Or hers,' thought Matthew Robertson, but he said nothing of this and set himself to placating his senior colleagues.

'I wonder what Shaw would have had to say about this one, Angus?' asked Ferelith one morning several months later as they sat in their lovely break-fast room, with the remains of a very hearty breakfast before them.

The great writer, who had died the previous November, would certainly have had some witty comment to make on the news item.

'Well, go on. Tell me,' said Angus. 'You have, as always, my undivided attention.'

'It seems,' said Ferelith folding her newspaper in a way that told him that she was incensed, 'that the great British public does not want to hear of momentous events like war or disaster from mere women. There are, therefore, to be no female news announcers on the wireless. There are to be no males with dialects either. I suppose *they* do know the difference between a dialect and an accent?' She moved her teapot, which was now empty, and half-filled her cup with the coffee left in Angus's coffeepot, a habit which had alternately delighted and exasperated him now for nearly five years, and went on, 'Were you asked if you would like bad news served up over your bacon and eggs by a man or a woman?'

'The question must have slipped by me: a busy day, perhaps.'

'I never cease to be amazed at a man's inability to deal with more than one thing at a time. That's what happened, of course. They asked men who were all doing something and therefore were unable to decide rationally on the answer to the question.'

'What about the women who answered?'

'Mere feeble-minded little women were not asked such an important question. Go to work, M'Lord, and send lots of nasty men to jail.'

'Yes dear,' said the Lord Advocate meekly and went upstairs to dress.

Left alone with his coffee Ferelith cleared a space and took her diary out of the briefcase which sat beside her chair. No court appearances today. A meeting at 9 a.m. with Simon, a committee meeting of the Edinburgh University Settlement Group at 11 a.m. and lunch with Maria di Rollo who was coming through from Glasgow because she was, she said, tired of waiting for Ferelith to visit her. This, of course, was complete nonsense since Ferelith was in Glasgow several times a month and saw the di Rollos on most visits. After lunch with Maria there was a meeting with Oliver Belanger who wanted to lead her on a rather nasty rape case he was defending. She would go from that to a cocktail party at the City Chambers and then just maybe, she and Angus could have a quiet dinner together. He would be in London for the next few weeks and they liked to stock up their memories of time together to warm them when they were apart.

She had cleared away her personal mail by the time Simon arrived. He was a happy man.

'The Fiscal said "yes", sweetness,' was how he greeted her.

'Yahoo.' Ferelith threw her arms around him and hugged his thin frame until he winced. 'How super. I wish Angus was here, and I can't let him know until that party for the Provost.'

'Rogers will probably be at that too – he's a big contributor to Festival funds – so watch no one spikes your drinks.'

'He won't come. Not even Tom Rogers has that much brass neck.'

'As we speak,' said Simon looking around for a clean coffee cup, 'lawyers and accountants are doing incredible things to prove that he is not in fact aware that he owns all those slums.'

For months Ferelith had been defending families who had been sued for non-payment of rent and she had been winning her cases. Slum landlords were being persuaded to upgrade their properties and to carry out running repairs. Evicted families were being rehoused, either in council houses which were springing up everywhere, or in privately owned buildings, but the biggest problem for the Law was to find the owners of the said proper-ties. Lawyers waded through forests converted into paper covered in legalese, trying to find the small print that led to revealing the actual owners of the properties. Address A would seem to be owned by John Doe, who was in fact merely a front man for X Industries, which were in turn owned by

L Enterprises, which were in turn found to be allied to an offshore firm called Lifeline Properties with a banking address in Jersey or Switzerland or even in one case, Brazil. Now the Procurator Fiscal had agreed that the creative accounting of one Tom Rogers, honoured business tycoon from Glasgow, could be investigated.

According to numerous reports in the press, Rogers knew nothing of L Enterprises and as for Lifeline Properties, he had never even heard of the company. Perhaps, he made bold enough to say, the Lord Advocate's wife should stay at home and have babies which would surely be a more suitable outlet for her undoubted talents than harassing a hardworking businessman who had devoted his working life to bettering the lot of his fellow man.

Ferelith, who had had several of these articles pointed out to her by *soi-disant* well-meaning friends, tried, in turn, not to let her personal animosity interfere with her investigation. She remembered Jane's conviction that marriage was a matter for the two people involved and no one else, and certainly not Tom Rogers, had the right to interfere.

Angus and I together decided not to have children, she consoled herself.

'It would be so nice to see someone like Rogers take the rap instead of the usual fall guys, Simon,' she said as Karen came in with a tray of fresh coffee.

'Don't hold your breath. His affairs are so convoluted that it will be impossible to unravel all the ends but I'm sure he was the one who told his underlings to lay off last winter.'

After the frightening incident on her very doorstep, Ferelith had been surprised that there were no further episodes. The anonymous caller had evidently decided that intimidation would get him nowhere and had stopped pestering Ferelith by telephone. Her windows had remained unbroken. No thug waited for her as she stepped from a taxi. By Christmas of 1950 she had begun to relax and now in the spring of '51 she hardly ever thought of the possibility of reprisals for her campaign against the slum landlords. It must have been obvious to the underworld that the judicial system was working and was backing Ferelith's efforts. One slum landlord had been convicted and was serving a prison sentence, and five more, whose abuses of their tenants were not quite so obscene, had been fined heavily and forced to modernize their properties.

Simon put another document on the table in front of her. 'The difficulty will be getting evidence gathered in the lead time given us.' He had gone on to another impending trial, and during the rest of their meeting they spoke no more about Tom Rogers and by the time she reached the City Chambers Ferelith had dismissed him completely from her mind.

She joined Angus, who had managed to get there before her, and they were having a discussion with several businessmen about the possibility of visits to the forthcoming Festival by both the Carl Rosa Opera Company and the Teatro San Carlo from Naples, when Rogers appeared. He had no compunction about joining the group around the advocate who would possibly be prosecuting him.

Angus withdrew from the group immediately, pleading a prior arrangement to speak with a newspaperman. Ferelith made as if to follow him.

'Oh, don't leave us, Lady Webster,' smiled Rogers. 'I know that you, like myself, have been deeply fond of grand opera for many years. We must persuade Travers here and Sir James, of course, to try for both companies. I've brought along a little cheque, Sir James, to help the Festival funds. What do you think, Lady Webster? Don't you agree that Edinburgh needs a purpose-built theatre? We should be doing some fund raising for a building fund. Maybe I'll start the ball rolling. You would love to see a new theatre especially built for large-scale productions of grand opera, wouldn't you, Travers?' He smiled at one of the men in the group who was known to be completely tone deaf, and who had admitted on more than one occasion that he thought sitting through any operatic performance should come under the heading of *cruel and unusual punishment*.

There was no way that Ferelith could leave the group without being rude and so she stayed talking and listening to the discussion for some time, admiring both Rogers's gall in trapping her and his obvious knowledge. She also felt sorry for poor Travers who, with the Director of the Festival Committee standing beside him, had had no choice but to agree that a new theatre would be a good thing.

Eventually she was able to make an excuse and she and Angus thanked the Provost for his hospitality and left the room. She was unaware of the look of venomous dislike thrown after her by Tom Rogers and she did not hear him ask a senior member of the Bar for Matthew Robertson's telephone number. She would not have been unduly concerned. She had little respect for Robertson's abilities, and no time at all for the man himself, but she had no reason to suspect that he actively disliked her.

In July a study told interested observers that women in Britain worked fifteen hours each working day and even more at the weekends. Ferelith, who was a perfect example of the study's findings, was too busy working to see the publicity on the findings or she would certainly have brought them to Simon's attention. She would not have told Angus, who was seriously disturbed by the amount of time his wife spent away from home.

'One might almost think you were unhappy at home,' he teased Ferelith on one of the rare occasions that found them curled up together on the same sofa reading and listening to music. Ferelith loved these times because they always ended in lovemaking. Classical music seemed to be a tremendous aphrodisiac: they always made love after concerts or operas, not after plays.

'I'm terribly unhappy,' she said, teasing him. 'Anyone can see that.'

'Then let's see what we can do to cheer you up,' said Angus, and did.

16

THERE WERE CASES that Ferelith took knowing that she was bound to lose. Losing is usually taken to mean that the advocate's client is found guilty and receives the full weight of the penalty of the Law. But if the client gets less than he might have received if he had been represented by another advocate, and perhaps less than he probably deserves, then the defending advocate can be taken as having won at least in a small measure.

Advocates do take cases where they know that their client is guilty and still they try to get them off. They also take cases where they know their clients are guilty and they do not want them to be found innocent but they believe very sincerely that everyone is entitled to a defence. Angus Webster and others like him had impressed this fact of the judicial system into Ferelith and her classmates. Everyone is entitled to a defence and to have someone represent him or her impartially.

One such case was the case of Harry Russell. Harry was one of the world's serious losers. Nothing had ever gone well for him. He had, like Ferelith herself, been brought up in an orphanage but his treatment there had not endeared authority to him or, it must be said, Harry to authority. After leaving school at the age of fourteen he had drifted in and out of prison for petty crimes and had spent the war years incarcerated for his part in an abortive bank robbery. Harry, it has to be said, was always the one left holding the baby – that is, the incriminating evidence.

In October of 1951 he was arrested for receiving and fencing stolen goods.

'Why on earth are you going to waste time on Harry Russell, Ferelith, with everything else we're doing just now?'

'Simon, come on, someone's got to help him.'

'He's guilty as hell. There isn't an honest bone in his body. Look at his record. Birching, birching, borstal, jail, jail, jail.'

'And jail again, I have no doubt, but that's not a record, that's a list of punishments, and doesn't it occur to you, Simon, that something goes drastically wrong with our penal system when it's dealing with the Harry Russells of this world?'

Simon poured himself another cup of coffee. 'Oh, spare me, Ferelith. He likes being dishonest.'

Ferelith held the sugar basin and watched with awe as he ladled sugar into his coffee. 'Perhaps he doesn't know how to be anything else, Simon. Has anyone ever taught him to be different, shown him that there is satisfaction in working for a living?'

Simon looked at her shrewdly. 'Are you all right, sweetness?'

'Yes, I am,' said Ferelith angrily. She knew exactly how Simon's mind was working. 'I'm sorry for Harry Russell. I don't think he's ever had a chance. I would like to represent him, maybe my high profile will encourage more people to think about reform. He needs rehabilitation, not punishment.'

Ferelith duly represented Harry Russell. She did not try to present him to the Court as an innocent man but eloquently tried to paint an honest picture of someone who had been born without a chance, and whose inherent weakness of character had led to his life of crime.

'But perhaps if he had been met by understanding, if he had been brought up to trust authority and not to fear it . . .' she began.

'Is my learned friend really trying to tell us that all children brought up in institutions are victims?' interrupted the Depute Procurator Fiscal. 'That they develop a propensity for crime? I'm sure you will agree, M'Lud, that that supposition is quite intriguing.'

Ferelith was furious with herself. She had laid herself open for such a silly remark. 'I am saying, as my learned friend well knows, that not all institutions have the highest standards. Not all guardians of orphaned children have the ability to spot potential. Children perhaps not academically talented' – poor Harry, everyone knew, was not the brightest of men – 'cannot possibly develop any potential they might have if their guardians are too pressured by sheer weight of numbers to give each and every developing child some individual attention.'

'I grows nice cabbages,' volunteered Harry, and was slapped down by the Judge for his impertinence in speaking out of turn.

Harry got three months penal servitude. 'Perhaps there will be a garden where you can develop your cabbage growing talents, Mr Russell,' said the Judge kindly as he sent him off to prison.

Ferelith was quite pleased with the result. She had felt sure that her client had been heading for at least six months and she thought too that the Judge's remarks about gardening might well be taken seriously.

On the 6th of January 1952, King George VI died and the Princess Elizabeth, a young wife and mother, became Queen.

'Another working mother,' said Ferelith to herself.

'If she can handle it, surely I should be able to do the same.'

'Poor girl,' said Angus as he watched the funeral procession, but why he was calling the slight figure in mourning a 'poor girl', Ferelith decided not to ask.

She was busy preparing a defence for a woman who had been accused by her employer of stealing a valuable piece of jewellery. Miss 'J' maintained that the jewellery had been given to her by her employer's husband in return for certain sexual favours, that her mistress knew this and was punishing her for her own husband's bad behaviour.

'I know what I did with Charlie, Mr Fairweather, wasn't right, Miss Gallagher, but he said he loved me and I couldn't resist him. I knew there wouldn't be a divorce – I mean nice people don't do that kind of thing – but I was sure he would take care of me.'

'Mr Fairweather denies both giving you the brooch and having a personal relationship with you.'

'Well he would, wouldn't he? She's the one with the money and he's terrified that she'll dump him.'

It was a sad, ugly story and not one of the three main protagonists came off well.

'I'll have to try to get Mrs Fairweather to drop the charges, Simon,' said Ferelith when she and Simon were discussing strategy. 'I think our client is telling the truth. He gave her the brooch, paid for with his wife's money – that's another example of creative accounting allowing one to believe what one wants. I paid for it. Ergo it is mine. Ergo, if she has it, she has stolen it.'

'Charlie sounds a right bastard.'

'Both women would be better off without him,' began Ferelith.

'Don't tell me a good Catholic is advocating divorce.'

'I'm not going down that path with you, Simon. Have you got the sales slip from the jeweller?'

He handed it over. 'Fairweather paid for it with cash. Didn't want his wife to see a cheque written for jewellery when she had not herself received it. He's a smart one.'

'But, of course it doesn't tell us who the piece was for and if we can't prove that we're nowhere with a defence. Mrs F asserts that her husband bought her the brooch and he says he did.'

'Their bed must be an uncomfortable place right now.'

'According to Miss J he was very rarely in his wife's bed: he was in hers.'

Together they peered at the newspaper photograph of Charles Fairweather.

'Hardly a Jimmy Stewart, is he?' said Simon.

'No, it amazes me that either woman fancies him, never mind both of them.'

Simon looked at her and laughed. 'Listen to us. Isn't it one of the wonders of the human personality that A appeals to B but not to C. I mean if we all fancied the same guy there'd be a right old mess.' He straightened up from the newspaper and looked at her ruefully. 'That isn't what I meant to say.'

Ferelith was saved from trying to find a suitable response by the strident ringing of the telephone. She picked up the receiver and Simon saw her face pale under her light make-up. 'I have nothing to say,' she said with as firm a voice as she could muster and hung up.

She almost fell into the chair beside the table. 'Simon, try to get Angus for me, please.'

Simon wasted no time in asking her questions but

proceeded to ring the Lord Advocate's office. Angus
was unavailable. Just as Simon hung up, the telephone rang again and this time Simon answered it.

'Tom Hardy. *The News*. Could Lady Webster con-
firm or deny this story for us, Mr Osborne. We have
been told that there is evidence to prove that Lady
Webster entered into an incestuous relationship
with her brother while they were at university
together in the early thirties.'

'I have known Lady Webster since the thirties and
there is absolutely no truth in this scandalous tale.
We will make a statement later,' said Simon and
hung up.

'Oh God, Simon. Who . . . ?'

'Rogers obviously, sweetness. He knows he's
going to jail but he'll make you and Angus as
miserable as he is going to be.'

Ferelith started up from the chair. 'Blair,' she
cried. 'He's had a dreadful year, Simon. I must let
Emma know so that she can shield him, if possible,
and . . . there's Jamie and Jane and Angus. This
horrible mistake will cost all the people I love.'

Angus was the next person to telephone. He had
also been approached by a newspaperman. 'Don't
worry, darling, and don't panic. The tabloids will
have fun with it and your tragedy will make a few
people gloat for a while but the decent papers will
print the story accurately and you'll get a sympathy
vote. Poor old Blair will be the main sufferer. You
know how he hates figuring as the wounded hero,
and now this.'

'Is there any way we can suppress it, Angus, for
Blair's sake? His lungs have been so bad this year
and I can't bear to cause him any more distress.'

'Ferelith, you did not knowingly enter an incestuous relationship with your half-brother. It was

the most appalling and heartbreaking tragedy and
I could kill Rogers. He's at the bottom of this: I can
smell him, but we are not going to let him beat us.
Now, I am not coming home. There is no need for
me to fly to your side before the end of my working
day: that will look as if we have something to hide.
You go ahead with your own work and my office
will issue a statement to responsible newspapers.'

More than anything Ferelith wanted to feel her
husband's comforting arms around her. Even after
six years she was surprised by the intensity of her
feelings for him, her need for him, but she knew that
it would be wrong for Angus to come home. Still, she
felt that she could not face the blaze of publicity on
her own. She would cancel all her engagements.

'And they'll wait until tomorrow or the next day or
the next, sweetness. Chin up. Ring Emma and warn
her and I'll get in touch with the Wintertons, but
then we are going out together, as usual, and you
are going to do a good day's work.'

Ferelith spoke at length to her brother and her
sister-in-law and then went upstairs to put on her
wedding ring. She never wore it during a working
day but today she felt she needed to feel some
contact with her husband. She looked out of the
windows of the second-floor library and wilted.
Already the street was full of newspapermen.

Well, get it over with, Ferelith, she thought to
herself. Maybe Sister Anthony was wrong and mud
thrown doesn't really stick. Eventually it can all be
washed off. And in the meantime there are people
depending on you to help them. Would their cases
be helped by the notoriety of their advocate?

The worst headline was even worse than Ferelith
had foreseen.

WAR HERO SEDUCES OWN SISTER

That came with some nice pictures of a very young Blair and a rather stiff graduation picture of her. On the same page was a picture of Blair in his wheelchair at Buckingham Palace and several shots of her with Angus.

'They'll wonder what he saw in me, looking at that graduation picture,' she said and wanted desperately to break down in tears, but she tried to smile at Angus who was suffering quietly but deeply, not for himself but for her. She could see the muscles in his jaw working, a sure sign that a usually quiet man was very angry.

'We will issue no further statements, darling. Everything has been explained simply, without hysteria. You and Blair were caught up in a tragedy, not of your own making. That, of course, is usually the way of tragedies. It's the innocent who suffer.'

Ferelith looked at the newspaper before her which had a picture of Jane taking Constanza to a children's party. Dirty tentacles were even creeping out to touch that lovely child. Furiously Ferelith crumpled up the paper and threw it into the fireplace. She watched it unfold in its deaththrows and saw little Constanza's face disappear in a burst of flame.

'And all because Helena Winterton wouldn't join her husband in India,' she said.

'You can't know that, darling, but if it's true then I'm glad that she didn't go because you are here.' He reached out and pulled her down onto his lap. 'I waited a long time for you, Mrs Webster, and I cannot begin to tell you what you mean to me.'

'Try,' she said, and he did.

There were other appalling headlines.

PROMINENT ADVOCATE AND BROTHER IN LOVE TRYST.
LORD ADVOCATE'S WIFE IN LOVE AFFAIR WITH BROTHER

These were the ones that really hurt and annoyed
Ferelith, especially when it was hinted that Angus
should resign. Some colleagues advised Ferelith to
withdraw from the public view for a while but she,
Angus and the members of their family besmirched
by the scandal, went gamely on behaving decently
and trying to return some decency to the lives
of those around them. She refused to give any
interviews.

'It's a classic damned if you do and damned if
you don't scenario,' said Angus, 'but although I
hate every moment of this, for your sake, Ferelith,
I think we are better to ride out the storm.'

'You must feel awful,' Ferelith said and tried
to smile.

'Of course I do. Why do you . . .'

'It's all your clichés, darling.'

'That's why they got to be clichéd: sometimes
they're the only words that work. Now come on,
business and life as usual.'

Ferelith managed to get the Fairweathers to drop
the charge against Miss J and she also persuaded
Mrs Fairweather to give her erstwhile employee a
decent if not glowing testimonial and a little nest
egg to tide her over until she could find a new job.

'Told you Fairweather was guilty as hell, Simon.
He and his wife deserve one another.'

'Frankly, I wouldn't put any one of the three on
my visiting list.'

'But you're such a snob,' laughed Ferelith.

'Someone has spent a great deal of money digging
up the past, Simon.'

Ferelith and Simon were taking a much-needed break from work and were having lunch together down at Gullane. When her mind was too full of her own and other people's trials and tribulations, Ferelith found that a brisk walk along a windy and, preferably, deserted beach was the best antidote. Simon had waited, snug and warm, in the lovely drawing room of their favourite hotel. He had made a point, after the war, of never getting wet unless he was in his bath and therefore he preferred to sit watching his old friend fight the wind, from the security of four tastefully-decorated walls. The fact that the hotel boasted an internationally acclaimed chef was an added inducement.

Now Ferelith came in, her hair wind-blown, her cheeks as pink as he had ever seen them. She looked, he thought, about twenty years old, but with an added serenity since her marriage that was extremely attractive. She smiled at him.

'There's nothing like a sea breeze for blowing away problems.'

He shivered. 'That's more a gale. Why didn't Angus come? I always feel he's a bit Spartan too: lots of ghastly vitamins washed down by exercise.'

She sat down beside him. 'I love you dearly, Simon, but if you think for one moment that you would be here if Angus was available . . .'

'Nasty,' he said and leered at her. 'It wasn't your undoubted charms that brought me galloping down here, sweetness.'

'I know. The chef. Well, let's order because I'm starving.'

'I do adore women who admit to enjoying their food but I must confess to believing that half the time you have no idea what you are putting in your mouth.'

'True, but today, I want to enjoy everything. No nasty snide remarks in this morning's papers: no letters saying, "Stuck-up hussy, nae better than me". Who helped him, Simon, if it was Rogers?'

'Your annulment is on record and you have to admit that even though you had no idea that you were brother and sister, your one-day marriage does make juicy reading. Decent people are heartily sorry for both of you and I think decent people make up the majority.'

'Oh yes, can you believe I even had a letter from Harry Russell to my office. It's barely literate but he says he knows I'm a decent woman and that he'll come and do the garden for me when he gets out of clink.'

'Great, your gardener with a checkered past can keep your mechanic, with a less than salubrious past, company.'

'Not if he only grows cabbages. Have you any idea how many cabbages are consumed in orphanages? Still, to be serious, we have had lots of supportive mail. Blair too.'

'How is he?'

'Remarkably well. He was like Angus, just dying to get out there and slay a few dragons, but he's calmed down and dear Emma has been so brave and supportive. It was a particularly nasty thing to do to us, Simon. Apart from Rogers, I really would like to know who hates me that much.'

Simon said nothing. He had an idea that certain disgruntled and unsuccessful members of their profession had been delighted to see Ferelith Gallagher's name being dragged through mud and would have been only too happy to see her retire.

'I'll never give up, Simon,' she said as if she could read his thoughts. 'I may never be the first female

Lord Advocate but I'll certainly be putting my good name forward for every advancement possible. I've worked too hard to be scared off by the Tom Rogers of this world.'

Brave words but sometimes Ferelith found herself thinking that it would be quite nice to have a good reason for staying at home out of the spotlight. What better reason than a child? Would having a baby not be the perfect fulfilment of her love and passion for Angus and his for her? No. Having a baby as an excuse for staying at home was no good reason.

I don't want a child, Ferelith told herself night after night as she lay beside her sleeping husband. Young people should have children. Angus and I are both too old, too set in our ways. I don't need a child. I need only Angus and I want all his love: I don't want to share him with anyone.

The love of a child adds a new depth to married love.

I can't give up my work. I just plain love being an advocate and I want to succeed. A child would get in the way. I wouldn't be a good mother. I have no experience.

Night after night Ferelith argued with herself and then punched her pillow irritably and went to sleep.

The scandal of 1952 went the way of all other scandals. By November no photographer was sufficiently interested in Lord and Lady Webster to photograph them as they went to Sadler's Wells to hear the new soprano sensation, Maria Callas, sing Bellini's *Norma*. After the performance they went to their favourite London hotel for a romantic late supper and to discuss the evening.

'How can you say she's wonderful, Angus? The top notes in that Casta Diva aria were so shrill they hurt my ears.'

'You have no musical soul, Ferelith.'

'I have no hearing either after that. I'll give you her dramatic power, darling, but nothing beats a decent tenor.'

'We'll have to agree to differ on that. I'm not going to fight about it when there are so many other nice things we could be discussing.'

'Like this Bentley-Craig case. I am so glad you don't have that to prosecute.'

'Would you want to defend them?'

Ferelith thought about what she knew about the notorious case that was gripping the public. Christopher Craig, aged sixteen, and Derek Bentley, nineteen, were accused of shooting a policeman.

'I think I would do everything I could to make sure Bentley doesn't receive a death sentence.'

'The Law states that everyone involved in a murder is responsible.'

'So you wouldn't mind prosecuting them?'

'Every prosecutor has to face uncomfortable decisions, Ferelith: every judge, every barrister. You know that. We don't do the job because it's pleasant. We do it because we believe in law and order. The policeman is dead. Nothing can change that.'

'But Bentley didn't shoot him.'

'He was heard to say, "Let him have it."'

'Isn't it possible he meant, let him have the gun?'

'Of course it's possible, but surely one would say, "Give him the gun, Chris," not, "Let him have it."'

'I think I'd rather talk about Maria Callas's top notes. Let's just enjoy our few days, darling. No law, nothing nasty.' She bent her head to concentrate on her lobster salad and it was some time before either looked up. The waiter refilled Ferelith's glass and as she looked at her husband over the top of it, she groaned. 'Oh no, it's impossible. You'll never guess who has just walked in – but it can't be him. He's in jail.'

'I can't turn around in a restaurant and stare.'

'A man has just come in with several friends and he looks just like . . .'

'Rogers,' interrupted Angus. 'He won his appeal, darling. I'm sorry. I didn't want to spoil our week-end by telling you.'

'Has he deliberately followed us to London?'

'That's paranoia, Ferelith. Come on. We'll go back to the hotel and have coffee and brandy in our suite and you can try convincing me about tenors.'

But the lovely weekend was ruined and the Websters left early next morning for Edinburgh and their never-ending workload.

1952 had also brought Ferelith an ever-growing list of juvenile crime.

'Would you wallop a child if you had one, Simon?' she asked one day. It was the kind of leading question she felt that she could not ask Angus.

'Depends, and depends what you mean by wallop. I don't think a good smack ever hurt anyone. Gets the message across, short and sharp. Why?'

'I'm getting so many of these vandalism things and I'm finding the attitude of the parents in some cases almost extraordinary. Do you know I have never represented a child who causes any trouble at all at home. Good as gold, helps Mum with the dishes and then goes out and breaks every window in every car in the street. Old Oliver thinks just bringing the little darlings into Court is enough punishment but I think all a court appearance does is fill them with curiosity. There's certainly no fear there.'

'You hankering back to the good old forties and the birch?'

'I see the same little blighters time after time now, Simon. A few years ago, one crime one punishment, and we rarely saw the same faces in the juvenile court. Look at this now. Four boys, all, according to their mums, "good as gold at home, he is", all nine or ten and all deliberately breaking car windows. What do you think would happen if the punishment was that Mum and Dad had to make good the damage?'

'Most of them couldn't afford it, so we're back at square one.'

'Well, something had better be done or we're heading for a great deal of trouble. Tell these mums, politely of course, that I wouldn't touch their boys' defence but this one now . . .' She handed Simon a brief.

'You're out of your tree. They're as guilty as this little lot.'

Ferelith paraphrased for him. 'Robin Hood and his merry men, robbing the rich, in this case the local poultry farm, but who are the poor in this case, Simon? Little Robin Hood, aged all of twelve says he stole the chickens. Why? How many chickens did he and his merry men rustle . . . ? Seven. Whose mum is going to cook seven hens? No, these were stolen to order and what we need to get is not these little villains but the person who is buying their chickens. I'll have a word with the Advocate Depute: we'll see if we can get them off with a caution and then we'll watch them like hawks.'

The Lord Advocate's wife did have power. The boys, obviously guilty, were cautioned and released and over the next few months leading up to Christmas it was found that they were spending quite a bit of time talking to a butcher in one of the better areas of the city.

A few days before Christmas they were followed as they made their laborious way to the butcher's shop. It is, after all, very difficult to carry four geese, five ducks, and two hens – the hens' keeper had already lost most of his flock in a previous raid – when you and your companions are only twelve years old.

Police Constable Christie arrested Mr Andrews, the butcher, when he saw him passing coin of the realm to the boys in exchange for the stolen poultry. Mr Andrews was further said to have been heard to declare the scheme 'a nice little earner' which is obviously what Robin Hood and his now not so merry men had also thought.

Lord Whitfield sentenced the boys to three months each in a Remand Home and Mr Andrews received six months at Her Majesty's pleasure for receiving stolen goods.

'I'd like to have been able to prove he actively encouraged them to steal, Angus,' she told her husband over dinner that same night. 'But it was his word against our little folk heroes'.'

'Perhaps he was telling the truth,' said Angus. 'After all, young Robin could easily have suggested the whole thing.'

Ferelith looked at him demurely over the rim of her coffee cup. 'Oh, no, darling, his mum said he was as good as gold in the house.'

17

A NEW ELIZABETHAN age was ushered in with incredible pomp and circumstance on the 2nd of June 1953, a day that Ferelith spent trying to save a woman caught shoplifting from going to prison. She did not succeeed. Her client had failed to mention to Simon, the instructing solicitor, that she had a suspended sentence already for failure to pay fines. Ferelith knew that her client had previously passed through the usual sequence – conditional discharges, probation orders but no one had told her of the suspended sentence and the Judge felt that he had no alternative but to impose a custodial sentence.

'Poverty is such a bloody trap, Simon,' she despaired.

'Lots of poor women don't steal, sweetness.'

'Oh, don't be so bloody patronizing.'

'Ferelith Gallagher, I never cease to be amazed at the language of so-called good Catholics when they are not getting their own way. She should have told us and we could have worked something out.'

'But why didn't she tell us? She couldn't make herself believe that she might go to prison. She stole because she's poor and she couldn't pay the fine because she's poor and now she's in jail because she's poor. I really loathe my job sometimes. What happens to the children?'

'There is a decent granny in this instance, who'll keep them for her.'

'And how old is granny?'

Simon looked around to see what there was to hand that his favourite advocate might throw at him. 'Granny is forty.' He did not need to remind Lady Webster of her own age.

She was only too aware of the fact that in a few short months she would be forty years old, the same age as the granny who was now bravely looking after her oldest daughter's children while that daughter was in prison.

'You'll be a Q.C. before you're forty, darling,' said Angus one night at dinner. 'You can pick up the baton of Dame Margaret Kydd and you can carry it farther, into even higher office.'

Ferelith had raised her wine glass and toasted him. 'And you'll be Lord Chancellor before then. Remember how we once talked of my taking silk before you became Lord Advocate and I haven't even got that far yet. But I would love to see you become Lord Chancellor: there's no one more able for the job.'

He had got up from the table and walked round to refill her glass. 'I'm not sure that I want that,' he said, putting his left hand with its broad, gold wedding band on her bare shoulder. 'It's important to me that you become a Q.C. but I really am quite happy with my career. There's nothing else in life that I want, except perhaps that you should be free of these whispers of nepotism.'

She put up her left hand to touch his hand that still rested very gently on her skin. The emeralds in her engagement ring caught fire from the candles and she watched them sparkle. 'We'll get them anyway, my angel.'

The pressure on her shoulder grew heavier for a moment and then he walked away from her to his own place. 'I want to protect you from everything, Ferelith, and I can't and that knowledge almost destroys me.'

'I was a law student when we met, and a lawyer when we married, Angus. I had already received everything nasty that life had to throw. Nothing that happens outside these four beautiful walls touches any essential part of me. All I want is for life to be as satisfying for you as it is for me.'

He said nothing but he smiled and toasted her again across the table, and Ferelith looked into his eyes and, not for the first time, wondered if she was being as truthful as she wanted to be. It was not satisfying for Angus. One thing was needed to make his life complete and he had never once asked for it.

His eyes were asking a question now and she answered by ringing the bell for Karen.

'I don't feel like coffee, darling.' She smiled at him. 'An early night?'

She rose and he got up and walked round the table to hold the door for her. Two minutes later Karen came up the stairs from the kitchen with the heavy silver tray she insisted on using to carry away dirty plates.

'I've got some lovely cheese,' she began before she realized that the room was empty. She lifted her head and looked at the ceiling above her head but she could hear nothing.

'I bet he was like Rhett Butler and just whisked her up the stairs. It was that dress, all that bare shoulder, just inflamed his passions,' she said, and then, since not even her fertile imagination could picture dull, quiet Angus Webster overcome by passion, she laughed and cleared the table.

Ferelith lay awake for hours after Angus's very

real and very satisfactory passion had died down and he had fallen asleep. His head still rested against her and she held him protectively as he slept. He was in his late fifties. If it did not happen now, it should never happen. But what would it do to her career? The only person to be pleased immediately by her decision, if indeed she made it, would be Father Munro, the priest of the little parish church she attended when they stayed with Blair and Emma. Deliberate contraception was, according to Father Munro, against the law of God.

The next morning, while she was still under the softening influences of the previous night's thoughts and desires and doubts, she made an appointment with her gynaecologist.

After he had listened to her he examined her thoroughly and pronounced her healthy. 'And as for having a baby, some would say that you have left it a bit late but if it doesn't happen now, Ferelith, it shouldn't happen.'

'It's in God's hands,' she said mockingly.

'And Angus's. All I will say is that if the two of you have a fairly regular sex life, save up for a day or two to give his sperm a chance to build up.'

'I'm going through to Ayr for a week.'

'Perfect. If there is anyone who will live like a monk for seven days it will be Angus Webster.'

'This is a highly embarrassing conversation, Jim.'

'Good heavens. You're an advocate. Don't tell me you haven't had fruity conversations about sex with hundreds of clients.'

'The sex life being discussed wasn't my own.'

'Men in their eighties have fathered children, Ferelith, and so it's unlikely that there will be a problem. If you don't want to tell Angus, and that's your decision, just be aware of your best chance for success.'

'I've left it so late that I might not conceive, Jim. If I tell Angus that I'm trying to get pregnant he'll be overjoyed and his distress if I don't will be just as powerful.'

She walked to her office feeling vulnerable for the first time since the early days after her first aborted marriage when she had half-prayed that she was pregnant and at the same time had prayed feverishly that she wasn't. She turned as if to go back to the doctor's office to ask him to put a coil back in.

I'm mad, she thought. I'm mad. I don't want a child. I'm almost forty. I'm too old. Angus is too old for disturbed nights and colic and teething and, oh God, toilet training. I went through all these arguments before and always decided that it was wrong to have a baby. I know Angus would love a child. I would love Angus's baby, my baby, wouldn't I, even when it got in the way of my career. Career? What a selfish woman I am. No, I'm not, I'm not. I told Angus I didn't want children. He agreed. And he's too old now.

Then she admitted to herself that, in all probability, Angus would adjust happily and that she was the one who would find the adjustment hard.

Too hard. It wouldn't be fair to a baby to have me for a mother. I want to be Lord Advocate. I do not want to be a mother and I can't be both. I can't be Lord Advocate either. The world isn't ready yet but a baby isn't my second prize. I don't want motherhood as a compensation. What have I done? It's not too late. I can have another coil fitted. Maybe I'm too old anyway. Maybe Angus is too old.

She blushed then in the street as she remembered how easily Angus had proved last night that he was not an old man but a man in his prime, a gentle man, a caring and considerate man who had never ever asked her for the one thing she withheld from him.

As usual she loved her time in circuit. Several times a year she travelled to conduct defences in various cities in Scotland. It was perfect when Angus too was in the same town but his position kept him more often in Edinburgh or London these days and she missed him dreadfully. In Ayr she stayed with her old friend from university days, Elspeth Baxter, who, with her husband, was a GP in the seaside community. They worked too hard all day, ate and drank too much each evening, and talked and talked and talked.

She said nothing when Elspeth told her that she and Michael had decided to have one more child, 'and even if it's another boy, we won't change our minds in a few years. Four is enough.'

'You said that about two and you said it ad nauseam about three.'

'Three is such an unsatisfactory number, don't you think?'

'Of children?' Ferelith asked drily.

'No. The numeral itself. It's so full of myth and legend. Three's a disappointment. The three witches in *Macbeth*.'

'You do realize that if it is a girl, you'll be all hot and bothered, terrified that the poor wee thing will feel all alone with all those big brothers and you'll decide she needs a sister, and you'll go on producing, trying to get your family all nicely symmetrical.'

'She can't produce without my help and four is *it*,' said Michael as he rose to offer them brandy.

'Thank God for that,' laughed Ferelith. 'No, not

for the brandy, for putting your foot down. We can't afford all these godchildren.'

'Just as well you two decided not to have any. Children are unbelievably expensive . . .'

Elspeth, her hands clasped protectively over her stomach, which was as flat as Ferelith had ever seen it, went on bemoaning the problems of parenthood. Ferelith switched off and sat comfortably on the couch, her bare feet comfortably tucked up under her and felt a ghostly fluttering in her womb.

I won't think about it, she thought. I won't think of the joy in Angus's eyes if I tell him one day that he is to be a father. And I won't pretend I'm tired when he wants to make love on Friday night when I get home because, whatever Jim says, I'm not going to cold-bloodedly save his seed for a big chance. '*Who is the patron saint of motherhood*? It has to be Mary, the Virgin Mary.'

'It's St Gerald, or is it St Jerome? I'm sure it's a man and a G or a J,' said Elspeth, and Ferelith laughed because she had asked her question out loud. It never occurred to Elspeth that Ferelith was asking the question for herself.

Despite her best intentions, she was as nervous as a new bride when she got home on Friday afternoon.

'You're jumpy, darling,' said Angus with concern. 'Too much chatting with Elspeth, I should think.'

'No, it was wonderful to be with them.'

'She's not a restful woman. I've never been sure what a dry old stick like Michael sees in her. Gosh, perhaps I'm the dry old stick. I'm ten years older than Michael.'

'Neither you nor Michael is dry or old. Michael is perhaps a little serious for his . . . gosh, he is a dry old stick, isn't he . . . but he's just right for Elspeth as you, Angus Webster, are right for me.'

He smiled. 'Shall we dine at La Dolce Vita tonight?'

La Dolce Vita had become his favourite restaurant because he said it reminded him of their honeymoon in Venice.

Ferelith thought quickly. She was tired. If they dined out, especially at the madly popular Italian restaurant, they would meet too many of their friends, eat too much food, drink too much wine.

'Hasn't Karen been looking after you?'

He looked a little guilty. 'Yes, and in fact I've already been to La Dolce this week. I took young Fiona' – a young solicitor in Simon's firm – 'on Wednesday night. We were both abandoned and she couldn't afford it on her own.'

Yes, he needed a child; it would save him collecting waifs and strays. 'We could stay at home then, darling. I'm sure I can find something, even spaghetti with a pesto sauce if you must have Italian.'

'Sounds great,' he said with alacrity. 'I'll open some chianti and I'll do some antipasto while you're making the pesto.'

Ferelith sighed and then smiled at his retreating back. She had meant to open a jar of pesto sauce. Now she was committed to measuring basil and pine nuts, garlic and oil, and grating parmesan. But it was worth it, and soon the heavenly smell of a really good Genoese pesto mixed with the aroma of prosciutto crudo, salami, and marinated artichoke hearts that Angus was arranging on a plate.

'We must go back to Venice, Ferelith,' he said as they sat at the table with the debris of the meal. 'Do

you remember that little place down the alley near
. . . oh, what was it near?'

'Santa Zaccharia.'

'You're wonderful,' he said and raised his wine
glass. 'Next summer?'

She did not immediately agree and he asked
again. 'Next year, darling, shall we try to go back? Of
course you know Italy so well and the world is full
of wonderful places and since the war, it's possible
to go anywhere. Goodness, how many times have
we said we must go to Paris. Unfinished business
in Paris, wasn't there, darling?'

'Yes, the Opera House. I couldn't afford it when
I was there.' Ferelith stood up. 'Let's clear away
for Karen, Angus. And yes, darling, I can think of
nothing I'd like better than to go back to Italy with
you. You still have to take me out in a gondola.'

She did not say next summer, she did not say, unless
I'm very busy, unless we are very busy, but he seemed
to be happy with her answer. Together they cleared
the table, rinsed the dishes and stacked them neatly
in the sink and then, their arms around one another,
they climbed the stairs to their bedroom.

By Christmas she had almost convinced herself that
she was no longer thinking about motherhood. She
was too busy: Angus was too busy. They were apart
a great deal and even though, when they were
together, everything was wonderful and very very
satisfactory, there was still no sign of a pregnancy.

'That's that,' she would say when she allowed the
thoughts to surface. 'Obviously I have left it too late
and really it's so much more sensible this way. How
could I possibly cope?' Quite happily, or at least with
resignation, she went back to the ever-increasing pile
of briefs.

In early December she had taken two days off to do some Christmas shopping in London while Angus was also there. She loved London for shopping and sightseeing, music and restaurants but did not look forward to moving there if Angus ever became Lord Chancellor. She kept those thoughts to herself.

The phone was ringing as she let herself into their Edinburgh house on Wednesday night.

'There's that bluidy phone again,' said Karen unnecessarily. 'It'll be Mr Osborne. He's been phoning every two minutes since yesterday.'

'Thank you, Karen.' She handed the housekeeper her briefcase and picked up the receiver trying to shrug herself out of her coat at the same time.

'Did it get into the London news?' It was Simon's voice. 'The Fiscal killed it up here, of course, but when he was found . . .'

'Simon, what are you talking about?'

'Maggie Sturrock. She knifed Bert.'

Ferelith stepped out of her shoes and sat down heavily in the chair by the telephone. Maggie. How long had she known Maggie Sturrock? Almost all her life, it seemed. 'Go on,' was all she said.

'The usual story of course. He beat her up yet again: all the neighbours testify that he was in grand form. Wee Charlie tried to hold him off, deflect his arm or something and he went for him. The boy said his dad was throttling him – his throat is heavily bruised – and Maggie went berserk, ran into the kitchen, picked up a knife and stabbed him . . . about thirty times.'

Ferelith felt sick and, for a moment, could say nothing.

'Are you all right, Ferelith?'

'Poor Maggie.'

'She wants us, you really. I'll find out when we can see her.'

'Fine.'

His voice was concerned: there was none of his affected femininity. 'Are you all right, sweetness? Is Angus at home?'

'Yes, I'm fine, just desperately sorry for the Maggie Sturrocks of this world, and no, Angus has one more day in London.'

'Rather him than me. Have a good stiff drink and I'll see you tomorrow.'

He rang off and Ferelith went into the kitchen where Karen was getting ready to prepare a meal.

'Don't worry about me, Karen. I had dinner with Lord Webster before I left. I'll have some cocoa and go to bed.'

She sat at the table and sipped the hot sweet drink from a cheery pottery mug she had bought in Italy. Had Angus been at home he would have realized, by her use of this old favourite, just how desperately upset she was.

Simon and Ferelith had been dealing with the tribulations of Maggie Sturrock almost since before they had qualified. Maggie had attended Dominic's cooking class at the University Settlement and Ferelith had first met her there. She had always been impressed by her courage and her willingness to try to better her lot in life. Unfortunately for Maggie, Ferelith thought, she had married Bert Sturrock because she was expecting his child and had lived with his violent abuse of her body, her mind, and her soul, ever since.

And God dammit, she thinks she deserves his abuse. Why? Because he had no respect for her because she had given in to his demands for sex 'to prove that you love me'. Dear God, do the Bert

Sturrocks of this world understand anything at all about love?

A more important question was whether or not the Prosecuting Advocate and the Judge and Jury really understood anything about domestic violence. Too often the police failed to act in cases that were labelled 'domestic'. There were firmly entrenched attitudes in society about the roles of men and women. Ferelith knew that if she were to ask ten advocates if they agreed that men had the right to beat up their wives and children most would say 'no'. But in Court it would soon be obvious that too many men felt that what happened within the four walls of a home was a matter for the people living there. Too many platitudes about such things as the 'sanctity of marriage' were mouthed daily. Men were often released with no more than a severe dressing-down from the duty sergeant. This had been the case quite often in the battles between Maggie and her violent husband.

'She asked for it,' was a perfectly adequate defence and several times Maggie had been told not to nag Bert about his drinking.

'If I leave him, Miss Gallagher, what aboot my weans? I cannae take them because there is naewhere fer me to go. Where could I get a job? I havenae even got a decent frock to wear. Who'd hire me and whit could I dae? All I've ever done is have bairns and wash dishes. I'd be worrit sick aboot Mary, my wee lassie. Whit if he turned tae her? He needs . . . it . . . regular,' she added with a blush as if ashamed to say something about sex in front of someone who, in her eyes, had obviously never been touched by it.

Ferelith had an unwritten but remembered catalogue of the ills suffered by Maggie Sturrock.

Bert was a waster. The only time in his life that

he had been employed had been for four and a half
months in 1941 when His Majesty had finally asked
Bert to do his duty. Bert's commanding officer had
very soon discovered that he had enough problems
with the opposite side without adding Bert to his
list and had thrown him out. Whereupon Bert had
returned to Edinburgh to limp around pretending
that he had been invalided out, to making life a
misery for Maggie and his children. Seven times he
had been thrown in jail for wife beating and every
single time Maggie had taken him back.

'Jist where am I supposed to go wi' five bairns?'
she had asked Ferelith again and again, not angrily,
merely with acceptance of the status quo. 'God alone
kens where he gets money but he aye seems tae be
able tae get us a loaf and there's aye tatties in oor
bit gairden and sometimes a cabbage or a Brussels
sprout. Wouldn't it be nice no tae ever hae tae eat
another Brussels sprout?'

Ferelith, who had spent seventeen years in an
orphanage where an unbelievable number of Brussels
sprouts had been consumed year after year could
only agree with her.

But now Maggie had had enough. Constant beatings of her own person she could, as she had
said often enough, 'thole', but abuse of her children? No. Maggie the lion had roared and she had
killed in defence of her young, but what would the
Law say?

'I kent fine whit I wis daein', Miss Gallagher. I
was that calm, I couldnae believe it. The bluid wis
rinnin' doon ma face but a' I could think on wis my
wee Charlie standin' up fer us and gettin' leathered.
He wid hae kilt him: the bairn wis blue. I hit Bert
wi' the knife the once but he didnae stop chokin'
Charlie an' I don't ken whit happened but I could

see masel lifting the knife and stickin' it in him and
liftin' the knife and stickin' it in him and there must
hae been noise but I couldnae hear nothin' and then
wee Charlie wis hingin' on my skirt and greetin',
Mammy, Mammy, and I wis fell tired and sat doon.
You'll no let Bert's family get my weans: they're a
bad lot. I'd raither they wis pit in a hame.'

Not calm, Maggie. Catatonic, decided Ferelith.
She did not know what she was doing. She could
hear and see and feel nothing. The action of her arm
had been an automatic response to the throttling of
the boy.

But Maggie Sturrock had accepted that she had
murdered her husband and for that *crime* she
expected to die.

'Not if I can help it,' decided Ferelith Gallagher
Webster and brought the whole might of her intellect
and training to work.

18

THE FACT THAT Maggie Sturrock had struck out in defence, not of herself, but of her son, weighed heavily in her favour. Against this was the knowledge of the surely unnecessary violence with which she had killed her husband.

'The first knife wound,' said a forensic scientist, 'would have been quite enough.'

There were over thirty wounds in Bert's body. According to her own traumatized son, Maggie had calmly, without screaming or yelling in any way, thrust the knife into his father again and again.

'I couldnae get her tae stop,' young Charlie, his throat still swollen from the brutal strength of his father's hands, cried to Ferelith. 'Mammy didnae seem to even ken I wis there. She looked at me that funny when she finally stopped and I think she jist stopped hittin' him because she wis exhausted.'

Added to the evidence of the thirty knife wounds was the unpalatable fact that Maggie had, according to many eminent and knowledgeable people, deliberately courted Bert's violence.

'Why did she take him back again and again?' asked the public, both male and female.

Maggie's doctor gave eloquent testimony to the misery of her existence with her husband but her very dignity and composure in the face of cross-examination acted against her. She was too calm, too unemotional.

'You knew what you were doing, Mrs Sturrock, when you wielded that knife and stuck it over thirty times into the body of your husband, and I say too that you enjoyed it,' said the Advocate Depute.

'I needed tae make him stop hitting the wean,' said Maggie calmly. 'There wis nae other way tae de it.'

'And you enjoyed it, Mrs Sturrock?'

Maggie looked at him out of thousand-year-old eyes. 'I didnae feel onything. I jist has tae stop him.'

Maggie Sturrock was not helping her defence at all. Ferelith, who had seen too many clients talk themselves into long prison sentences, decided to try a new tack. 'We'll have to try to persuade the Jury that in the face of severe provocation and real fear for her son, Maggie was temporarily insane, Simon.'

'According to most judges and juries, temporarily insane people do not deliberately go into the kitchen to get a bread knife.'

'But they do.'

Ferelith ran her hands through her hair. She was tired. This case was taking more out of her than any other. Her whole being wanted to get Maggie off and every day she could see a death sentence getting nearer and nearer to her client.

'God, I wish I wasn't so tired, Simon,' she said and he noted the dark shadows under her eyes and the loss of weight.

'You're taking too much out of yourself, Ferelith. When did you and Angus last go out somewhere nice for a quiet dinner?'

'I dine quietly with Angus every night that we're at home together,' said Ferelith which was not really an answer to the question. Sometimes she felt that she and Angus were doomed to spend the rest of their lives passing one another in doorways as one came in and the other went out. 'You know he'd be the last person in the world to try to stop me doing my best for Maggie. If only I get get the Jury to see that she is traumatized by the fact that she murdered her husband —'

Simon interrupted. 'Can't you get her to break down, relive some of the beatings? If she comes across scared and desperate, she'll get the Jury on her side. Right now she's not making a very good impression.'

'Why, in the name of all that's wonderful, should she have to . . . why should she have to sell herself? Can't you see that she's pulling resources out of some inner place she didn't even know she had to help her deal with this. She's distancing herself from the murder, from the years and years of brutality and fear, in order to be able to stand up there in the witness box just to hear herself being described as "unnaturally calm and composed". Did you hear Fenton suggest . . . ?' Ferelith stopped to compose herself and took a sip of water.

'Ferelith, why are you letting this case get to you so much? You're making yourself ill.' Simon was on his feet, his usual indolent pose gone.

'I'm not ill, Simon,' said Ferelith putting the glass back on the table. 'I'm fighting mad. He suggested that she liked being beaten up. He told her that if she hadn't enjoyed it, she would have left Sturrock. What banana boat did that Neanderthal man come up the Clyde on? She stayed for her children. Can't you stone-age men get that through your thick heads? There was nowhere for her to go and she stayed to protect them: she took years and years of rape and beatings for her children.' Ferelith broke down and started to cry, great sobs that tore at her. Simon took one look and went to the telephone to ring Angus's office. Then he put his arms around Ferelith and held her until the paroxysm of crying had stopped.

'I'm holding you to stop you throwing something heavy at me, sweetness. Angus is on his way here to take you home. No, don't argue and don't struggle. I'm stronger than I look and it would be so dreadfully embarrassing if anyone came in and found us rolling on the floor in a parody of immortal passion. You need a good night's rest. Angus agrees. I'll talk to Maggie's doctors and see if we can get some sympathy for the abuse.'

'"I'll talk to Mrs Sturrock's doctors", Simon, not Maggie's. She is entitled to some dignity. Women don't like strange men calling them by their Christian names and they certainly hate the old school "Sturrock" or "Gallagher".'

She looked at him, her friend, her dear friend. 'Why do I attack you when I'm angry, Simon? My best of friends. Anyway, not even her doctor, and he's sympathetic, knows the extent of the abuse, Simon. Women who are being beaten up hide the evidence. They pretend they've fallen downstairs. They don't go to the hospital unless they're so badly beaten that something is broken or they're bleeding so badly that they're frightened of dying and leaving their kids. She never told her doctor about the times Sturrock raped her.'

'Ferelith, he was her husband. A husband can't rape his wife. I mean . . . marriage, he's entitled . . .' Simon flustered in the face of Ferelith's obvious contempt for his opinion. 'Aren't wives supposed to submit to their husbands? Doesn't it say that in the Bible?'

She stood up calmly and looked at him. 'Dear God in Heaven, Simon, if a decent man like you

thinks a husband can do anything he likes to his
wife . . .'

'I didn't say that.'

'You said a husband cannot rape his wife. Rape
is violence, Simon. It means to take by force what
has been withheld. Most men will say, "Maybe
tomorrow?" if a wife says, "I'm too tired", or "I
don't feel well" or "you're drunk", but not the Bert
Sturrocks of this world. He took what he wanted
whenever he wanted. He raped her in front of
their own children, Simon. And then they wonder
that violence and degradation are self-perpetuating.
God, if only there was one decent relative to keep
the children. That will be held against the poor
woman too.'

The door opened before Simon could ask her what
would be held against her client and the Lord Advocate came in. Ferelith's defences crumpled again and
she went into the haven of her husband's arms.

'I think she's fighting the flu, Angus,' said Simon.
'Take her home and feed her hot lemon and honey
with a shot of whisky. She did that to me once when
I had plumbed the depths. Works a treat.'

'Sounds wonderful,' said Angus. 'I'll have some
too. Come on, darling, you're letting this case get
to you and that is no good for you or for your
client.'

'Do you know what one of the newspapers printed
this morning, Angus? "Is Maggie Sturrock a good
mother? If she is, then we don't want her to hang
because she should be there to look after her children. If she is a bad mother, then it doesn't really
matter." We're talking about someone's life and
we're saying "it doesn't really matter". Excuse me,
I have to go to the Ladies before we go home.'
She pulled herself from her husband's arms and

hurried out and the two men were left looking at one another.

'This case is really getting to her, Simon.'

'I've known her over twenty years, Angus, and I've never seen her as emotional as this. What is it about Maggie Sturrock that has got to her like this?'

'She feels helpless. There are no tricks she can pull, no playing to the gallery, and Mrs Sturrock's attitude isn't helping. Maggie killed him: she admits it and she is showing no remorse. If she could just be made to work on the susceptibilities of the Jury. I know there are too many men but men have sympathetic natures too. If only she'd say something like, "I never meant to kill him."'

'But did she murder him and does she deserve to die?'

'An eye for an eye?'

'The fact that the children are in care and have been in care so often is a strike against Maggie. Her children have been in care, ergo, their mother is a bad mother and they are better off without her. I wish we could make more of psychiatric evidence: if we could prove that she was criminally insane or had some other mental disorder.'

'I'm sure the day is not far off when the psychological state of the accused will be important but right now it's a kind of mumbo-jumbo world that no one understands. To me it's obvious that Maggie was operating in a state of diminished responsibility. Nothing has come up to show her as a violent person: she never even spanked her children. Bert did too much of that. But Ferelith is having a hard job convincing those eleven men and four women that Maggie did not know what she was doing when she ran into the kitchen for a knife. Why not the rolling pin or a broom? Why did she deliberately open a drawer and take out a knife? And why did she go on and on knifing her husband? Because she was not in her right mind.'

'What would you do? How would you handle the defence?'

'Ferelith has the instinctive feel of a good jury advocate. She'll get them on her side and she'll get them on Maggie's if she can persuade Maggie to emote more. There are, as you know, Simon, so many unspoken prejudices in a case like this. Ferelith naturally empathizes with Maggie. She understands what motivates her. If anyone can get her off, Ferelith can.'

'Well, thank you, M'Lord.' They had not heard Ferelith return. She looked a little better with slight colour in her usually pale cheeks. 'Let's go home and have some scrambled eggs and then I'll spend some time working out how to explain Maggie's detachment to the Jury. It is so frightening how little time there is to deal with life and death.'

'You are going home to bed, Mrs Webster,' said Angus severely. 'Please, darling, you will be unable to help Maggie if you tire yourself out. You have spent more hours than necessary on this case as it is.'

Ferelith pulled away from his arm. 'How can you say that? Simon thinks men are entitled to do what they bloody well like with their wives and you think your wife shouldn't get too tired defending Maggie Sturrock. Dear God, what chance does she have of justice? I'll go home, Angus Webster, because I want to go home, not because the two big strong men in my life are telling me to go home, and after I have made some scrambled eggs, I will work on my client's defence and I will take as many hours as it takes.'

'Sitting up in bed comfortably,' suggested Simon. She ignored him and stalked out.

'You're a braver man than I am, Simon,' said Lord Webster as he hurried out after his wife.

A light supper and an early night seemed to do wonders for Ferelith's health.

The *Mens Rea*, the advocate's term for the state of mind of the accused at the time of the incident, had to be explained to the Court. That is, Ferelith had to make the Court understand Maggie's intention. To succeed as a defence to murder, she had to be able to prove that Maggie acted in self-defence and in defence of her son. The Jury might be prepared to accept force, even leading to death, if they could be made to believe that stabbing Bert was the only way Maggie and Charlie could escape death themselves. The insurmountable stumbling blocks were the number of blows struck and Maggie's detachment. Ferelith strove to show that years and years of brutal conditioning had made Maggie Sturrock accept her husband's brutality. She did not seek it, she did not enjoy it, but she saw no way out of the vicious cycle. Eloquently and movingly she painted a vivid picture of a woman who, as a young and idealistic girl, had acted wrongly.

'She loved Bert Sturrock: she, like many other innocent and loving young women, gave in to the pleas of her young man for sex to prove, in his words, that she loved him. Some of you might say that was wrong: you might think it immoral. Was it not immoral for that young man to ask such a pledge? Should he not have said, "I will prove my love for you by staying chaste with you until we are married." Maggie gave in and she paid the price and she went on paying it for year after year of degradation and brutality where she herself came to believe that she was no good, that she did deserve Bert's violence. And then, on that fateful night, when most happy and loving families, no matter how poor their circumstances, were looking forward to the joyous and loving season of Christmas, Bert Sturrock subjected his wife to a vicious beating, a beating so severe that a young boy dared his father's anger and brutality to try to save his mother. And what happened to that brave boy? His father, his father, ladies and gentlemen, tried to strangle him to death. And Mrs Sturrock saw her son turning blue and something inside snapped, not because of the beating she had received, but because of this innocent and brave boy. In her own words you heard her say that she saw nothing, heard nothing, was aware of nothing but her child struggling for his very life in the hands of the man who had given him that life, and in that state of consciousness she went to the kitchen and she took a knife and she stabbed and stabbed her husband until she heard her boy cry, "I'm safe." Who among us would have acted differently in the defence of the baby we had nurtured in the womb? Maggie Sturrock killed her husband, ladies and gentlemen, but she did not murder him.'

She sat down wearily in her chair and Simon looked at her anxiously as, with trembling hands, she sipped water from a glass. He watched as a very subdued jury left the room to begin their deliberations. What were they thinking? What would they decide?

It was Maggie Sturrock who consoled Ferelith. 'You're no looking weel, Miss Gallagher, and I want tae say now, afore they come back, that naebody could hae done better fer me. I killed him, lassie.

I'm no proud that I've taen a life but it's all over fer me now. You ken, Mr Osborne, this time in the jail has been the longest time in thirty-five years that naebody's belted me one. It's my bairns. They'll be fine in care, won't they? Naebody'll be on at them for whit I did, will they?'

Ferelith looked at her. The weeks in jail had actually been physically beneficial to Maggie. She had lost some weight, probably because her diet was slightly better than that which she was used to.

I wonder if she ever made any of the casseroles Dominic taught the girls to make, Ferelith thought, or did she lose heart for sensible cooking too?

The neat blue dress that Ferelith herself had bought for her client sat well on her frame and the colour suited her blue eyes. A shadow of the pretty young girl whom Ferelith had first seen all those years ago was visible now in the ravaged face.

She's even standing taller these days and has that been bad or good? Bad probably. The Jury would have preferred her to look more cowed, to be unable to meet the advocates' eyes.

'Jury's back, Miss Gallagher.' So soon. So soon. The Court Officer was already at the door.

Ferelith felt her stomach flip over with dread. She wanted to retch, to be violently sick. She breathed deeply and looked at Simon.

'My God, Simon, they've been gone twenty minutes. How can they decide in twenty minutes? I take longer than that to decide what to wear in the morning.'

They walked back from their waiting room and as always, Ferelith was conscious of the many people, innocent and guilty, who had walked these corridors in fear and trepidation, throughout the years.

They were back in the courtroom. Ferelith and
Maggie took their places, Simon just behind for support. The Judge came in with the Court Official and
the mace and then for a few minutes Ferelith experienced what she felt Maggie must have experienced
when she had killed Bert. There was a swimming,
humming noise in her ears. She knew she was doing
what her long training had taught her to do but she
was acting like an automaton: she saw the hazy
figures of the Jury and the Judge and the Advocate
Depute and all the court officials. She was aware
of the mace, that great symbol of regal authority
hanging on the wall behind the Judge, but she could
hear nothing.

And then Simon was helping her into her seat
and Maggie was standing there with her children
around her and they were laughing and crying and
flashbulbs were popping and then Ferelith knew.

'Not guilty?' she asked in amazement and still
with that far away voice as if this was all happening
to someone else, 'but they couldn't possibly find her
not guilty.' She grabbed Simon's gown. 'They found
her not guilty?'

'Not proven,' he said and in front of any interested spectator, he kissed her. 'You won, Ferelith,
you won.'

19

ON THE 10TH of January 1955 the contralto, Marian Anderson, became the first black singer ever to sing at the Metropolitan Opera House in New York. Angus, who had been on a courtesy visit to the Supreme Court of the United States, was so entranced by her voice, her age, and her achievement, that he had to telephone Ferelith from New York to share his experience with her immediately rather than to wait for his return. He telephoned every day when he was away from home anyway and this time he was anxious to contact her because he had been worried about her health over Christmas and the New Year and had been on the point of cancelling his trip when the Not Proven verdict had come in.

'I'll rest at home for a few days, darling,' Ferelith had persuaded him. 'Go to New York. I'd adore to come with you, I'm madly jealous, but maybe next time.'

'When I get back we'll talk about that holiday we were going to have. Somewhere for some sunshine or Paris or anywhere else you want to go?'

Now he tried to convey to her the excitement generated by the national acceptance of the great contralto.

'It was the *Masked Ball*, darling, Verdi. She sang Ulrica and it was electrifying. Toscanini says hers is a voice that comes along once every hundred years and I feel privileged to have heard it and in the

States in the Met. Let's not go to Italy after all for our holiday. Let's try to find out where she's singing in the summer. She tends to do concerts . . .'

Ferelith listened to the bubbling excitement of his voice and her heart lurched with love and happiness. 'Why are you so excited by one singer and a contralto at that?'

'Because the United States grew up a bit last night: that's exciting. She's black, sweetheart, and there she was accepted as a singer and a great one in a country where blacks and whites can't sit on the same bus. Where children of different colours can't sit in the same classroom. Her glorious voice was like a breath of clean fresh air. You remember how we heard Toscanini yelling *vergogna* at the orchestra when we were at Pietro's ordination? Well, no one was shouting "shame" at anyone last night. The place went wild.'

'And Angus Webster went wilder than anyone.'

'I behaved,' he said mock sternly, 'with my usual magisterial decorum but I did send flowers. Have you any idea of her age? She's sixty this year. It's taken her all this time to be acknowledged, to succeed. I thought you would be delighted for her. And since you, at forty, are a mere child, I thought, when I get home tomorrow, we could talk about your application for silk.'

'That'll be nice, dear.' Ferelith smiled and he could not see the smile but he sensed it.

'You have wanted to take silk for years, Ferelith, and especially after the Sturrock case, you are bound to be accepted, not as my wife, but on your own.'

'Yes, Angus. We'll talk about it tomorrow.'

Lord Webster was not at all happy with his telephone call. Lady Webster, on the other hand, was delighted with her half of it.

But we won't be chasing Marian Anderson this summer, Angus Webster, no matter how wonderful she is.

Angus's flight reached Edinburgh in mid-morning and Ferelith was there to meet him.

'You're glowing, darling,' he said as he kissed her. 'Either it is this cold frosty air or the rest since the end of the case has been just what you needed. I was so proud of you and I want you to be the first female Q.C. and, why not Ferelith, the first female Lord Advocate?'

'That's nice, dear,' she said again and he looked at her strangely but said nothing. 'Nice that I'm glowing,' she said, a hint of laughter in her grey-green eyes.

What colour were they? It seemed to depend on her mood and the weather.

'You seem to have put back a little of the weight you lost, darling. I'll tell you now that I was really worried when you were defending Mrs Sturrock.'

'Oh, it was nothing. Fatigue, worry. Everything is fine now. I shall amaze you with how healthy I am.' She turned and led the way to where she had parked the car.

'Do you want to go into the office?' she asked when Angus had stowed his suitcase and his duty-frees and the countless magazines he always seemed to accumulate on journeys. 'I thought you might like a nap first and then we could have a lovely lunch at La Bella Napoli.'

'Only if a nap is a euphemism for what I hope it is.'

She smiled that tantalizing smile again and turned the car into the road leading out of the airport.

'You are behaving very oddly, Mrs Webster,' he said finally. 'I was actually surprised to see you this morning: I thought you might already be up to your ears in a new case.'

Ferelith slowed down at the approach to a roundabout and appeared to give her full attention to the difficulties involved in steering her course safely.

'I'm glad you have lost your fear of this car,' Angus went on as Ferelith had not answered him.

She had learned to drive in Angus's powerful Jaguar but she drove as seldom as possible. Usually Angus drove, as he actually enjoyed it, but Ferelith preferred that he not drive after a long flight.

'It's a nice car,' she said. 'Had you thought of changing it?'

'Why on earth should I change it? The mileage is remarkable for its age: it's not as if we go any great distance in it. Don't tell me you've seen something you'd prefer? I always thought a car for you was merely something that took you conveniently from A to B.'

'And so it is. We'll talk about it after your nap.'

'Our nap?'

'Wicked old thing, you. You'll have to think of a good excuse for Karen.'

'Give her some shopping to do – as far away from the New Town as possible.'

'I'm only teasing you. I've given her a day off to hit the after-Christmas sales. I'm going to ring Simon after lunch too, darling, to ask him to dinner. He had to have Traviata put down and he's really desolate.'

For Edinburgh the road from the airport was fairly quiet and they were soon at home.

'Apart from your opera programme, did you bring me anything?' Ferelith teased when he abandoned his attempts to unpack his suitcase.

'I didn't bring you my programme. I'm keeping that for myself. That's an "I was there" programme. I brought you some nylons from Saks on Fifth Avenue.'

'Is New York as exciting as everyone says it is?'

'Nowhere is exciting when you aren't there, my darling,' said Angus and proceeded to prove to their mutual satisfaction just how very exciting windy Edinburgh could be.

Later they drove down to Tollcross to the restaurant and Ferelith surprised her husband by asking for champagne.

'To Marian Anderson,' she said when the waiter had poured the first glasses and left them alone.

'Miss Anderson,' agreed Angus.

They drank.

'And to Baby Webster,' said Ferelith looking over her glass at her husband.

'To Baby Web . . .' he began and then he put his glass down so abruptly that the champagne spilled over on to the immaculate white cloth. He looked at his wife.

Her lovely eyes sparkled at him assuring him that he had heard what he had hoped he had heard. He leaned across the table and grabbed her hand making the stones in her engagement ring bite into her flesh. She did not feel the pain.

'Ferelith, but you can't . . . we agreed. We've taken steps.'

'I un-took them, Angus, months ago.'

He lifted both of her hands and kissed them very gently.

'You're going to have a baby?'

'We're going to have a baby and, oh Angus, I'm thrilled and terrified but mainly thrilled, in fact ecstatically happy.'

'Oh my darling girl, so am I.' They sat holding hands and just looking at one another. A baby. Neither could quite believe that this miracle was going to happen. Angus looked at his wife and saw her as he had seen her only an hour or two earlier. He would be much gentler from now on: he would take great care of her.

'You wonderful, wonderful girl,' he said.

'Woman, Angus. I'll go along with wonderful woman.'

'Should you be drinking alcohol? And you need food. Shall we order?'

'Yes, I should be drinking my celebratory glass of champagne and yes, I need food.'

Angus summoned their waiter and soon Ferelith's favourite antipasto was on the table between them.

'The car?' he said.

'Not a family car.'

'You are right. Let's get one of those marvellous estate wagons.'

She laughed and speared a marinated artichoke.

'It's only one baby, not a rugby team.'

At that glorious thought he leaned back in his chair and put his fork down. 'We have to go home. I keep wanting to do crazy things like kiss your feet and that is definitely not acceptable for a Lord Advocate.'

'It is in the privacy of his own home, but I'm starving. I've worked very hard this morning,' she said archly, 'and I have to go home and prepare a nice dinner for Simon.'

'No, you mustn't strain in any way, darling. We'll eat out or I'll ring Simon and tell him to come back in . . . how long?'

'In six months. So no holiday in Venice, and now you know why I couldn't get excited at the thought of a second honeymoon. I couldn't tell you until I was quite sure. Venice will wait. We can even take the baby. But we can't cancel poor Simon. He's awfully upset about Traviata and I cancelled our meeting this morning to fetch you from the airport. I'll have some work to do after dinner and you can catch up on your sleep.'

Angus signalled to the waiter to remove the antipasto. 'Just salad for Lady Webster and *linguini con funghi* for me and a tossed salad. And water.

'Ferelith Webster, you are avoiding my eyes. You are going to tell Simon that you are resigning?'

'No.'

'No. You mean not yet, not for a few weeks yet. When did you find out? Who told you? I mean, how does one . . . this is silly but I've never been . . . intimate with a pregnant woman before?'

'I should hope not,' she teased and then took pity on him. 'I went to see Jim a few days ago and I guessed for myself on the last day of the trial. All the fatigue, the nausea, I put it down to overwork, to stress. And then I came in after the Jury came back and there were such strange things going on in me and around me and I felt the baby move. Jim says he's too small but Jim isn't pregnant and he's never been pregnant. I am and the baby, our baby, introduced himself. He said, Mummy, I'm so sorry you've been feeling awful but I'm here now and we'll be fine. And he was right. I started feeling better and I want to share my joy, our joy with everyone. We'll ring your sister, then Blair and Emma, and Jane and Jamie, and all the di Rollos and Elspeth. Some doctor, Elspeth. She thought I was talking about her,' she said cryptically, but he was not sufficiently interested in Elspeth to ask for an explanation. 'Then we'll tell Simon and maybe old Oliver but then we'll keep it a secret until I've finished the work that I have on hand.'

'Ferelith, a pregnant woman can't practise at the Bar.'

'Why not?'

'It's not done.'

'Why not? Finish your linguini and we'll go home. I'm perfectly healthy, Angus. I'm a teeny-weeny bit old to have a baby and I will take no more instructions until after he's born but —'

'After he's born?' Angus interrupted. 'Ferelith, my wife is not going back to work. It's unbelievably unsuitable.'

Ferelith touched his hand gently. 'Finish your linguini, dear, and we'll discuss this at home.'

Angus called for his bill and for the waiter to remove his unfinished meal. He did not speak until they were in the car and heading home. 'I will not allow my wife to work in her condition and that is final, and I will not allow my daughter's mother to go out to work either. It is totally unsuitable.'

'How do you feel about your son's mother taking silk?'

Angus was so angry that he stalled the car at the west end of Princes Street; and because he was angry he flooded the engine and took so long to restart the car that there was a huge tailback of honking cars. It did not help that the policeman on duty at the corner recognized him and tried to ease the situation.

'Sometimes I can almost understand what drives men to violence,' he said through clenched teeth as they reached their home.

'What a dreadful thing to say. Scratch a liberal and he's every bit as outdated and prejudiced as anybody else.'

'You're being childish.'

'And you're being medieval, prehistoric. "My woman doesn't go out to work."' Ferelith hurried up the steps and threw open the door and almost slammed it closed again in her husband's face. 'I'm furiously angry,' she said unnecessarily.

She could see Angus withdraw. She had seen him do it over the years in Court but he had never yet done it to her. They had never had a flaming row. Neither of them was prone to shouting and raging. Now her anger frightened her.

'I suggest that you lie down and rest,' he said quietly and she could see how hard he was trying to control himself and she almost capitulated. 'Your condition . . .' he began and she exploded.

'My condition? How dare you, Angus Webster. You are like every other arrogant male. You don't like what I am saying and so you take refuge in stupid stereotypes. We should have moved on from the Ancient Greeks who gave us the word hysterical and stuck it as a label on every mother who did or said something her lord and master didn't like. My womb is not governing my actions: I am not affected by the cycles of the moon.'

She stood at the foot of the stairs trembling with anger and misery and looked at him. He did not look any happier than she. Poor Angus, she thought. He has wanted a baby so much and now I tell him there is to be a baby and I spoil it by fighting with him and he's afraid to say anything to me because he has always felt there was something holy and mystical about pregnancy and there is, dear God, there is, but he has to realize it's a perfectly natural state.

'You do know that Simon's Traviata was a Fidelio until she had kittens and he saw that he was a she. She had them perfectly happily and easily.'

'Don't be childish, Ferelith: you are not a cat. You are my wife and I don't want you exhibiting yourself and your condition in court.'

'Exhibiting myself?' She almost choked. 'That antediluvian gown that advocates wear would hide anything. No one will even know I'm pregnant. I don't intend to go into labour in court number eleven but I will finish the work I have agreed to do and if you don't like the idea, you can . . . you can . . .'

She could feel the words 'Get out' forming themselves on the end of her tongue and she swallowed them and ran up the stairs to the sanctuary of her bedroom. She sat down on the bed and looked at herself in the wardrobe mirror. At the enormity of what she had almost said she started to cry and she did not hear Angus open the door and cross the room to her. He held her, sobbing, in his arms until she was quiet.

'I think my perfect mix of cerebral and emotional has gone somewhat skewwhiff. This was supposed to be the loveliest day in our marriage.'

'And it is.'

'If I give in.' Ferelith looked at him and took a deep breath. He was not going to like what she had to say but she could not be dishonest. 'Angus, I still intend to apply for silk. Don't you see, advocacy is the perfect job for a mother?'

'Why do you want to work at all? You don't need to work.'

'Oh darling, I do. While I'm useful, I want to work. The baby will change things. I'm not the same woman now that I was three months ago. In six months' time I will be a mother and I'll be changed again. Maybe my aspirations will change but I want to leave the options open. Sweetheart, I'm like your

wonderful Marian Anderson. I've changed things
for the better, and she's not finished and neither
am I. Can't you understand?'

'No, but I'll try.'

'That's all I ask.'

Angus was unhappy about Ferelith's decision to
continue working but in the days and weeks that followed he was amazed by her energy. He delighted
in her slowly changing shape and made countless
plans for their unborn child.

Ferelith did not announce her pregnancy to her
colleagues but she did announce her intention to
apply for silk. This was a courtesy not always
given by all advocates. After all if one was rejected
and had not made a general announcement it was
sometimes possible to lick the painful wound of
failure in private. If one did announce, one knew
that one's hopes and aspirations, one's talent or lack
of it, one's education, experience, in fact everything,
would be a hot subject of discussion for weeks if not
months.

Ferelith decided to make her application public.

'A woman?'

'Well, there is Margaret Kydd.'

'Then that's enough surely.'

'Is there no end to her ambition? Old Webster had
better look to his laurels: she'll be after his job next.'

'I hear Ferelith Gallagher has applied for silk.
She'll get it, of course. I mean if one only had the
Lord Advocate to put in a good word . . .'

'Nonsense, she's a damned good advocate and
she's done her time. Brilliant in Court.'

'Brilliant? She's an assertive, aggressive, unfeminine woman and Webster should be ashamed of
himself to allow it.'

And steadier heads tried to discuss why it was perfectly noble for a man to be assertive and even aggressive in the defence of his client but not permissible for a female.

Aware of all the arguments Ferelith sailed through her pregnancy on a cloud of euphoria.

It became generally known that the Lord Advocate and his wife were to have a child and Ferelith experienced another change of attitude in Court on the few times she appeared before her voluntary withdrawal from public life.

'I was so frustrated, Angus, I could have wept,' she said one night at dinner. 'Old Ironsides has been particularly hostile to me since I first appeared before him and today he behaved like my uncle. He almost said, "There, there, lovey, sit down and put your feet up and I won't argue with you." And his Lordship stopped proceedings when I took a sip of water to ask me if I was tired. He actually said, "We must all remember your condition." My client didn't know my "condition" as he called it until he said that and now she thinks I'm a fallen woman. "You really understand where I'm coming from," says she.'

Angus, who had met no prejudice of any kind in court or out of it, tried to sympathise.

'You are absolutely delighted that I'm the little pregnant wife at home now, aren't you? Admit it.'

'I'm absolutely delighted that my wife is *enceinte*.' began Angus.

'You Victorian, you. You can't even say pregnant.'

'Of course I can. I merely wanted to point out that his father has a smattering of learning. Actually, Ferelith, I want to rent a bus and watch it drive around Edinburgh with a banner up that says, "Ferelith Webster is pregnant and I did it."'

She got up and went to him. 'Darling Angus, you are pleased and proud and you won't mind if it's a boy or a girl.'

'I would have difficulty if it were anything else,' he teased her. 'Ferelith Webster, you continue to make me the happiest and proudest man in the world.'

'Oh, it's nothing,' she said. 'Now put your hand there and feel him kick. Definitely a rugby player.'

They sat for some time communicating with one another and their unborn child and then Ferelith jumped up. 'I forgot to ring Pietro. Everyone in Edinburgh knows I'm a fallen woman but not the man who is going to baptize the little treasure.'

James Gallagher Webster was born very easily on the 21st of June 1955 and it was a few weeks before his mother had time to read the papers. She scoured the newspapers that referred to the date of her precious child's birth and found that after a two-day trial, a jury of ten good men and two good women, had taken twenty-five minutes to find one Ruth Ellis guilty of murder in the first degree. Mrs Ellis was hanged at Holloway on the 13th of July, just a few days before Jamie was baptized.

July 13th was also the day on which Lady Webster was told that she had been awarded silk and would now be a Queen's Counsel.

'Well Jamie?' asked Ferelith and at her voice the baby opened his eyes and looked up at her face. He continued to suck and she watched him tenderly. 'This is the most beautiful time, Jamie my love,' she told him. 'So much tenderness flows from me that I feel the world should be able to see it. I love you so much – and your daddy. Daddy is the nicest man in the world, Jamie, and I hope you will grow up to be just like him.'

James Gallagher Webster burped loudly and regurgitated some milk and his mother laughed.

'Not an accepted way to conclude an argument, young man, but effective, I must admit.'

'Am I disturbing you two?' Angus stood in the doorway of the baby's room.

Ferelith smiled at him. 'Come and join us. We're having a mother to son talk and he told me what he thinks by spitting at me. I told him I wanted him to be just like you and he thought I meant I wanted him to be a lawyer: he hates the idea.'

Angus took the baby and expertly began to burp him. 'What does he think of having a working mother?'

'I haven't asked him that yet. Where did you learn to get rid of wind?'

'Not in the Court of Session, although perhaps thumping one or two people on the back might be rather a good idea,' said Angus, giving the baby back to his mother. 'I'm a quick study. I'm going to try a nappy as soon as he's finished.'

Ferelith smiled at her husband who was looking absurdly young in his pyjamas and not at all like a Lord Advocate. 'Nappies are serious business.'

'So is being a father. When you go back to work . . .'

'I haven't decided yet,' said Ferelith quickly.

'Oh, I think you have, darling. I saw your face when you read about the Ruth Ellis case. I saw your face when I called you Ferelith Gallagher Q.C.'

'I want to be Jamie's mother.'

'I gave the matter a great deal of thought. Advocacy is actually quite a good job for a woman. If he's sick you can stay at home with him and remember, I want to be an involved father too. Sometimes I'll be free to look after him.'

Ferelith bent her head over the baby to hide the ready tears. 'Oh Angus, I still want it all, not today, not until Jamie is weaned, but I do want to continue.'

'That's what I want too. You're a brilliant advocate and there are people out there who need you.'

'More than this precious mite?'

'Differently. And he has a father who is now going to send his mummy off to bed while he struggles with his first nappy pins. Go on, I won't stick the pins in him. We're going to have the first of many man to man chats.'

Ferelith kissed the drowsy baby and handed him to his father. 'Did I ever tell you that I love you very much, Angus Webster?'

'Not nearly enough. We'll get back to that later. Goodnight, Ferelith Gallagher Q.C.'

'Ferelith Webster Q.C.'

He looked up from his struggles with the pins and looked solemnly into her smiling eyes.

'Yes, we like that, don't we, Jamie? Ferelith Webster. Q.C.'

BUTTERFLIES IN DECEMBER

Eileen Ramsay

It was her beloved father who first made the observation: that graceful, intelligent, independent women like Lucy Graham were as rare as butterflies in December. Lucy was determined to realise her ambition of becoming a doctor – but in one of the poorer districts of Dundee another bright young woman held on to the same dream. For Rosie Nesbitt, the path to her goal would be more of a struggle, demanding sacrifices from those closest to her and testing her resolve to the limit.

As pioneers in their field, it was perhaps inevitable that their paths would cross. And when they do, their chosen career isn't the only thing they have in common: the party at which they first meet is hosted by Kier Anderson-Howard – a potential husband of Lucy's – but whose attention is clearly centred on Rosie.

Lucy may have burnt her bridges with the man she had sacrificed to her career. But as the Great War approaches, Lucy's life encompasses further sorrow and joy with the re-appearance of a long-lost figure from the past – a figure she'd been resigned to losing forever . . .

General fiction
0 7515 1649 X

THE DOMINIE'S LASSIE

Eileen Ramsay

As daughter of the local schoolmaster – the dominie's lassie – it was only natural for Kirsty Robertson to become a pupil teacher at her father's school near Arbroath. It was the first step on her road to qualification; the first step on a road that would lead her through both heart-rending difficulties and overwhelming joys – and not all of them academic . . .

The year is 1908, with Kirsty in the full flush of her teen years and the Great War still a distant menace, far over the horizon. Before long, however, the trenches in France would claim the attentions of the two young men closest to her: Jamie Cameron, an old schoolfriend, and Hugh Granville-Baker, son of the local squire and object of her seemingly unrequited fantasy since their very first meeting.

As Kirsty endured her own problems in her struggle to qualify, little did she know how the fortunes of these two men and her relationships with them would come to shape a lifetime.

General Fiction
0 7515 1132 3

Other best selling Warner titles available by mail;